A Tide for Drowning

For Richard

A Tide for Drowning

Dick Durham

Prologue

The tide along the coast of East Anglia is easy to calculate. During the flood it runs for six hours in a South-Westerly direction, during the ebb the reverse happens.

The sailors of old had a rhyme, which gave a snapshot of the tide at different locations:

High Water London Bridge
Half ebb in the Swin
Low Water Yarmouth
Half flood at Lynn

FIRST EBB

June 6

HW time 06.54 (am) Height 4.83 m   HW time 19.11 (pm) Height 4.73 m

As the sea receded Adele watched a peeler crab raise its claws like a prize-fighter and, using expert footwork, scuttle away backwards. That the falling tide should reveal a black scarecrow with outstretched arms, fixed the crustacean's armoured eyes on the intruder while it settled in a draining rivulet and, fists still raised defensively, buried itself in a cloud of silt.

It struck Adele as ludicrous that something so tiny should be prepared to put up a fight, but it was a creature of alternative worlds, tide-in, its submarine terrain was a murky, gravity-less wash of waving weed and safety. Tide-out it was a scuttle over an exposed desert.

As the water continued to shrink away to a white horizon of distant North Sea, it revealed Adele's open prison: a vast plateau of sand puddled with the reflection of fluffy, non-moving clouds. The early morning light was soft and the world motionless under the stilled sky.

It had been quiet for days, not a cats-paw of wind had stirred the sea lavender over the salt marsh or puckered the filmy neap tide as it slid slowly across the great sands. The country was in the grip of searing summer high pressure weather and the beacon which pinned Adele to the dried sea-floor, stood shimmering like some mirage in the heat. It was isolated in the sand, at one time a gibbet-like warning to mariners that any nearer and their keels would be joining it, but now it was obsolete: the shoals it once marked had shifted, forming humpbacked sandbanks in the channel, rendering it useless for navigation. From the beacon's legs, cross-beams and braces, fronds of fleshy bladder-wrack hung like brown grapes unmoving in the airless, stopped world.

Now the tide had gone out completely the rising sun emerged from the mud as a perfect orange disc and immediately began to warm Adele's rubber suit. Unable to move her bound arms and shackled legs, she craned her neck and looked at the little book gaffer-taped above her head on the nearest barnacled pile.

It was a tide table, which revealed that the fallen sea, which, at its height had reached her midriff, had a 4.83 metre range. The afternoon's tide was predicted as having slightly less height: 4.73m. The following morning it would climb again to 4.77, but make slightly less in the afternoon: 4.69m. For the next three days this pattern would continue, slightly higher tide in the mornings and slightly lower in the afternoons. But after that, as the moon ballooned into its waxing gibbous phase, the pattern reversed: the North Sea would lift more swiftly over the sand and start to pick up: higher in the afternoons each day until high water on Wednesday 11 June. By the time it reached Adele's mouth it would have a further 0.7 metres to climb before peaking.

She had six days before she would drown.

———————

Two miles west, on the shoreline, the rising sun was already moistening black scabs of tar on the planks of an ancient weatherboard hut, its windows wide open to snare a hoped-for sea breeze. Into the new day emerged Jackson Smith in his shirtsleeves. In waders he squelched out onto the Dengie Flat, a collapsible easel in one hand and a holdall of brushes and paints in the other.

Jackson used the vastnesses of the Essex mudflats as a stage for his life studies. At least that's what he said. The fact that the old wildfowler's hut, which he rented, was the only house for miles around and was an hour's drive from his home, served another, more furtive, purpose.

He placed figures in all manner of poses across the brown sands he painted, but somehow they always looked out of place, stuck on like felt figures in a child's picture. Perhaps this was because in reality the Dengie was deserted, but then again it might have been because his figures were motivated by Jackson's loathing, and not his sympathy and therefore, disembodied from humanity, were left just as gargoyles in space. He painted ugly representations of people who were better painters than him, people who were better connected than he was and people simply better-looking. He would paint his enemies treading in dog turds, throwing up in drunken stupors or in a state of unflattering undress. Why all these people would be 'on the beach' mattered not to his clichéd way of bohemian-received wisdom: such considerations were 'narrative' and he was not a story-teller. He was much deeper than that. His targets, anyway, were unaware of their representational fame, as Jackson had never been 'hung'. At least, not in any gallery. In a lifetime of daubing, his sole claim to fame was that he had once got a picture accepted in the annual sop to parochial talent at the Royal Academy's summer show. Unfortunately, though accepted, it went straight into storage. It was after this 'success' he became Jackson, jettisoning his birth name, Brian.

As the sun rose higher in the east the Dengie was turned into a shallow glitter, a mirror sprinkling with light, and then there was a scream. What was a scream doing on a still, perfect summer's morning in a coastal wilderness, all on its own? If it was a scream it had the effect on Jackson of suddenly reducing the desolation to something human. Momentarily Jackson felt as though he was in a giant room.

But not a gull wheeled in the warm sky. The Dengie was lifeless, empty. The universe mostly orbited around Jackson's ego. Any one of his senses could be stimulated, but if not immediately backed up with secondary empirical information from another, the information remained unconsidered. Like a scream in the middle of an uninhabited wilderness. Instead of stopping to ask what on earth he had just heard Jackson trudged on, still fizzing with his own reality: resentment.

He taught innocents at a nondescript local art college and as his once raven black hair turned a dirty grey and his once sexually attractive leanness failed to prevent his chest hollowing and his back forming a slight hump, worked even harder at bedding students in his studio, although only those without the wit to see through his paintings. His wife knew what he was up to and was simply grateful the marital bed was for slumber alone.

But to keep up appearances Jackson still had to turn out his large boards of Essex mud-banks inhabited by alien figures.

He squinted at the distance - a Sahara of tide-deserted, sparkling mud - and as his eyes passed over the Buxey Beacon, something registered and he turned back. There was a subtle change to its shape. The filigree of light through its splayed legs was obstructed on one side. Yes there was a shadow on the east side, a large sack maybe. But a sack wouldn't stand up like that, he absent-mindedly didn't notice.

It mattered not, today Jackson was going to use the Buxey Beacon to crucify his latest victim: a fellow painter who had secured an agent in the West End. It was almost too much to bear. This man could actually draw and although drawing belonged to coherence and therefore communication, ergo 'narrative', people wanted to buy his bloody work.

Jackson unscrewed the butterfly nuts of his easel's legs and set them up on the ooze. He placed a board already prepared with the khaki-

9

colour he thought mud looked like and started making rapid upright strokes in black, a third of the way across the horizontal just as he told his students to do. Soon he had a stark Buxey-shaped crucifix standing alone on a plane of Essex mud.

Adele could see the rising sun had lit the distant sea wall, a dun brown line topped with green. She could see a speck against it. A moving speck. She had saved her energy but now was the time for screaming.

Perhaps he was just too far away. There was no sea breeze to carry the plea and it dissipated into the hot summer's morning. Nothing like that belonged out here. What fickle sound reached his ear did not belong out here. And he was pleased to exercise his artist's scepticism. Not for Jackson the melodramas of the superstitious. The Dengie was a place of historic violation, that he knew, but ghosts? Ghosts were recruited for narrative vehicles, ghosts were for story-tellers.

Next squeezing a gobbet of red and white onto his palette, Jackson worked up a garish pink and draped a human-shape over the cross-bar. Cleaning his brush on a rag, but also 'accidentally' brushing a small smear on his Levi 501s - people would know he was a painter from his trousers if not from his trip-tych - the artist tapped on little flecks of vermillion dropping like feathers from the figure's hands. 'The stigmata of capitalism,' Jackson muttered to himself.

So intensely had Jackson worked on his crude oil he had failed to notice the tide slipping in through a shallow swatchway behind him. The first he was aware of it was when it suddenly pooled his muddy footprints, overflowed and slid towards the easel's legs. He packed up his equipment and splashed back to the sea wall.

'The stigmata of capitalism,' he repeated as he returned to his hut, 'I like it.'

———

In poor light Lady Adele Moulding's narrow face suggested a youth now lost to her: what had once been lean and aquiline had become goat-like and long in tooth only, but, in poor light, it aroused men's libido still. Combined with her carefully looked after figure she was not wrong in considering herself desired. The trouble was this fading potential had long stopped pleasing her husband. This she knew, of course, yet never thought of changing her allure from the purely physical to something more cerebral. In fact such thwarted ambition served only to make her catty to other women and rude to men she felt were likely to interest her husband in spending any time away from home. She was pointlessly possessive and ineptly controlling. Although she knew this pushed her husband further away, she could not help increasing the distance.

So in spite of the high-minded 'distractions' Sir Keith talked about, it was into the periphery of life that Lady Adele grazed. She could only focus on what was trite, superficial and ephemeral. She was not stupid and knew her existence lacked gravitas, especially since her childhood upbringing in the Catholic Church had denied her her powerful sex drive resulting in her rejection of religion which, as crutches to oblivion go, she was beginning to regret kicking away.

She had hoped to nail down Sir Keith with their three children and had been successful until they left home which they did so in a hurry sensing the void.

Now she was left with all the TV channels money could buy, and all the technology to archive them. Yet she despaired of anything to watch, trying and failing to enjoy populist reality shows, which so exercised her younger friends.

'Read a bloody book,' Sir Keith would admonish, but the only books worthy of national attention seemed either to be about schoolboy wizards, or sexual fantasists and while her friends loved talking about them she found them a poor read.

'Get some new friends,' was Sir Keith's advice, but making friends from outside the privileged circle of fund-raising events she attended was easier said than done and her contemporaries were an unwelcome reminder of her age.

Her husband had started his working life selling pre-packed plastic raincoats during the summer vacation from public school. For although he'd had what was called a privileged education, his father believed in instilling the work ethic and any money which young Keith had control over, he had to earn. It had stood him well financially and also kept him 'focussed' or narrow of mind right up until late middle age when he began to sense the emptiness of the counting house. But this had in no way halted his ostentation, in fact it now, perversely, fuelled it. What had at first been a firework display of have was now a conflagration ignited by self-parody. He'd picked a detached Victorian merchant's villa in a small town west of London and then added a quarry-load of Welsh slate to line the front garden which had been completely excavated and dumped in landfill in order to create a car park with 'kerb appeal' for his stable of four automobiles. That was the old Sir Keith. The new, enlightened, Sir Keith had later added coping stones around the huge parking lot substantial enough to support individual Cypress trees in Grecian-style pots.

In their early days together Adele was not happy with her husband's flair for drawing attention to himself, epitomised at Christmas time with the 300 cards they sent out sporting a rather poor artist's stylised etching of their home with Santa Claus astride the ridge tiles, but as she was not prepared to deny herself the trappings of success, provincial limelight was unavoidable. 'It's ridiculous to expect anonymity and drive around in a black Merc sports,' said Sir Keith, 'the only people who will ignore you will be those pretending they don't want one, but even they will have *seen* you. If you want to be anonymous join the poor people and get the bus into Richmond.'

On the night of her disappearance Adele had driven from home with the roof of her two-seater car open. The hot summer air blew around her. Adele's sense of the erotic was old fashioned: she did not believe stockings should stay up without assistance. Hold-ups suggested hosiery that was over-engineered: a tourniquet around the thighs. Also, no man – or woman for that matter – could know she was not wearing tights. But her suspenders: 'pingers', as Sir Keith

13

dismissed them, could be detected under the close-fitting, light, woollen cream dress. The stockings themselves were the most expensive denier available from Mayfair, their glossiness so delicate that Adele wore washing up gloves over her red talons to ease them on. As she looked at her pretty painted toes through the sheen they excited her as though they were someone else's feet. The shade was just respectable, although with her legs crossed and a stiletto dangling from the hanging foot, the heel reinforcement revealed they were black.

As she changed gear she could feel the silky summer air around her figure in place of her disinterested husband's clunkily-ringed hands. She allowed the hem – already above her knee – ride up a little further and was pleasantly shocked at the appearance of lean shining limbs working the pedals. She adjusted the driving seat back a notch too far so that her legs had to stretch their full length to control the car. Her red, sling back high heels were cast casually on the passenger seat, the expensive rash of their make was suggestive of crocodile, but in fact was the skin of an eel, a creature still waiting anthropopathism by a wildlife charity and therefore not protected.

At the Richmond Bridge traffic lights she ranged alongside an overworked bus, shimmering heat-waves throbbed out of its engine grill and a good-looking youth with a shaved head, ashamed to be travelling on pensioner's transport alongside a Cougar in a convertible, looked down from the grimy window at Adele's prone form, her legs held in articulate readiness over the pedals – like an artist's drawing doll - for the lights to turn green.

Sir Keith was going straight to the Mansion House from his Canary Wharf office and would meet Adele in reception. Because of his wife's continued battle to stay young and beautiful she rarely drank more than a single glass of 'fizz' as her younger friends called sparkling wine. So she would drive them both home after the dinner. A chauffeur was always on hand but Adele held out the forlorn hope that her husband, if not succumbing to her physical allure, would appreciate her doing something useful. In any case it was Friday and if Ron, Sir Keith's driver, was engaged so close to the weekend there was always the chance some male-only activity would be arranged for the following day and she'd be left with nothing but 200 TV channels.

The dinner was at 7.30pm by which time the City would be a ghost town, the trains of Fenchurch Street, Liverpool Street and London Bridge, between them having emptied the monied canyons of all suits until Monday. London would be left to rave on west of the Aldwych, so finding a street parking bay would be easy. As the black faux leather roof expanded back into saloon-mode, Adele used the driving mirror to wipe on some more fuschia roll to her lips. She noticed a dirty white van pull up in the bay behind her. 'There's absolutely no problem parking on the street, once Le Weekend grips the City,' she said to herself, after pursing her lips to compress the carmine.

She walked from Bread Street the few hundred yards to the Mansion House, buffeted by fetid air being dispelled from granite-faced City buildings as their air conditioning systems fought to chill the summer heat.

Inside Mansion House she could see Sir Keith away across the main hall sipping a glass with an old crony. As she walked towards him he was smugly pleased with his wife's appearance.

'I wish my wife would wear some fun clothes,' said Sir Ted Smart, the old crony, 'she always used to.'

'Nonsense, Ted, Alice *is* fun, she doesn't have to dress like a clown.'

'You know very well what I mean, dear boy, I want her to look a bit flighty. She always used to.'

'For goodness sake Ted we're at the Mansion House not in your wife's boudior.'

'She won't even do it there anymore.'

'What?'

'Wear, you know, appropriate clothing. I mean look at Adele she looks stunning: stylish, sexy. Alice says she refuses to be dressed by me. Refuses to be an object. Tells me I should be more subtle and not expect her to be a floosie.'

'May I present …my wife,' said Sir Keith mockingly, 'Sir Ted, Lady Moulding.'

'Hello Ted, how are you? You're looking well.'

'Not as well as you Adele, my dear,'

'Ted thinks you look sexy.'

'Really? And what do you think?'

'I couldn't possibly comment.'

A tall, heavy woman, handsome in a way that suggested in her youth she would have been voluptuous to the point of being overripe, joined the trio. Her cleavage was impressive but alas too much sun worship meant its fleshy tracery had to be veiled in netting.

'Alice, always a pleasure. How are you?' said Sir Keith.

'You know how I am you old fraud, still basque-less in Belgravia, frightfully frigid and dry as a nun's cunt. Are you pouring or is he?'

They were seated at linen-covered tables, girl-boy, girl-boy and across from the same gender arrangement but with strangers. Sir Keith found himself opposite a young woman called Sam with a stylishly cut sloping blonde bob which she continually fingered back over an ear as though it was an unwelcome intrusion, but which acted as a coquettish device enabling her to reveal an elegant neck.

Sir Keith was always more comfortable sitting down. His lack of height was compensated by the expensive black tie ensemble he wore for the Mansion House dinner but only until he was joined by a taller man. Standing up he was an emperor penguin among women only. Seated he could colonise.

'Sir Keith, CEO Metrobanc,' Sir Keith thrust his hand across the table to the blonde.

'Oh hello. This is Gervais Ritchie of NDL…'

'How do you do, sir? But it's you I'm talking to, Sam. Not often we get the pleasure of dining with exotic young creatures. What is it *you* do?'

Adele and Alice exchanged mirthless smiles.

'I'm the PRO, for Gervais,' said Sam

'For the bank, Sam, for the bank,' said Gervais.

'Yes, for the bank,' she added.

'I should have thought publicity was the last thing they're seeking these days' said Adele.

'We want to promote the brand going forward...' said Sam, before Adele intervened, 'Strange way to describe the future, it sounds more like a tank than a bank.'

Sam smiled nervously her neck a perfect cylinder of fecundity, a pedestal for her lovely young head, which she admired as much as anyone else, as anyone else could see from the way she variously tilted, shook and poised it in mock attention.

'Why won't you lot lend anybody any money? That's what I want to know,' Adele continued as Alice poured more champagne.

'Difficult times, my dear,' said Sir Keith, 'difficult times. Everyone has to tread much more carefully now.'

'What you mean no more hunting for hill-billies in the Everglades or wherever they live and putting them in half-Nelsons until they borrow enough cash to pay for a shack instead of a trailer?' Alice joined in as her husband chuckled.

'Something like that,' said Sir Keith, 'but then I'm sure Sam is the new face of banking. No more toxic deals...'

'Going forward,' interrupted Adele whose neck was already flushing with the effect of just one glass of bubbly.

Sir Keith's pride in his wife's appearance had waned with the addition of Sam to the party. He looked at her reddening neck, circled with age lines as symmetrically as an oven ready joint of beef is with string.

'Yes, indeed, going forward and it's about that: the future, in the case of homo sapiens getting older, that we are here tonight,' said Sir Keith, changing the subject, 'a fund-raising dinner for Alzheimer's research, so cheers.'

'Cheers,' said Alice topping up Adele's glass again, 'who was Alzheimer? Sounds like some crank Austrian philosopher.'

'German, Alice, and he was a psychiatrist,' said Sir Keith, 'so do you have anyone close to you who is affected with the condition, Sam?'

'I don't think so.'

'She's not old enough to have relatives old enough,' said Alice, 'make the most of it my dear. Old age does not come by itself.'

'Going forward,' said Adele laughing, 'and why does a bank need to advertise anyway?'

'It's not so much advertising, it's more brand awareness,' said Sam, 'we want people to know we are there for them.'

'And I'm sure you are doing a great job, Sam,' said Sir Keith re-filling her glass.

'Well if it's confidence you are trying to create I would have thought PR is the last thing you need because people don't trust it,' said Adele proffering her glass to her husband's stewardship.

'Steady, darling, remember you're driving.'

'I'm fine. I'll match it with coffee.'

'It's unlike you to have more than a glass.'

'Public Relations is a lot of bullshit,' said Alice, intervening, 'it's the company employing someone to lie for them so they don't have to do it themselves. Spouting corporate virtues, damage limitation when things go wrong and littering the postal system with unread kindling.'

'Well we only operate online,' said Sam.

'Or the ether with unopened emails.'

'Come on Alice give Samantha a break she's only just starting out,' said Sir Ted.

'Oh take no notice of me, dear, it's nothing personal, but it's a fact, post-modern PR was invented by Joseph Goebbels and look what he was selling.'

While his brand was being defended a disinterested Gervais Ritchie was pecking at his smart phone trying to get in touch with his boyfriend while cuffing his gelled quiff into place.

Sir Keith couldn't quite bring himself to offer Sam a business card. It was too obvious and he would never follow it through anyway, there would never be any cover-up required and so with nothing ever to hide his lust shone through.

'Well I expect to hear great things about you, young Sam and you might want to consider some freelance work with Alzheimer's research. We need someone to pull together all the different interested bodies.'

'You're very kind, Sir Keith, it's certainly something I'll bear in mind.'

'She's got her work cut out trying to re-brand exploitation,' said Alice.

'Yes and she's definitely not interested in your body, darling,' said Adele pouring Alice, Sam and herself another glass of champagne.

'Boom boom.' said Alice.

Sam let her glossy blonde bob fall forward over half her face, then flicked it back, laughing.

Sir Keith's forwardness with Sam was now thrown. His wife's master stroke at pouring a glass for Sam had formed an alliance of gender which discomfited him.

At a stroke his tepid abuse of authority was undermined. And, strangely, he began to find his wife erotic. If Sam liked her it would be the closest he would ever get.

As he watched the three women talking he became convinced Sam was holding his wife's gaze for longer than was required for acknowledging trivia.

More champagne was delivered to the table and all glasses re-filled. Sir Keith's interest now had shifted to the chemistry taking place rather than the legal requirements of motoring.

'Two hundred and eighty quid for dinner is a bit steep even in the Mansion House. Where the hell does all the money go?' said Alice.

'For research into Alzheimer's, Alice. It could benefit you one day. It could benefit us all one day. One day, statistically-speaking, it will benefit two of us at this table.'

'You may well be right but it's more likely to benefit your business before me. I'm already brain dead anyway, ' she poured herself another glass and topped her companions up.

'How many are ga-ga in your homes?'

'About 80 per cent of our residents, over 70, have dementia of one kind or another.'

'So that has to be good for business?'

'I don't think it's helpful to see it like that, Alice' said Sir Keith trying to hear what Sam and Adele were giggling about.

'Oh come off it Keith, I know I come over as some raddled old radical who can tell it like it is because I'm "privileged" …'

'But you are privileged, darling' said Sir Ted laughing, 'you were born into it, my dear, it's only not privilege if you work for it, like Keith does.'

'As I was saying brain dead people are good for your business because they are your business. Let's face it who, of sound mind, would choose to live in a threadbare guest house which smelled of faeces?'

'I won't ask you to work on our profile, Alice,' laughed Sir Keith, 'look, our homes are all registered with the local authorities, checked by them and closed by them if there are any improprieties.'

'Whatever an impropriety is it doesn't cover dreary old dumps full of zombies kept half alive by a neo-colonial slave trade in Filipinos who live in even worse housing.'

'Atta girl Alice, give this new money boy what for,' laughed Sir Ted, pouring out more champagne.

Sir Keith smiled wanly: 'It's true that most of our care force are from the Philippines and they want to be here and we're very lucky for that. Their national characteristic appears to be compassion.'

'And ours is, find cheap labour at all costs, or rather to save as much cost as possible. Keith I don't doubt you are right that they want to be here, but that's because their country is an even worse cuckoo's nest than living in one of your care homes.'

'Well you're often shopping in Regent Street why don't you take it up with the Philippine Embassy it's just off the Haymarket.'

'Bingo – brilliant touché dear boy. Give it to her Keithy.' roared Sir Ted enjoying himself enormously.

'You should have been trepanned years ago dear,' said Alice silencing her husband, 'Anyway the point I'm trying to make is that if the people they are obliged to look after are brain dead then their job is a lot easier. Like the old mental asylums: as soon as there's any reason to give the inmates a liquid cosh of hard drugs or a short, sharp electric shock it was taken up. But if they come to you in a comatose state in the first place...'

'Yes, but dementia is not a comatose state. At least not in the sense that the sufferer is brain dead, as you put it. They are more like an active volcano, they appear to be asleep or inert but they can explode at any moment sometimes for an apparent reason: ie they fight against being bathed or dressed, but at other times for no apparent reason,' said Sir Keith, 'They can be very violent... You are enjoying the champagne, girls?,' he turned to Sam and Adele who were now allies.

Sam laughed and threw her hair back behind her ears again, flexing her beautiful neck again.

'She has a neck like a swan, darling,' said Adele admiringly.

'Indeed, she does,' said Sir Keith.

'You have a neck like a swan darling,' giggled Adele.

'But why no necklace?' said Alice, 'as a woman's neck, like her hands are parts of the female form which are bare to the world, they are a chance for libidinous decoration...that is until you are over the hill. Then you're stuffed.'

'Why's that?'

'Because although we can ruffle our necks with chiffon, our hands are the dead giveaway as we can't wear gloves at dinner, my dear,' Alice stared, a plump and spotted hand gripping the champagne flute, 'so make the most of it.'

'Where's the loo?' asked Sam.

'Come on, I'll show you, I've been in this Masonic morgue as many times as I've had hot dinners here,' said Adele.

Sir Keith watched them walk away on their heels. Sam laughing and leaning in towards Adele, her left hand just steadying herself on Adele's behind.

Sam was flattered that the CEO of such a well-known bank was attracted to her, and excited with the impropriety of familiarity shown by such a big fish's wife and deeply relieved her PR role was no longer under scrutiny.

The sheer luxury of the ladies loo, its Breccia marble like glossy, petrified pepperoni, the polished Cube-shaped taps, the immaculate mirrors made her feel important. Her companion was important and sharing such an intimate space with her made Sam feel sexy.

Their ablutions finished they stood side by side washing their hands and looking at each other in the mirrors.

Adele used a paper towel to dry each of her fingers. They were long, articulate and taloned. Sam watched the reflected image of the hands moving across to her mirror and then around her. Gently, they embraced. That was the last gentle act. Now they were all out sucking each other's tongues, caressing each other's neck, back, rump.

'In here,' Adele said, and guided Sam into the disabled toilet, where she locked the door and lowered a nappy-changing unit from the wall.

'On here.'

Sam sat legs apart on the nappy bed. Adele got down on her knees, ran her hands up each of Sam's thighs. Her knickers were a bulbous promise: pink gossamer stretched over a black bush. A rush of lust seared through Adele's blood: Sam's blonde hair was unnatural, her real colour now revealed. It excited Adele that Sam dyed her hair. That Sam wanted to look even more desirable.

The knickers were damp, Adele pulled them off, sucked the gusset. The salty tang she then carried to Sam's mouth. They kissed furiously. They kissed through the knickers, then Adele plunged her tongue into the shocking pink and Sam came quickly in a series of jerks. Adele licked up as much of the juice as she could then returned to kissing.

25

'If Keith wants to taste you he'll have to kiss me,' she whispered and they both laughed.

'Let me taste you, darling,' said Sam, but Adele had already come and simply pulled off her black leopard patterned knickers and pushed them into Sam's mouth.

They kissed again running their tongues over the silky material. Then they swapped underwear, brushed themselves off and re-joined the dinner.

Sir Keith detected their bond.

'You two seem to be hitting it off well.'

'Your wife is good fun, Sir Keith,'

'And Sam is young and sweet and gorgeous enough to eat. Being around people like you make us all feel younger.'

'Make the most of your lambing days,' said Alice knowingly, 'no-one wants to go down on mutton.'

Everyone stopped, then everyone laughed and Sir Keith felt marooned. And confused. He wanted Sam. He wanted his wife. He wanted both.

Taking the lead from his wife he became braver. Why shouldn't he be informal, too, with this attractive young guest?

'Sam, you've made a difference to my wife. She's having fun, she's actually enjoying a fund-raising dinner, which has to be a first. I wonder can you work your magic on me, too?'

'She hasn't got a wand big enough,' said Adele.

'I'll do my best Sir Keith,' Sam added, thrilled at the prospect of a potential career change.

'Keith, please. Call me Keith. Let's leave the knighthood at reception.'

'So, roll in the red carpet, eh?' said Alice, 'that's not very chivalrous, trying to hide your armour, it's almost as tacky as taking your wedding ring off from nine to five, hoping to pull during office hours,' said Alice.

Sir Keith smiled. Alice was always like this.

'You are on top form, Alice,' he said.

'It's difficult sustaining a conversation for long with a new target of the opposite sex without mentioning something of your domestic arrangements, I know I've tried often enough,' said Alice.

Ted cackled. He relished his wife's provocation.

'You can talk around it for a while, even try waffling about a partner, which unfortunately is not ambiguous enough.'

'Fascinating, Alice, your take on office romance,' said Sir Keith.

'You always know when your husband's cheating on you because all of a sudden he wants to have it off with you. Something's made the old goat realise it's not just an overflow pipe for claret.'

'No dear, no dear. It wasn't that,' said Sir Ted spluttering with laughter, 'I simply reactivated our boudoir department in order to camouflage my illicit life, but of course I hadn't reckoned on your brilliant analytical mind and it completely backfired on me,' tears of laughter ran down his cheeks.

'But in Keith's case Sam knows who his partner is even if he's forgotten himself,' said Alice.

'Poor Keith,' said Sam, 'he is just being nice to me. I think he's very charming.' Sam's chance of manipulation had come. She boldly looked Sir Keith in the eye and held his gaze just a second too long to be decent.

Sir Keith's blood rushed about.

'Thank-you Sam at least someone here has a sense of propriety.'

'Oh he'll be nice to you, don't worry about that,' said Adele, worried at the new front opening up, 'but you'll have to come through me first, SIR Keith.'

Sir Keith looked at his wife, the woman who had, just a moment ago, been an object of desire because of her chemistry with a young, attractive, unattainable woman. Now he knew Sam's lust was for reflected power. Now any misbehaviour coming from Adele would give him the excuse he needed to move in.

'And I'm taking Sam clubbing later,' said Adele.

'Clubbing?' said Sir Keith, 'you mean there's somewhere left that'll take you as a member?'

'Very droll, dear, but I'm not talking about the sort of establishment where they dust antlers and iron the Daily Telegraph. I'm talking more Soho than St James.'

'Do you like dancing, Sam?'

'I do Sir Keith. All girls like to dance. Why don't you come, too?'

'She's just being polite. My husband's not a boogier are you SIR Keith?'

'I'm a fast learner and with youth to teach me the moves…'

'I've got no room for you in the Merc. You'd better alert Ron although I don't suppose he's ever accessed the pages of his A to Z north of Pall Mall.'

'It might be safer if Ron drove you and I took Sam in the Merc…'

'Me ? Ride shotgun with your precious Ron? He'd never get over it and more to the point nor would I. No thanks. Sam's coming with me.'

'But you have had a few glasses, dear. Would Sam feel safe driving with you? What do you think, Sam?'

'Sam is coming with me. I'm perfectly OK. I've never felt more focused and there's coffee being brought round now.'

'I'm in your hands,' said Sam coyly looking alternatively at Sir Keith and Adele.

'He wishes…' said Alice.

'I never drive without a drink in me…far too dangerous otherwise,' cackled Sir Ted, 'in any case you try finding a chauffeur who'll put up with the Lady Alice. Pass the port.'

'Why don't we get a taxi?' said Sam.

'Good idea,' said Sir Keith, 'the clampers don't come out til after nine in the morning, so the Merc'll be all right where she is.'

'Public transport, Keithy?' chortled Sir Ted, 'whatever next?'

'What is it about cab drivers makes them think we're all crypto-fascists?,' said Alice, 'one whiff of Chanel and they assume I share their deluded ramblings about immigration.'

'Oh my God that's so true,' laughed Sam, 'and you never know whether to, like, focus on their face in the driving mirror or the back of their head when they're talking to you?'

'They're born brain dead, but maybe there's something about doing the knowledge that makes them receive their wisdom by rote, too. I just tell them I've got a Romanian chamber maid who sells the Big Issue on her days off,' said Alice.

'So a cab it is, then,' said Sir Keith, 'if I say we're all UKIP members we should get one straight away. Goodnight Alice,' Sir Keith pressed his lips to her fleshy cheeks, 'and goodnight Ted.'

'Goodnight, old man, no need to kiss me, too,' chortled Sir Ted.

Although it was close to midnight by the time the trio emerged, the great metropolis still held the day's heat within its naked infrastructure. The relentless, hard, sunshine of the last few days, which City workers were finding oppressive, had been absorbed by the City's stonework, the Corinthian columns of the Mansion House were actually faintly warm to the touch, the cobbled drop off area to the west of the great edifice was still emitting heat like the stones of a South Pacific beach oven, and the night air was balmy.

'Where are we headed, then?' said Sir Keith, 'to which one of your flesh pots darling?'

'Ronnie Scott's.'

'How cool is that,' said Sam.

'Sounds like a plan, I'll hail a cab.'

In spite of the warmth, Anglo-Saxonic habits die hard and Adele felt she would need her light summer coat, which she'd left in the car, before the night was over. She also knew its well-tailored cut showed off her figure and with the collar turned up her hair was always bunched up and ruffled in coquettish disarray.

'I'm going to get my coat,' she said, 'I'm parked a few minutes away. You two go on ahead I'll see you there.'

'Adele? You're not going to drive are you?' said Sir Keith.

'I just want to walk for a bit, pick up my coat, get my second wind. Then I'll jump a cab, too. I'll see you there. OK?'

'OK. If you are sure.'

'Sure I'm sure. Sam can't possibly walk in those heels. I'll catch you up.'

Sam smiled coyly. She angled her right foot momentarily. Her glossy royal blue five inchers were lashed to her slim feet with just the hint of bondage from only two straps, one around the ankle the other across the top of her foot. Her long toes appeared to be clasping the front of the soles.

Adele walked eastwards into the warm night. She could hardly bear to keep the image of Sam's feet in her head. She was very excited. She thrived on sexual jealousy. She was thrilled that Sam wanted her body and equally turned on that she wanted her husband. Or at least was seduced by his prestige. 'I can still pull,' she thought delightfully as she walked away into the warm night. She would return to Sam and Sir Keith looking a million dollars.

From a single UPVC window – which could never be opened fully – there was a cell-like room with a vista of stained drainpipes, drooping moss-filled gutters, and a whirring air-conditioning unit surrounded by a sea of paint-spattered asphalt, broken only by curlicues of razor wire over roof lights. It was a panorama of the metropolis repeated a million times. Windows in the greater part of multi-occupancy Greater London were for light, not views.

Rod McKay heaved in his bed trying to find a cool patch of pillow in which to bury his booze-heated head. A well-muscled arm dangled over the mattress conducting what cool air there was into his dehydrated torso. Around the bed a morass of crumpled foil take-away food boxes, empty Old Speckled Hen bottles, and cigarette packets, covered a threadbare paisley-patterned carpet.

His mobile phone throbbed its way across the bedside table and fell into a half-finished box of king prawn massala.

A large fist retrieved it and pressed the answer button.

'Shit, I'm covered in Paki juice,' he muttered, 'No nothing. What's up?'

Detective Inspector Rod McKay was being briefed on his next assignment.

A banker's wife had gone missing from her Canary Wharf apartment.

'How do we know she's missing?' asked Rod, wiping the cold curry on a used serviette.

'Should have been at a dinner with her old man last night'

'So she's missing after one night? You're having a laugh.'

'No, she's missing all right. The dinner was a charity supper at the Mansion House, she was excited, never been before, she'd bought a new outfit.'

'Well my missus wouldn't give a shit about that not if she'd had a better offer from some toy-boy.'

'But Mrs McKay hasn't gone missing, well maybe missing from your life, but that's hardly a mystery disappearance.'

'Steady, son. OK, I'm on it.'

Rod had no bedclothes to throw off they were already on the floor. Using his feet to clear away the detritus of nutrition he dropped onto a patch of carpet and pushed himself up and down 20 times. He accepted he would never do anything about his gut, he enjoyed beer too much for that, but he was proud of his biceps, although he'd resisted the vogue for covering them in Celtic scrollwork.

Since separating from his wife, Erica, who had custody of their eight-year-old son, Freddie, Rod hadn't too much cash left to spare on his weakness for sharpish suits and had been reduced to hunting in charity shops for discarded fashion labels. You could get last season's Jasper Conran in good condition in Mencap, British Heart Foundation or the animal rescue shops, in central London. Although he avoided Oxfam like the plagues they were trying to eradicate,

'It's like open heart surgery of the wallet in here,' he once told an astonished purple rinser in South Ken.

None of the suits were a perfect fit and the one he pulled on this morning had to have the too tight waistband pulled up into the soft tissue above his hips.

His two-bed, ex-council flat was back in his native Bethnal Green, about the last manor yet to become desired in the relentless gentrification of the capital. 'It'll never become trendy as long as my arse points at the ground,' Rod would say, 'the rag-heads will take care of that, Mohammad bless 'em.'

His car, a Toyota sports, he described as a 'poor man's Porsche', but was fast, easy to park and not worthy of covetous attention from envy scratchers.

His 'partner in crime' as he described his Metropolitan Police 'inferior' as he also described her, was Dippy Daud, a Somalian refugee who had worked her way up through Hendon Police College and lived in neighbouring Bow.

Dippy's most striking physical characteristic was a large bush of copper, corkscrew hair: 'People only want me for my hair,' she'd say self-mockingly, having read in an out-of-date women's magazine, some dial-a-doctor interview about female manes. Apparently men were strongly attracted to women with 'frizzy, reddish hair' because they sub-consciously thought it was pubic. However crackpot the psychology it had struck a chord with Dippy.

'All you gotta do is fasten some bling round your neck and people'll think your changing the guard at Buckingham Palace,' was Rod's cheery take on his inferior's hair.

'Jump in we're off to the city of glass,' said Rod as he picked Dippy up from her flat, 'and mind your barnet on my headlining.'

'What's the story?'

'Some banker's wife's done a runner. Master of the universe he maybe but in the safety of his own home he holds no sway. She was s'posed to have been at a posh nosh with him last night but has "disappeared"'

'Christ, so she's not even been gone 24 hours. Is this really worthy of investigation by top cop Rod McKay?'

'Yeah well she ain't no refugee from the Dark Continent. I mean if she was a pirate's daughter from, say, Somalia, we'd give it a month before checking it out. And don't take my lord's name in vain, use your own prophet when blaspheming.'

Dippy laughed, 'But nevertheless this is not a schoolgirl we're talking about. What is the risk assessment for an urbane banker's wife?'

'Low, but the reason we're even bothering, is that this banker is the banker for one of the assistant commissioners.'

'Neat.'

They joined a long queue of glinting traffic jerking towards the A12. Cars crawled over flyovers, cars crawled down into tunnels, cars crawled sideways into their lane from slip-roads. The hot, still summer's day was warped with heat from the metallic ants.

'Look at this lot, repeated over and over again in every road in every metropolis the world over and you tell me humankind is having no effect on global warming,' said Dippy.

'You make sure you unplug your laptop when you're not using it. We need off-set for the third runway at Heathrow,' said Rod, 'look at that: a top of the range Beamer, 0-60 in 4.7 seconds, top speed of 140 miles per hour, and he's just a snail crawling along the highway. Potty, in it?'

'At least it'll have air-con.'

'Air-con? And you're worried about global warming? Imagine on every road in every metropolis the world over in mid-summer. All shunting along sucking in the air that we breath, scrubbing it, washing it, squeezing the heat out of it, rubbing it with crushed ice and then blowing into the oxters of some hedge-fund merchant to stop his Charles Tyrwhitt minging, and what's left over we get to inhale?'

'I bet you don't unplug your laptop.'

'I don't have a laptop. I have top-lap,' Rod tapped a forefinger on his temple.'

The thing you were not supposed to notice about Sir Keith Moulding was his chin, or rather lack of it. He had trimmed a sparse goatee just below his lower lip but the white-ish bristles dropped from his mouth straight to his neck.

He was a small man in his early sixties who kept his hair cropped close to his head, a style more suited to a much younger man and a much younger head. Large freckles and age spots showed through his hair as a result. He dressed like a much younger man, too. But a much younger man who was out of date. Polo neck jumpers under formal jackets, trousers cut too close in the leg, which made his air-sole Chelsea boots bulge from his profile like surgical shoes.

A natural meanness with money coupled with a smart head for figures had seen his rise through the banking world. And he was well thought of by the board for not spending too much on business contacts. This had started long before when he was the head of a commodities department. Every time a deal was celebrated with a champagne lunch he'd get one of his staff to foot the bill: 'Would you oblige? Only I've left my credit card in my other jacket.' The put upon staff member never baulked at the request, for it would be signed off on expenses – by Sir Keith. But, of course, it resulted in accounts seeing high-spending staff and a boss who never spent a penny of company money, or his own for that matter. It also meant that there was no competition when it came to promotion.

As a man who was without a sense of humour he laughed publicly at the obvious to demonstrate he had one. He would be one of those to laugh out loud and clap in the theatre – although just a split second after others who got the joke first. He secretly loathed staff who were naturally popular among their peers, but nurtured them hoping their charisma would rub off. 'Your part in office morale is not to be overlooked,' he would tell them. But when the charisma failed to transfer he would dream up some disciplinary measure to use against their character in a bid to stifle it. 'You're very entertaining but you are stopping others from working.'

Ashamed of his wife for being a contemporary: he felt when people met her they realised how old HE was – he was dissatisfied at home and continually lusted after younger women at work sensing that with an abuse of status he could enjoy an affair. Yet he was too mean to risk it. His staff could see all this as clear as daylight and he was known as Bob to staff. Banking over bonking.

As Rod and Dippy entered his glass-walled office in the sky, Dippy noticed he had 1950s photographs of Ava Gardner and Marilyn Monroe in diaphanous clothing framed on his desk. As soft porn it was respectable because it was retro. It was a rather sad statement, one which Sir Keith believed said he had experience of beautiful women.

'Adele was very excited about the dinner,' said Sir Keith, 'I'd bought her the last cream dress from Reiss.'

'Reiss?' asked Rod.

'Yes the High Street clothing chain. Not what I would have considered the best, but that's what she wanted. That's what they all want isn't it?'

'Not sure what you mean'

'A minor royal's choice of this season's summer dress,' said Dippy, 'it was in the Standard. They're selling out apparently.'

'Oh. So has she failed to turn up before?'

'No.'

'What, ever?'

'Well we had our set-to's years ago.'

'Set-to's?'

'Yes, you know, the sort of thing. When the first glitter of marriage wears off.'

'Please explain.'

'Look, that was ages ago. We've been married 24 years all that's in the past.'

'The past has a habit of lurking around.'

'Well I can't see as it's relevant to now.'

'I understand that Sir Keith, but I've got to seek out any little wrinkles. Here you are a man at the top of his game, married, successful, dinners at the Mansion House, but when something unpredictable happens in a well-ordered life, something you do not understand, I ask where are the seams, where's the conflict?'

'All part of the great tapestry of life sort of thing?' said Sir Keith in a weak attempt at a joke. He was admiring Dippy's magnificent mane.

'If you like. So what happened years ago when the first glitter of marriage wore off?'

'Well I would carry on with the lads a bit. You know, in the pub too long, on the golf course too long, weekends away sailing. Adele hates sailing. I admit I carried on as though I was still a bachelor and there were times when Adele would simply take off. To teach me a lesson.'

'And have you been carrying on with the lads recently?'

'No, no. Two of them are dead – through booze – I myself drink very little these days and Adele and I, we are content.'

Rod looked down on the river some 30 storeys below. A silver ribbon of the Thames winding away into the heat haze over

Dagenham. An ant-sized tug was towing a lighter eastward, even from this height the brilliant sunshine picked out its wake in sparkles.

'That's nice,' said Rod, 'but a woman wants more than contentment.'

'Women want more, men want more. We always want more because we don't realise that most of daily life's little rituals are simply distractions, distractions from our time, because inspector, in the end, that's what we really want: more time. More time that is when we are really alive, when we are young, when we are having good sex, when experiences are new. That's when we want life to go on forever, at those times. When we get older we are happy just to be content.'

'Very profound. So this dinner, this dinner at the Mansion House, was that a new experience?'

'Not really Adele, had been before several times, but she enjoyed having somewhere to go where she could dress up.'

'So for her it was like being young again?'

'I suppose so. As I say she wanted a new outfit...although that's back to distraction again!'

'And the dinner, what was that in aid of?'

'In aid of Alzheimer's. It was a charity dinner to raise money for research into the causes of dementia.'

'Very worthy'

'Yes it is.'

'But still an occasion to dress up for ?'

'Of course.'

'Do you have a camera, Sir Keith?' asked Dippy.

'In common with the rest of the world, I do, yes. Would you like me to take your picture? A glamorous young woman like yourself should be recorded in her prime.'

'To sit me alongside Ava Gardner? I don't think so But what about your wife? I thought all execs had photos of their wives on their desks?'

'She hates having her picture taken.'

'Well we're gonna need some sort of image,' broke in Rod, 'now she's gone missing. If you're happy she hasn't gone AWOL again like in the old days, then it might suggest she's disappeared against her will.'

'Well done, he's very good isn't he?' Sir Keith said to Dippy.

'The best,' she said.

'We'll need a toothbrush as well. Toothbrush or hairbrush.'

'Good grief, he IS taking this seriously. Does that mean to say Adele may only ever return as an unidentifiable corpse?'

'Forgive me Sir Keith, but YOU don't appear to be taking your wife's disappearance very seriously.'

'I'm sorry. I'm trying too hard with the metro-man about town stuff. No, please, forgive me, but I've always wondered about DNA. How the hell is a jury supposed to consider evidence if they can't examine it? You can call in a boffin but it's only his word against whoever.'

'Same is true for all witnesses, Sir Keith, they take the stand give their account. This is cross-examined and the jury make of it what

41

they will. But let us hope it does not come to that in your wife's case.'

'Indeed.'

It was strange how London did not feel alien to Dippy Daud, a credit to its long-standing cosmopolitanism. The same could not be said for much of England beyond the capital, however. Yet even the growing popularity of UKIP had not unsettled Dippy, in fact she secretly sympathised with their sentiments on immigration. But then she'd come from a broken land where the rule of law was a gangster charter: everyone was equal under the barrel of a semi-automatic, except the men holding the guns, of course, but even they were equalised... by other men holding guns.

Before the civil war, her father had worked the reefs along the Puntland coast with lobster pots. As a child she'd often gone out offshore with him in his simple open boat, which was dragged up on the white, flour-like sand at the end of each trip. Dippy could still recall a sense of wonder as she watched her first blue-shelled, crustacean hauled up through the sun-penetrated clear water in a basket. It was as though her father had gone shopping at sea! The creature clawed myopically at the sunlight before being dropped into a well on the boat.

Such largesse had attracted other, more powerful fishing boats, as law and order broke down in the country and Dippy was increasingly left at home as her father and other fishermen welcomed those with guns aboard to help them scare off the foreign raiders.

Such a move was never going to end well and when some of those protecting the catch boarded a raiding craft to retrieve their lobsters and returned instead with crates of beer, nets of frozen meat, cameras, watches and mobile phones, the piracy began. Within months the foreign fishing vessels themselves were taken and their crews ransomed.

The idyllic world of Dippy's childhood had gone forever and she left the increasing chaos of northern Somalia for London where a well-established ex-pat community existed to help her make a future.

Grateful for a stable community and embarrassed by the bad name the Somali community was getting, thanks to a few violent drug dealers and an ill-informed press, she used her natural athleticism and her acquired sense of justice to work her way through Hendon Police College to become one of the first Somali nationals to join the Metropolitan Police.

Other women in the force warmed to Dippy's sociability and coveted her tall litheness, seeking out a flaw in her well-proportioned figure, and were satisfied to find that her feet were too long for such slim legs.

Rod was very proud to have an 'ethnic' as a partner and believed Dippy brought a sort of chic credibility to his street charisma.

'How many bangles did your tribe shackle round your neck to get your head that far from your shoulders?' Rod asked when first introduced.

'Enough to pay for my passport.'

Rod's superiors were nervous about their inspector's knockabout treatment of Dippy's origins, but even more unsettled by Dippy's nonchalant reaction as, although both officers had completed and signed off their online diversity training modules, no one was certain this would protect the force from any future legal claims of racist behaviour. They need not have worried: after the serious lawlessness Dippy had experienced in her home country she found such accommodation quaint.

'Fancy a drink, Dips?' Rod asked at the end of the day. He asked it at the end of every day, knowing that Dippy didn't drink and that his evening would not be hampered with her acceptance.

'Go on then.'

'You're not supposed to say, Yes'

'Well I'm distinctly underwhelmed by an old knight making a pass at me, so for once I'm going to take you up on your offer. I need to know I haven't lost it quite yet.'

'So you want to be chatted up by a toy-boy, eh? And there was I thinking I was the invisible man. All is not lost.'

'What do you make of Moulding? He doesn't seem overly bothered about Adele's disappearance.'

'Nor am I. She hasn't been gone long enough to warrant more than going through the motions. Standard checks.'

'Yes but it's out of character.'

'According to him. But supposing he's right, then it could be no more than mid-life crisis. She's buggered off with someone else, that's her crisis. He's not bothered, that's his crisis.'

'Isn't he a bit past mid-life?'

'People have crises at all times of their life. Look at you for example. You're having a drink with me.'

They drove into Fleet Street and Rod parked down a side road. Even though the   great newspaper offices had scattered a good many years ago, Rod felt comfortable in the former street of ink. And many of the old hands wandered back, especially to the Snooker Club, a basement-drinking den where deadlines were suspended, as journalists arrived in daylight and left in darkness. Or sometimes even daylight. Next day's daylight.

Some, the jobless, came because, like elephants they wandered back to the watering holes of history. Tricked by the ephemera of their trade they had not noticed their own lives slipping away as they lived in the hectic moment: pouring their all into the edition. Only to start all over again the following day. As they laboured at fish and chip wrappings, the bigger story: their own span went unreported until they became obsolete. The intensity of all those fast-moving days had camouflaged the slow-moving decades and suddenly the only way to make sense of their own story was to look back. Like the bound newspapers in the British Library their lives were as archive.

Others, still employed, returned because many police officers giving evidence in court still drank in the place, after all the Old Bailey had not moved.

The wedding cake tower of St Brides Church soared like a stone missile almost directly over their heads as Rod and Dippy walked down the alleyway behind Fleet Street, descended the worn steps into the little lane which curved down at the foot of the high graveyard wall and then disappeared into the bowels of the City through a doorway and, still descending, via a creaking wooden staircase into a drinker's dungeon, called the Snooker Club.

Dippy's eyesight took a while to adjust from the bright summer sunlight to the dingy, cellar-like bar. The darkness was interspersed with pools of light thrown over vast green tables from large triangular hoods suspended above them. Different coloured balls like molecules in a science construct clicked against each other as formally-dressed men summoned uncharacteristic concentration before poking them with long sticks.

'I thought the only people who wore ties these days were funeral directors,' said Dippy.

'And coach drivers,' laughed Rod, ' but these guys are dinosaurs, the few who survived the volcano of digitalisation.'

'Seems the ash is yet to clear, don't they know they're s'posed to smoke outside?'

'This is the lost world of analogue man. And Bernie wouldn't have a bar if he told them to puff on the pavement. Going to join me in a pint?'

'No thanks, just a lime and soda, but what are they doing here anyway, Fleet Street's finished?'

'You can get away with using two fingers on a computer keyboard, just as you could on a typewriter, but you don't survive long in newspapers unless you can bring in stories. Contacts provide stories and these old farts have contacts. Me, being one of them. Plus they've got the Bailey across the road and the High Court just up the street: the judiciary is still a fund of stories.'

'Scoop McKay, eh?'

'Who's the bush baby, Rod?' the query came through coils of smoke as a tall, lean man in a dark suit, leant on a pool cue while his opponent took a shot.

'She's Dippy, the sexiest cop in the Met, Bob.'

'Well I can see that, but what's she doing with you?'

'I told Rod I'd never seen a prehistoric monster, so he promised to show me one,' said Dippy.

Bob leaned over the table, took his shot then straightened up, pointed at Dippy and smiled.

'I think you've pulled,' said Rod.

'That's a shame.'

They sat at a long wooden table on upholstered bench seats and Rod ordered bowls of chips, and more bottled ale. Dippy spun out her soda. She could hear the unmistakable sound of somebody snoring. As her eyes got used to the dark she noticed a crumpled figure at the far end, chin on his waistcoat, one hand gripping his beer glass on the table in front of him. His suit jacket had rolled up newspapers

47

stuffed in the pockets. He was fast asleep. Dippy looked on in astonishment: sleeping was such a private act. A time to abandon the constraints of social behaviour, yes, but not in public.

'That's Jimmy McGlone. Don't wake him up unless you want to lend him a pony,' said Rod, 'once the court corr for the Evening Standard. Spent most of his working life at the Bailey. Made redundant two years ago, but with no wife, no kids and no room for them anyway in his basement in Bermondsey, he spends his evenings at the Snooker.'

'Still wears a tie, too.'

'Yes, he comes into Fleet Street every day as though going to work. Still pops in and out of the courts at the Bailey as well. The commissionaires let him in as they have done for years.'

'What does he do that for?'

'He needs to be in the know. His life has been spent breaking news. He would be the first to break the news from Court One, dictating his perfect shorthand note down the phone. And then 40 minutes later, seeing the lunchtime edition, still warm, emblazoned with his name, being snapped up by office workers.'

'Hot off the press, eh?'

'Indeed. It's like a drug to these guys. Then next day they need another fix of ink. Even though, in Jimmy's case there's no more by-lines for him. But he can still come into the Snooker and tell the lads what's happening in court. He's first, you see, first to break the news to someone. Anyone.'

'Isn't that rather sad? I thought Englishmen retired to their gardens?'

'Is it any sadder than gardening: nurturing plants that just take longer to die than newspapers? '

'At least you're in touch with the seasons.'

'Newspapermen don't notice seasons. What's a season, 90 days? That's 90 by-lines, 180 if the edition changes just once a day. What a flower show! Such intensity. Jimmy senses the day he stops breaking the news will be the day his life ends. Anyway he's Scottish and hasn't got a garden.'

'Very deep, Rod,' said Bob, his game of snooker finished, 'you're wasted in the Met. Drinks?'

'Aye,' the slumbering Jimmy woke up.

'Might have known that would resuscitate you. Ready for more mouth to glass?'

'Aye.'

Bob Packer returned to the table with a tin tray and dispensed the drinks. Bob was a newspaperman too expensive to pay off, surrounded, in the office, by much younger colleagues on half his salary working twice as hard who never went to the Snooker Club. But in spite of that he still brought in the stories. Tips, backgrounders, collect photographs. All from contacts – mostly police officers, but also Customs investigators, snouts and freelancers who trusted him to put them down for a credit.

These people did not write emails. You had to talk to them. Make notes.

Because his salary reflected the glory days of the unions, the management had tried to get rid of Bob by ensnaring him into accepting 'confidential' advice on alcohol abuse from the Human Resources team. He had seen straight through the ruse and despised the management. He didn't think much more of the editor, who loved his copy, but who failed to stand up to management pressure to rid themselves of high salaried employees. But none of this made Bob embittered he knew it was the way the world worked. It simply made him loath sophistry, of which he was more than capable himself, and instead embrace a reductionist demeanour.

'So, what are we missing?' asked Rod, 'what's happening in the world of the Express?'

'Hamas have fired rockets at Israel. Boring. A coach crash in Kazakhstan has killed nine school-kids. Boring. The Queen has eaten a puffin heart on a visit to Iceland: hold the front page. We've sent the Bristol corr to Lundy Island to try and eat another to get inside Her Majesty's buccal cavity,' said Bob, 'so when she visits Somalia what should we stock up on?'

'Camel yoghurt take your fancy?'

'Is that what made your hair curl?'

'You should try some, though I'm not sure once hair's gone grey it can curl anymore, 'Dippy laughed.

Bob smiled and pointed his forefinger, again.

'Porking Packer, you'll get nowhere with my deputy. She's smart as mustard old son.'

'It's fair to say I've reached the age where the only messages I get are from my service provider, but you can't blame a man for trying, Rod.'

'Now you've reached the age of invisibility why not use it to lech over younger meat?' said Rod.

Bob turned to Dippy: 'Where have you been all my life?'

'In the nursery,'

'Well said, lassie, well said,' spluttered Jimmy, cackling into his beer, 'I've never seen you lost for words, Bob. Hee, hee'

'It's all right for you, with your new lease of life.'

'Oh?'

'Yes, Rod. Our Jimmy's in love. What's her name again?'

'Marguerite'

'Is that Margrit, or Margaret?

'Marguerite. She's from Ostend, originally.'

'What's she doing over here? No waffles in Bermondsey.'

'She came over in the war as a young nurse. Married. Had family here. Husband died years ago and family all moved away. Here I've got a photo.' Jimmy pulled a scrotum-like purse from an inside pocket and unfolded a creased print. A large woman with grey hair and spectacles had beefy hands with strange puffy ends to the fingers, rather like a tree frog's, folded over a red print dress.

'That's madam. I know she's the size of a young silverback, but she's great in bed keeps me warm in winter...'

'That's lovely,' interrupted Dippy, 'there's no need to apologise for her,'

'And the flies off me salad in summer,' continued Jimmy much to the delight of Rod and Bob.

51

'She's good in the kitchen, too,' Jimmy continued, 'although she enjoys confectionary in an unconventional way.'

'Do we want to know this?'

'I don't think so but you're going to hear it anyway,' said Bob, 'he's engaged the loop again.'

'He's just being affectionate,' laughed Rod, 'he's a lovely fellow when you get to know him.'

'As Marguerite's no doubt discovered,' said Dippy. 'I think I'll leave you lot to your old speckled men,' she added.

'Must you go?,' said Bob.

'Take no notice of me lassie,' said Jimmy, 'or him.'

'Dippy, have another soda and I'll run you back to Bow.'

'No, it's fine. I know when it's man time. Seriously I've got stuff to sort.'

'Well I don't mind telling you now she's gone,' Jimmy went on, 'Madam likes it eaten out of her.'

'Dippy has shown intuitive timing,' laughed Rod.

'I've heard it all before, Rod, another beer?' said Bob

Jimmy was now excited: 'And she loves this English chocolate she says the Belgian stuff's too dark and poncy. She likes the commercial stuff, Kit-Kats and Yorkies and suchlike. But I introduced her to the Snickers, you know the one with the nuts in. She went crazy and later on when I was giving her one I felt something on me old pelvic gladiator and when I pulled it out there was a peanut on the end.'

Rod exploded a mouthful of old hen across the table.

'You filthy old git. Well, I s'pose it's better than dolly's hat off, dolly's hat on.'

Always better when someone else does it for you, Rod…as you well know.'

'Anyway what's going down at the Bailey, Jimmy?' asked Rod.

'It's very quiet. There's a long-running fraud case, which stops every other hour for legal argument. Not a bad murder in Court three, but no-one's covering it. It's just another domestic. The big let down for Bob was the youth club paedo who was acquitted.'

'Yeah, weeks of work on a backgrounder spiked,' said Bob, returning with more bottled beer.

'What was the story?'

'Evil youth club paedo lured wheelchair kids to sex den with ice-cream,'

'Not bad'

'It wasn't bad until today…he walked, so it went from a splash and double-page spread to a single column and that only after a quick re-write: Youth worker cleared in ice-cream bait case vows to help disabled.'

'Tame.'

'Agreed. If only the jury'd had a chance to hear the background…'

'Shame.'

'And what about you? Detective Sergeant Rod McKay of Scotland Yard, whose collar should be burning this afternoon?'

'More a case of hem-line than collar. Apparently some banker's wife's gone missing, according to the banker anyway.'

'Which banker?,' asked Bob, 'anyone famous?'

'Nah. There's no story in it for you. He's a bit of a chinless wonder. Sir Keith Moulding.'

'Never heard of him,' said Bob.

'Hang on that's a name I recognise,' said Jimmy, 'doesn't he own a string of old folks' homes?'

'No idea Jimmy. She only went "missing" early this morning so I'm not busting a gut on it, we haven't run checks on his background yet.'

'Yeah, I'm sure that was the name. I remember George – you know old George Grover who covered the High Court? – telling me about a visa hearing. A whole load of illegals working at care homes and several of them were employed by Memory Lodges PLC, which are owned by a Sir Keith somebody. I'm sure it must be your Moulding because old George was saying he was a banker as well.'

'Yeah well, where there's dung, human or otherwise, there's dough, I guess,' said Bob.

'The only person shitting himself in court was this Sir Whathisname, according to George, he was facing some serious financial penalties. But in the event got off on some technicality. It was an arse-covering exercise .The illegals were all deported, nonetheless.'

'Your like the frigging Law Society Gazette, Jimmy.'

'Years of practice, dear boy. Top up?'

'Malpractice, I think you mean. Yeah why not?'

Hervey Lamb called himself a fisherman. But the handling of nets, beam trawls or lobster pots were a complete mystery to him. He ran an angling boat, with twin outboard engines taking people who used rod and line in the name of sport to places quickly. He was a dilettante man of the sea because the estuary waters, to some extent, were safe and easy to access. The river was a place where the novice could learn by his mistakes. If you ran aground it was mud you hit, not rock. If the wind increased suddenly you were mostly under the shelter of land, the estuary being on the leeward side of England. The prevailing westerlies hammer the coasts of Ireland, Wales and Cornwall first. By the time they get to the east they are spent. And if the weather came in from the east he had 80 HP to call upon to whisk him back to sanctuary.

As for navigation, like so many modern mariners, Hervey had no need of chart, pencil and dividers, although he still had them aboard. He was a child of the digital age and embraced any piece of kit, which offered him a short-cut. His boat bristled with antennas, which provided signals for his electronic chart plotter, his fixed GPS, his AIS system by which ships found and identified each other, and his radar. He also had back up, hand-held GPS. He had made himself an expert with all these systems, not by reading the manuals, which was too linear an approach for a lazy mind, but by trial and error in use and by talking with others who had them of which there were many all buying and selling, trading and exchanging on 'FleaBay', as he called it, and other sites. His pals in the gaming shops of his teenage years, when weekends and evenings were spent in his bedroom committing electronic genocide, had shown him how to cannibalise the anatomy of receivers. 'Meteorites pock mark the satellites, but spotty geeks put a dent in the system,' Hervey liked to think.

His father, Joe, disapproved of his only son being spoilt by his mother's continual gifting of digital war games. 'He won't be able to fight his way out of a mulched burger box with all that junk,' he would say and obliged his son to spend as much time in a local boxing gym as he did on his games console. And, quite quickly, Hervey proved he could at least take punishment if he was not so good and handing it out.

He moored his boat up a lonely river, which meandered behind a marshy islet used by the MOD for testing all manner of weaponry. No-one could see what sinister goings on were taking place down behind the seawall, but red flags were flown on operational days when new shells were tested by being fired out over the empty sands towards the sea. Locals had long got used to the far off puffs of smoke followed seconds later by either a dull crump or a splitting bang depending on the range being shown to the prospective foreign buyer or the wind direction. These guns, their ordnance and materiel were on sale only to those who could sign end-user certificates to guarantee their use as defensive weaponry to back up rather than defeat the ballot box. That the Sunday newspapers quite often ran stories about British servicemen being killed by bombs and bullets manufactured by companies awarded gongs by Her Majesty for export excellence – a case of unfriendlies using friendly fire - were mostly ignored by the residents living in and around Foulness. The place provided jobs and stopped time. Foulness and its environs' perceived charm was imbued with a reassuring stasis. 'It hasn't changed since I was knee-high to a shell case,' Hervey would tell his customers as he ran them off into the North Sea for tope or bass. Occasionally the natives of this isolated corner of Essex were reminded of the game-changing power being tested in their midst. Once many years ago a shell mis-fired and came in over the village demolishing a garage, fortunately without harming anyone. More recently a sperm whale had got itself stranded out on the vast Maplin Sand where it expired.

Diggers were sent out to bury it but there was not enough time between tides to entomb the beast in the estuary mud. Next the local butcher and his assistants went out in an attempt to cut it up, but they too found themselves still sawing as the tide returned. In the end the MOD blew it up with a few coils of Semtex.

'You could smell it for months,' Hervey told his anglers as they chewed impassively on their sandwiches, half watching the little bells pegged on their rods. It was a story he trotted out when the fishing was not so good.

The old boat-building shed from which Hervey operated, was owned by his father Joe and had been built 100 years before. Its blackened

57

planking had sagged over the years, not helped by the removal of great oak knees, which angled between the sides and roof of the shed. These had been crudely chain-sawed off when a rumour went around the tiny hamlet, that they had originated from the Beagle, Charles Darwin's old ship which had incongruously ended her days here as a Coastguard vessel and was now under the marsh. The owner of the shed was a man who knew the value as well as the price of everything. He was one of a kind of ex-London entrepreneurs whose basements had been used for the shortening of shot-gun barrels, the tools of his trade, until the metropolis had become inviolate. Although there were no longer bobbies on the beat, it was not possible to bribe a CCTV camera. So Essex is where he and his ilk had drifted. A run-down old boatyard was not so different to a run-down old haulage yard. It was great place to store stuff, keep some heavy plant and come-in handy salvage. Old cars on flat tyres sat alongside trailer loads of old boats on flatter ones. If a mooring root was required the car would be jacked up, a wheel removed, filled with concrete, chain embedded and dropped out in the river with a buoy attached.

The lock-ups held welding gear, cutting equipment even an ancient foundry. The boats were hauled out of the river by means of heavy lift chain pulleys shackled to a gantry, wheeled down to the low tide edge and towed out again by an old tractor once they had been floated into position. On the Solent such an arrangement would have been condemned years ago. But Gunfleet Boatyard's workers were all the sons or cousins of the owner. Hervey, being the eldest. In summer they could be seen, shirts off, riding dirt bikes up and down the sea wall or throwing dinghy paddles for a large Rottweiler called Moose.

In the winter they wore trapper's hats and burnt driftwood, old ropes, even abandoned trainers on a huge brazier. It would take a very bold Health & Safety officer to try and make Gunfleet Boatyard comply with working practices. It was the perfect realm for Joe Lamb.

There was just one hitch, it had a public footpath running right through it.

Joe had let the brambles grow up around the signs, had erected a padlocked farmer's gate at the boundary of his land and, of course, Moose, had the freedom of the city.

On the whole it worked because the sort of pursuits which would bring folks out to such a desolate place were enjoyed by the petit bourgeois. Only people not fighting to make a living 'wasted time', as Joe saw it, rambling or twitching.

Joe's wife Betty lived in a care home, which Joe didn't visit any longer ever since the day he watched her like a little monkey, arms and legs hanging away from her body, as she was swung through the room on her lifting harness and deposited gently onto her automated reclining chair. Her trousers and cardigan could not hide the fact that her limbs were skinny from under use, making her large-boned skull look top heavy. Her short white hair was kept regularly washed and was lovingly combed back over her ears, this combined with the fact that her breasts had shrunk to nothing more than empty sacks of skin gave her the appearance of a shockingly premature school-boy.

As a resident of the optimistically-named Memory Lodge, Betty had spent the last three years, in front of a wall-sized flat TV screen tuned to daytime light entertainment. Nobody really knew what to do with dementia sufferers, but for someone whose synapses were swaying precariously like a spider's web in a breeze, daytime TV was unlikely to increase the mental Beaufort Scale and blow them away.

She had been deposited there by her son Hervey because his father could not cope any longer. He'd done his best as a 'sandwich family' as the Daily Mail had dubbed those whose parents had reached their second childhood before their own offspring had stopped playing with toys.

Hervey, who visited his mother once a week, had decided that Filipinos had nothing of the 'inscrutable East' about them. You could read their faces. And when Hervey ventured gently as to how long, er, people with dementia went on, invariably the carer's eyes would fill with tears. They did not want to talk about Betty in that way, they had formed a relationship with her, one that did not require verbal communication. The people looking after her now were probably closer to her than even the mother, she still called for, who died some sixty years before. But although he took comfort from the carers' attention to his mother, Hervey still felt a sense of guilt about abandoning her in a strange land. He was uneasy about what might be happening to her in his absence. When leaving he would stand at the doorway and wave goodbye, then stick his head back around the door-frame to see if his mother was still focusing on where he had just stood. If she was he would wave again and disappear. Then pop his head back round and wave and wink again. This he would do until his mother's gaze would eventually meander somewhere else: to the wall-mounted TV, the Fleur de Lys patterned carpet, the framed Vetriano print. Then he would leave.

Hervey had a faith in the Almighty, which did not extend to the Good Lord's subjects. Hervey never took anything – except the Gospel – at face value. He trusted nobody not even the family GP and deliberately eavesdropped the doctor while on the phone to his surgery before he accepted his mother's diagnosis.

At first Hervey thought the best way of fighting off his mother's disease was to pull her up on her misconceptions. 'How can you have a mother? You are 86', 'Your mother died in 1947', 'You can't go home to Mummy, she's sold the house.' He even drove Betty round to her childhood address to show her the new occupants coming and going. Occupants, which did not include her mother. At the time it seemed to work but as soon as she was back at Memory Lodge she would start calling for her mother once more. Hervey began to realise that questions were like a physical assault: Betty did not have the apparatus anymore to be able to answer them. It seemed that questions made her aware of this. Questions were a kind of ABH. Even the sort of rhetoric used in everyday conversation caused her confusion and mild distress. Questions required answers and answers are a cognitive process. Being battered with questions: How are you? What do you mean? What did you say? Which one?, only served to make Betty aware of her inability to make any sense verbally. Whatever perceptions she had were locked in her mind and could no longer be expressed.

So Hervey took a different approach and just went over old ground, repeating memories: the name of her childhood dog Buster made his mother's eyes light up. Soon Hervey was meeting Ethel – Betty's mum – and asking if he could take Buster for a walk in the woods. Betty smiled. This was a film recorded before the camera packed up.

And yet in spite of all this every now and then Betty would suddenly make sense, coming out with a sentence from nowhere like the swirling drums of a fruit machine displaying three cherries. But in the next minute, she would be back to random snippets which could be categorised as nothing more than miscellany.

But then one day Betty started talking again. Hervey had gone along on a Sunday morning as usual, with a bunch of yesterday's flowers from the Co-op. There was no point in wasting good money on fresh cuttings, she never smelled them any more.

As he entered the conservatory area where Betty and the other residents sat, the wall-mounted TV was broadcasting a children's magazine show about a visit to an aquarium. 'Fish live in their own poo,' said the presenter. No-one in the room was watching the show. Most heads were looking at their laps, wilting like sunflowers on a cloudy day. Except old Lucy who was staring, mouth open as usual, like a monitor lizard trying to cool down in the desert.

'What a job: collecting whale snot,' said the TV presenter as a mammal vet next appeared on the show.

Hervey surveyed the scene from the doorway and was surprised to see his mother was focusing on him. Unusually she had recognised him without hearing his voice first.

'Hello, mum.'

'If there's one thing I want, it's to get back to England,' the first sentence she'd uttered in months.

Hervey knew by now it was better not to contradict his mother so instead of saying 'You are in England' he said: 'Why's that mum?'

'You've got no idea what it's like here,' she said.

'Where's that, mum?'

'Don't you start. Germany, of course.'

Betty had, in the past, accused her carers of being 'torturers.' The harness they buckled around her with which they lifted her onto her hoist, she had seen as a 'torture chamber'. She had shouted at them when they undressed her. Images of neatly stacked clothes, shoes side by side had disturbed her: 'You will not strip me,' she had yelled. And when they lowered her towards her bath she had lashed out with her fists and screamed: 'Murderers'.

Personal care had become difficult to administer. Her remaining bottom teeth became a continuous ridge of sticky plaque, her toenails curled and her fingernails, though painted pink by the visiting manicurist, were full to capacity underneath.

Her husband had long before stopped visiting. A man who had lived by physical domination, he could not face the way of all flesh especially his own. So when she became violent Hervey had been called in and told that a course of sedatives might have to be administered, but he fought that. He spent many hours reassuring his old mother that she was not in prison, that her carers were not trying to punish her, that the webbing they fitted around her was to help her move.

Eventually as she deteriorated and the routine of the home became ingrained, her constitution became institution and she succumbed to a state of passive equilibrium.

'You've got to help me get back to England, Hervey. I know what'll happen, they'll get bombed and I don't want to die under rubble.'

'But mum no-one's going to get bombed.'

'Of course they're going to get bombed.'

'Who are?'

'The Hun.'

'Mum I'm not going to let anything happen to you. You mustn't worry.'

'No just get me away. Even if they're not bombed they will kill me. They are trying to kill me.'

As a youngster Hervey had often dreamed about killing someone. When he woke up the fear of being caught did not fade away immediately and he wasn't sure if he had killed or not.

Who can say what makes a man want to kill another? Actually *want* to. Greed, jealousy, advantage, revenge, all motives which can lead to the act. But holding the act as motive itself is strange, but perhaps not unfathomable.

Hervey was the second child born to a travelling family who were stationary. That is to say they were Romany stock, who no longer 'travelled'. The Gipsy caravan of popular myth was in fact a three-bed council house which the Lambs had been obliged to go 'respectable' to get. No more hunter-gathering of the ducking and diving kind. No more unpaid rented accommodation, moving on one step ahead of the bailiffs. No more purchasing brick effect wallpaper to 'repair' old ladies' chimneys with. No more red wool tied to the gates of homes with expensive dogs worthy of stealing. Joe and Betty, were about to become young parents so they went on a housing list, signed up for benefits, and before long were living in a two-bedroom, terraced home owned by the state. For old times' sake Joe soon burnt the wicket fence as kindling on the living room fire and had the front garden denuded of grass from the DIY industry carried out on two semi-cannibalised cars, covered in oily tarpaulins. He was good with machines and soon had the electricity meter rigged. To the master bedroom, where he kept bundles of cash, he fitted a hasp and padlock to the architrave. There was only one key, which Betty was allowed to use, but only when Joe was in the house. From the two motors Joe produced a runner, an old Vauxhall, and started operating a one-man taxi business. His prowess with mechanics led him around various car-breaking yards and later he started his own on a parcel of unwanted marshland, which eventually became the Gunfleet Boatyard.

Hervey's elder brother Nobby had an ugly face. It was just a slope of brow and long nose as though his skull was the shape of a Norman helmet. His eyes were oily, unsmiling and carried threat in every gaze. And yet he was soft, sentimental, friendly and kind. The ugly baby had been over-loved by Betty who was suffering a little cherish-fatigue when the better-looking Hervey arrived, and she was tired too from her 'homework'; electrical components which could be fitted together in a simple repetitive task and which became the innards of moving soft toys which she assembled each night while watching TV.

So unloved Hervey spent the evenings after school on the allotment at the back of the house. In a ruined shed was a broken glass box, which contained a stuffed trout. It was Hervey's pet and he 'fed' it moths, which he captured under jam jars before pinning them in front of the varnished fish's mouth. He liked to watch them flutter.

When Betty gave birth to a baby girl, the young mother was shocked when the six-year-old Hervey said: 'Do we really want her?' and realised that she should have paid less attention to the soft toys and more to her second son. To make up for it she bought him a puppy Doberman pincer, which Hervey called Julian after a posh boy at school whose middle-classness Hervey unwittingly coveted. Now the lonely Hervey had a creature with which he could bond. He was unremitting with his cuddling, stroking and petting of the puppy, which responded happily until it matured when it preferred to doze

66

rather than nuzzle. But Hervey still required a reaction so he started winding the beast up until one day it bit him in the face and was put down.

Hervey was pleased. It served Julian right.

From a young age, although tough, stocky and not to be messed with, Hervey was reluctant to uphold his self-respect solely with his fists. He was, after all naturally intelligent and had inherited his mother's humour: 'Where I live the ice-cream van comes round even on Christmas Day,' he once commented to his fellow grammar school contemporaries with a kind of grim disgust at what he saw as the cheapness of council estate life. He didn't really care about 'belonging' but did not revel in being an outsider either. He referred to himself as 'Lord Lino,' his mother's ironic phrase used about a neighbours' airs and graces adopted after being the first on the council estate to get his hallway floor covered. Hervey said he came from a long line of 'landed pikeys.' Other people's land. Those around him took care not to laugh too loud.

His stoicism impressed his classmates when on one occasion a charismatic art school master, Mr Batchelor, called Hervey out in front of his schoolmates and had him receive a slipper across his backside for being disruptive. Hervey had envied the teacher's popularity and had set out to undermine it. Now it was a showdown.

'Ouch' Hervey mockingly announced to the class.

'Bend down again, boy,' commanded the teacher.

He slippered him again, harder.

'Yaroo,' yelled Hervey laughing.

The teacher set at him again, again Hervey made faux calls of complaint.

By now the room was hushed. Clearly the assaults were painful, but equally clearly Hervey made light of them.

'Straighten up,' the teacher snarled, 'hold out your right hand, palm upwards.'

Hervey did so and received the full force of the slipper across his hand.

'Ouch,' he said.

Again and again Hervey was hit across both palms. By now tears of pain, which he simply could not prevent, were rolling down his cheeks. But he refused to stop entertaining the class. Mr Batchelor realised only too well that a Rubicon had been crossed, his relationship with his class had changed forever. In exasperation he ordered Hervey to go back to his desk.

'Of course, Sir,' said Hervey.

The story spread throughout the school and Hervey became a legend among his contemporaries, and a target among the teachers. Now wary of him the school closed ranks and it was left to an ex-forces PE teacher, Jim Laidlaw to teach Hervey a different kind of lesson to that provided by the curriculum. Mr Laidlaw was well respected in the school. Smartly-dressed, slim, fit, the ex-paratrooper cycled the six miles from his home to the to school each morning and over his cape still proudly wore his maroon beret.

Hervey didn't much care for physical education. He felt he didn't need it. Life at home was Spartan enough, his father a hard taskmaster, his mother producing austere meals, his siblings fighting for space around the hearth over the stolen coal. He was hardy enough and felt cross-country running, rugby and soccer simply a means of wasting personal energy. Hervey handled all these pursuits with ease but did not cherish them and was happy underperforming. He performed unnoticed.

So when Jim Laidlaw suggested he joined his boxing gym, he was surprised, but flattered.

For a whole term Mr Laidlaw taught Hervey how to box. He told him he was a star pupil. And just before the summer recess a boxing ring was set up in the assembly hall and three different weights from three different years were 'on the ticket'.

Hervey, as the main event, would be fighting Mr Laidlaw.

Only Hervey's youth carried him through the six-round bout. He did not land a single blow, but needed all that he'd been taught simply in defence. The skills of the older man, paid for by the British taxpayer and learned and practiced over two decades, were more than a match for the tyro. As his face started to swell up, and his midriff started to feel as though his organs had been par-boiled, Hervey suddenly felt marooned in a public arena. His training bouts with his teacher had never been so unremitting. He had never been hit so hard. Hervey was shocked at Mr Laidlaw's aggression, shocked at how serious he was taking this sporting bout. But he refused to give in. And he did not go down. Mr Laidlaw was hurting him, making mincemeat of him, and once again the audience was hushed. The fete-like atmosphere from the earlier bouts had ended, the friendly cheering abated. Even some of the teachers were looking anxious. And then Hervey realised. It was a set up. This was to humiliate him. Pay-back time. He was learning a real lesson now: never to trust anyone. It spurred him on. He redoubled his efforts just to stay upright and it was working, everyone could see Hervey was completely outclassed by an expert bully, but this fact meant that although he was losing the bout he was wining the battle.

Beginning to tire, the older man came in close: 'Where's the pikey now you need him, eh, Lamb?' he whispered. But Hervey smiled.'Yaroo' he yelled at the crowd and the boys went wild. They cheered, they shouted, they stamped their feet. Mr Laidlaw came in harder. Hervey deliberately dropped his guard and received three blows to the head. He could no longer feel the punches. Instead in a bloody slur, he shouted: 'Ouch'.

The crowd exploded with support.

As Mr Laidlaw and Hervey sat in their corners seconds before the last round the whole school started chanting: 'Her.. vey, Her..vey, Her..vey'

The teaching staff were powerless to stop the cries and were now beginning to hope they would mean Hervey survived the last round without serious injury. It had not meant to go this far.

Mr Laidlaw tore across the ring pummelling Hervey's torso as Hervey staggered away. But he did not go down. 'Ouch, ouch, Yaroo, Yaroo' he yelled in a red spray.

'Come on Gipsy, call yourself a fighter.'

Only when the final bell sounded did Hervey finally collapse and then only onto his stool.

When the embarrassed ref read out the points win by Mr Laidlaw the whole school instinctively shouted: 'Ouch, Ouch. Yaroo, Yaroo.'

Hervey learned from this triumph that he could take punishment, but he intended that no-one could take advantage of his resilience again by training properly at a local boxing gym.

Before he was in his twenties he had even fought in a handful of semi-professional bouts.

As role models went his father Joe treated Hervey as an equal. That is to say as a competitor. Even as a little lad, Hervey was seen by Joe as just another portion of stew not coming his way. At the age of 12 Hervey discovered the £8 he'd saved up from a paper round and kept hidden in an old book in his bedroom, the cash he counted every night hoping to save enough for a drop-handle-bar bicycle, was one night, missing. His father had used it for a drinking spree.

Later in life, as a working-man, he had loaned his father £2,000. He never got that back either. But he admired his father's ruthlessness. He believed Joe to be stoic, not soft, like Hervey. Compassion got you nowhere. Trusting people was just being stupid. Everyone had an agenda, that was life. You couldn't believe a word anyone said. Hervey started eavesdropping on his mum and dad, it was the only way to find out what was really going on, what they really thought. When that threw nothing up he wondered if they knew he was listening. Or if they had a kind of code.

Later he was the same with girlfriends. Especially if anyone else was around. He would feign tiredness and lie on the landing trying desperately to hear what was being said, hoping for a clue among the laughter that would reveal he was the subject of the mirth. He would get aggravated at silences. Were they whispering? Mouth-reading words and pointing? Then conversation would drift up to him once more. Or laughter. And he became disappointed that his own paranoia was not being converted into evidence.

A desire to punish became an overwhelming motivation in his life. He returned to the early solace he had discovered at Sunday School and retreated into the Bible where, with some judicious interpretation, he found much to justify a personal Holy War against those who would do him wrong.

Perhaps he could have, should have been loved more by his care-worn mother, but as he looked at her now, at her thinning white hair, her hideously toothless mouth and her food-stained blouse he did not hold it against her. Now that she was the one in a wheeled chair and not him, he felt only sadness. That was his love for his mother: sadness.

One of the carers in her navy blue nylon coat arrived with some soup for Betty. 'How are you Betty?' She moved a chair beside Betty's recliner and sat with the food and lifted a spoon towards the old mouth. But Betty refused to open it.

'Come on Betty. It's your favourite. Chicken soup.'

Betty's lips remained compressed. The carer's hand dressed in a Latex glove lifted the spoon towards Betty's mouth and gently touched it against her lips, hoping to tempt her appetite with the flavour. She swung her head to one side.

'Come on, mum,' said Hervey, 'you must eat. Here let me try.'

Hervey managed to get his mother to swallow a spoonful.

'It's good eh?' he said and handed the spoon back to the carer. Betty hadn't noticed the utensil was back in the hands of the carer at first. But upon taking the gruel she spotted the Latex glove. Now she shut her lips with the soup trapped in her mouth.

'Come on Betty swallow.'

'Come on mum.'

She spat the soup out, 'Get away Gestapo,' she yelled. For a frail old lady the volume surprised even Hervey.

'Beasts, murderers, get off me. You dare touch me.' she shouted.

Hervey wondered if the carer might have more success if he was not there. His presence might be emboldening his mother's mad outbursts. So he left the room and stood by the door, peeping around the frame. She stopped yelling and started taking the food. But he was also suspicious. Was there anything behind her ranting? She was supposed to have stopped all that. In any case it only happened when she had to be man-handled to be undressed and bathed. Sure he was Google-aware that Alzheimer's suffering went in stages and that early on those afflicted became aggressive even violent, but there had been something so adamant about his mother's outbursts that they seemed to go beyond ranting.

Memory Lodge had been by far the best care home the Lambs had found in their local area. The first one Hervey inspected was a dingy, poorly lit, late Victorian pile, badly converted into little, over-heated, human-sized cupboards joined by cold corridors. The second was so chronically understaffed that the smell from collapsing bowels made Hervey gag. He didn't even cross the threshold. Memory Lodge, however, was like a scruffy guest-house: a bit worn at the edges but bright, friendly, bustling. When Hervey told the manageress Betty was 85 she said: 'Just a baby then. We've got them living to their mid-nineties here.' Which hadn't really been the news he wanted to hear, but as soon as he recognised within himself such predatory hope, Hervey felt guilty and vowed to 'be there' as much as he could for his old mum.

Now he wondered whether others might not have suppressed their antipathy to his mother and allowed their true feelings to surface. The carers with their smiling, compassionate, Filipino patience appeared beyond reproach. But what if this was just a mask? What did they do to any resident who was awkward when no-one was there to witness it? Who would believe the confused ramblings of the mentally deficient, anyway? The blue Latex gloves they always wore had been distressing to Hervey at first. It seemed the carers wore them as though they were feeding untouchables. As though they might catch something. But of course the reverse was the case: they were worn to prevent the spread of bacteria from carer to resident. Dirty hands can be a killer to the vulnerable elderly. Everyone knew fingers carried microscopic germs.

'And prints,' Hervey suddenly said aloud.

He sought out the manageress, Edna Dawson, and explained that while he knew his mother was quite possibly delusional, she had after all mistaken the legs of a table thrown up by a night light as shadow on her bedroom ceiling for a giant spider, it was his duty to check on her welfare.

'Of course, Hervey, of course you must always come and see me if there's anything worrying you. I would if it was my mother.'

'She keeps talking about how "they" are trying to kill her, how I must get her away. It's kind of mixed up with wartime stuff...you don't think there's anything else to it, do you?'

'It's all in her mind, I'm afraid,' said Edna, 'It's a foreign country to them when they first arrive. Then there is an obvious foreignness as most of our carers are from the Philippines, as you know, and their English is not easy to understand. They do sometimes talk too loud to make up for this. This can unsettle some residents and it certainly irritates Betty as there is nothing wrong with her hearing. I think she is also fearful of the uniforms.'

Hervey smiled. Men in uniform had only ever meant, in the Lamb household, unwanted attention from authority.

'Also Betty's a fighter and will lash out for no apparent reason at times. But then in the next minute she is sweet and smiling,' said Edna, 'She is popular with all the staff as she is a such a character.'

Hervey felt there was a certain hollowness to her words, but said nothing. Memory Lodge was open to visitors at all times. Hervey was in the habit of turning up on Saturday afternoons. He decided to pay an unscheduled visit.

Joe Lamb had never lost the lustrous blackness to his thick hair, which, even in maturity, he kept combed back over his collar in a D.A. or duck's arse, as it was known in his youth. It included a buoyant quiff over his forehead. He was a bit of a dandy in his younger days, always sporting a smart mohair suit. And his love of winkle –picker shoes was something of a fetish. He was forever checking his flashy Billy Fury-style look in the driving mirror of his taxi, which he kept immaculate. The long hours of night work he put in had seen him quickly upgrade from the old Vauxhall to an almost new diesel Mercedes and it was while on the rank in his new motor that he picked up a fare which took him out of town. Three large men got in, all sat in the back, and the biggest one, a little drowsy, sat in the middle. They wanted to go to Crays Hill, which was a good 28 miles away and Joe asked for a deposit up front, as was his custom for lengthier journeys.

'Don't worry, drives, you'll get paid,' said the spokesman of the trio, a mean-looking man whose electric blue suit – which Joe could not help admiring – was a tight fit around the shoulders.

'I normally take some cash up front on out of town rides,' said Joe.

'Listen, cacker, the cash is at the destination. But I'm telling you, you'll get paid.'

Then the big man spoke in a slurred voice: 'I'm your guarantee, moosh. What's your name, drives?'

'Joe.'

He had little choice but to take the fare. It was all part of the cab driver's lot and Joe was philosophical about it. These were three of his own: gipsies and not to take them would cost more in damage to his taxi than a lost fare.

At Crays Hill they turned off the arterial road and Joe was instructed through a rat run of bungalows until the street petered out to a tree-lined unmade lane.

'Down there, drives'

'Look guys I'd rather just drop you here. This is a new motor and I don't want to risk bottoming out on any potholes,'

'You'll be fine, drives, just take it slowly.'

Reluctantly, but with a slow anger rising, Joe drove down the rutted lane for a thousand yards until it opened into a large area of open country surrounded by woodland. In this open glade were dozens of caravans – a couple of them burnt out – and cars littered the site in various states of cannibalisation. Engine blocks, tyres and car seats sat on the grass and incongruously in the middle of the area stood two very grand looking, houses.

'Here'll do,' said the blue-suited man and Joe pulled up. Two of the men immediately jumped out and dragged Joe out of the driving seat as crowds of men, women and children ran towards the car.

Joe struggled trying to land a pointed toe in the crutch of blue-suit, but the men laughed and lifted him off the ground.

'Put Joe down, now,' roared a voice. It was the slightly drunk bear who had been in the middle of the back seat.

Joe was allowed to stand and ushered into one of the mansions by the bear.

'They're only playing with you,' he said, 'nobody comes onto the site unless they are invited. I'm Amos Cory,' he pushed out a large paw, well washed, but with engine oil in the creases. 'This is Glenda, my sister.'

A slim, dark-eyed woman, who looked like a pretty witch, smiled.

'I know what the fare is to here from Southend Victoria. So here's forty quid for your trouble.'

Joe pocketed the cash. It was a result, but he was more interested in Glenda and gave her a smile as Amos packed his suitcase away.

'Southend Victoria, that's right by Argos where I work,' said Glenda archly.

Joe smiled at her again and was ushered back out to his taxi, which was surrounded by the mob.

'Make way for Joe,' shouted Amos and Joe got into his Merc. All the windows had been opened but apart from that the car was untouched.

'Now give him a tip,' commanded Amos and a shower of silver and gold coins rained into the car from all sides.

'Now go, Joe,' Amos said and Joe drove back out of the glade and onto the highway. He didn't stop until he got home. When collected up the coins he'd received a further £30.

Glenda was to become Joe's concubine not that such an arcane phrase was known or even used by the Lamb family. For many years Glenda was a secret, living her life at Crays Hill Farm with regular visits from Joe on Sundays, Thursdays and Fridays when he worked nights. Betty had him for the rest of the week when he was on days.

Joe's double life was revealed to Hervey when, returning home one day in his late teens, he found his father's natty suits, shirts and underpants strewn in the front garden and his beloved winkle-pickers, their toes cut off, impaled on the palisade fencing opposite which prevented the children of the local primary school, spilling into the Lamb's garden. A confrontation from Mrs Lamb was a force with a fury no known human had ever managed to endure. Joe's wardrobe could be replaced, but when Betty, armed with a claw hammer, turned her attention to the Merc he rapidly confessed to his dalliance although not to the fact that he had sired another son.

The legitimate need to nurture, cherish and raise a child had not been at the forefront of Joe's mind when he'd engaged in the effortless act of procreation with Glenda. So he'd chosen a name he hoped might address any lack of self-esteem the boy might suffer and in any case Gascoigne had been one of Joe's sporting heroes.

Over time habit and survival reconciled Joe and Betty helped by the fact that the sexual heat the adulterer had felt for Glenda cooled as she grew more witch-like than pretty. The eventual physical removal of Crays Hill Farm itself conveniently helped wipe the memory of Joe's indiscretion from his mind. It was cleared by the local council, as it had been built without planning permission, and Glenda returned, along with many of her clan, to her native Sligo taking her pre-school child with her.

———————

Lucy had joined the devils again. A desultory slashing of the wrists had secured enough attention from accident and emergency to make up for the love she was missing elsewhere. Her father had turned up and demanded she be moved to a private ward.

'I want the best for my daughter,' he hectored at which poor Lucy screamed: 'I don't want the fucking best.'

His second daughter was a complete mystery to Maurice Muir, a wealthy old money man who had used the cash to make new money with a successful helicopter upholstery business. Whatever the Latin was for 'specialise to accumulate' it should have been the family motto emblazoned on their heraldry alongside the upright trout and strutting pheasant.

Lucy had wanted for nothing. A Millfield education then a finishing school then into a digital web-design agency in Brick Lane, as a resource manager. What on earth she saw in Hervey, Maurice could never fathom. It was the only thing the two men had in common. But there was something real about Hervey. She was sick of her parents' lie of a life: dad virtually lived with his secretary, mum slowly drank herself into oblivion to drown out the betrayal, and she found her friends superficial and the people she worked with phoney. She had come across the menacing figure of Hervey one day while lunching at St Katharine's Dock. He had come up the Thames to collect an unusual party of City boys who wanted a jolly up on the river.

She watched Hervey assist the party aboard not succumbing to their jovial bonhomie and attempts at instant intimacy: 'Mornin' Skips what's the weather doin'?'

Among the regular collection of bystanders which always gather around harbours watching the movement of craft and the Japanese tourists brandishing their native Sonys to video tape the opening and shutting of lock-gates, Hervey sensed one spectator in particular. A tall girl with long, naturally orange-brown hair was leaning on the dockside chain fence. When Hervey stepped onto the pontoon beneath the fence to slip his mooring lines he looked up.

'Fancy a day on the river?'

That had been three years ago. Since then Hervey virtually lived in her North London flat at Bounds Green, only staying away to tend to late night angling parties when he slept on his boat or occasionally in the old shipwright's shed. He was too ashamed to bring Lucy down to the Gunfleet Boatyard where his father now pottered around breaking old cars. The boatshed stood empty of boats, but Joe used the seaward end for hanging hares or wildfowl to cure. The blood of these creatures dripped into a bucket, but had also, over the years, congealed around the nails used for their suspension. The bloody nails, the oaken beam, thrilled Hervey, who added an upright stake to the frame, and when no-one was watching, knelt to pray. He was too embarrassed to reveal his Faith to his metropolitan girlfriend and his makeshift chapel was strictly for private worship. Hervey's unorthodox Christian beliefs were not for sharing and revealed only when he was in the role of Christian soldier.

But in summer the pair made trips out on the boat, which Lucy loved. He would pick her up from the public floating pontoon at Gravesend. They explored the rivers and creeks of the Thames Estuary and twice made crossings of the North Sea. Once into Zeebrugge and up to Bruges and another time to Dunkirk. Lucy preferred the home waters jaunts. The open sea was in turns daunting and boring even though it did not take the powerful boat long to reach the continent. Once Hervey realised he didn't need to impress his posh, classy girlfriend with trips abroad, he was happier with the coastal excursions, too. It cost a lot less in diesel for one thing. On the boat, away from anyone else this unlikely couple bonded. Lucy found the detritus of World War II: the rusting gun platforms, the sunken munitions ship still filled with shells, and the sinister looking wreck of the Mulberry Harbour section which had never made it to the Normandy beaches, fascinating. The estuary was a place of mystery with its flat coastline marked with leaning, decrepit beacons, obsolete spider-legged lighthouses and winking buoys.

Out at sea Hervey relaxed his possessiveness and even started taking his prize partner for granted. Lucy, able to step down from the pedestal he put her on relaxed, too. She liked being part of the furniture, not revered.

But out at sea was as good as it was ever going to get. They couldn't stay afloat forever. Weekends and holidays over, shore life beckoned with jobs and mortgages and back on dry land their relationship ran in parallel lines of daily requirement, ruts of aspiration. Hervey kept his boat in Limehouse Basin when he stayed at Lucy's. It was a lot cheaper than St Katharine's Dock and Lucy loathed anything that smacked of City money and privilege.

Even though she gave him no reason to worry about her loyalty Hervey resented Lucy's workmates, and friends, envious of their easy relationship with his girl and acutely aware he did not belong in their world. Conversely he respected her father's antipathy towards him. Hervey was not jealous of Mr Muir. He was not a threat. Lucy couldn't stand him and so, perversely, Hervey always spoke well of her father. Always entreated Lucy not to be so hard on him, encouraged her to return his calls, get in touch.

Their sexual behaviour was complex. Lucy found Hervey attractive and did not hide her lust. She came on to him regularly and wanted to enjoy the abandonment of being dirty. It turned her on because she thought that was what turned him on. But Hervey did not want her to behave like that. He wanted her to be the unattainable woman, which he had managed to attract. But he also wanted to besmirch that. He wanted to fight her into submission. He wanted to violate her. The whole edifice of his fantasy collapsed if she made the running.

However Lucy enjoyed sex like a man does. Sex in and of itself not in the context of emotion or higher feelings: sensuality not spirituality. She was aroused easily: the width of a man's back, the deliberate promiscuity of youth, the freak-sized thighs of rugby players on the TV, would excite her. She enjoyed sex as a dog does, anytime, any place and unashamedly, although not with anyone. She was loyal to Hervey although he fretted about her sexuality because it fired her whole being and people warmed to her instantaneously because of it. She made everyone feel they were attractive. But this was completely natural.

'Your trouble is everybody thinks you're up for it,' said Hervey.

'That's not my problem.'

'No but I worry about you. I don't want some one taking advantage of you if you've had a few drinks.'

'What you really mean is you want to control me,' teased Lucy.

'No I don't.'

'Yes you do. You don't like me seeing other people. I don't mind you being like that. I like it. It makes me feel special.'

'I don't mind you seeing other people.'

'Yeah, but you don't like my friends, or rather you don't like me having friends.'

'Leave off. What are you talking about?'

'You get twitchy if I have a late night with the girls.'

'I worry about you, that's all, what's wrong with that?'

'You've got nothing to worry about they all know who my lover is, the mysterious Gippo, tough guy Hervey, the boxer boy. They're all terrified of you anyway.'

'I don't want them to be terrified that's absurd.'

'Oh I do, I love it.'

'And I don't mean I'm worried about that anyway. It's just that you are engaging, you do like a drink, it can send off the wrong message. And I do like your friends,' said Hervey plaintively.

'Yes, darling you like the ones that aren't erotically charged. You don't mind me going out with the ugly sisters they are not sirens. But you can't stand sexy Carol.'

'What have I ever said about Carol?'

'Nothing, you don't have to. When I come in after a night out with Carol and all the lights are turned off and you're in bed pretending to be asleep what you don't know is I've already seen your little face at the darkened window pane checking out the taxi,' she teased.

Hervey didn't like being played. It made him feel insecure, but it also powered up his libido. Lucy stood in heeled leather boots, which came halfway up her calf. Her legs were covered in purple tights, which took over Hervey's eye and carried his gaze a good way until they disappeared under leather shorts. At the crucial part there was a convex bulge.

'You're looking great,' he said.

'I know. I'm going out with Carol tonight, as it happens.'

'Well there's a surprise.'

'Meaning?'

'How come you never wear sexy gear when you're with me?'

'Oh, so now I've got to have your permission before I dress?'

'No, not at all it's a fair question. You dress up like a tart whenever you are not going out with me and you drink heavily and you stay out til the early hours is it any wonder I may occasionally look out the window worrying that you are getting home OK?'

'Yes, but once I've got home OK why are you calling up the cab firm to find out where I've been?'

'In case it's a dodgy manor,'

Lucy's top left one shoulder uncovered far enough to reveal a pink bra strap edged with black lace.

'Yours is the dodgy manner. Hervey you want me in flat shoes when I'm with you. Remember? You want me in long skirts when I'm with you. Remember? You want me to be this dumb deb. But that's what my father wanted. His idea of female allure is to have his daughter in sensible shoes and a check skirt staring winsomely out of Country Life. I did wear sensible shoes, a check skirt and I did stare winsomely out of Country Life. I was on sale just like the fucking houses. It's no different to an arranged marriage. But less honest.'

'Your father just wants what's best for you.'

'No he doesn't he wants what's best for himself. You would never believe the arseholes that read that shite. They're not looking for a spouse they're looking for a sponsor. Penniless wankers relying on posh accents to get them a comfy existence. They think you come with a stately home. It's not the damsel they're after it's the castle.'

'What's Carol after?'

'She's always on the pull, trying to find Mr Right, but she hates going hunting alone, thinks it makes her look a slut. With me she can have a laugh, pretend she's not interested in a potential admirer and play hard to get.'

86

'How very complicated. But if it's her on the pull why do you have to go dressed to kill?'

'Come on, women always want to look like they can compete, even if they're not after anyone. They are not going to go out with pals looking stunning while looking like frumps themselves it's just unnatural.'

Lucy enjoyed stretching Hervey's libido to breaking point. When she returned in the early hours she allowed him his pretence of sleep, but climbed into bed alongside him cocking a stockinged leg against his prone backside. It was all he needed to save face: she had 'woken' him up. Jealousy was his most powerful sexual stimulant and Hervey was never as huge as when he lay abed wondering where she was, who she was talking to, who was making her laugh...

Lucy loved such nights. She could party and flirt and drink knowing that back home in her warm bed was the badass Gipsy lying snorting in frustration like some crazed bull.

Hervey would lie there a meat missile between his heavy thighs, but he had the discipline not to fire it until he could go inter-continental – from his sovereign territory into hers. He would lie there throbbing in an agony of expectation. Checking the clock: 12.30, he'd stuff her mouth first. 0100, no just mount her. Then he would nod off. The longer she was out the more suspicious he became, the more he coveted this woman, but also the harder would be the violation. 02.30. 'You're gonna get it up the fucking arse you bitch.'

What he didn't understand was just how much Lucy craved his anger, how she stayed out deliberately to get the best sex of her life.

It was just an erotic teasing game. What she didn't understand was just how dangerous this game was. Because Hervey was waiting for a time to take violation further. He wanted her to be 'at it', and not loyal, then he could really let loose.

He had gone through her handbag many times, as she lay sleeping off her girlie's night hoping to find evidence of betrayal. He didn't know what he was looking for, but bar bills, the odd phone number scrawled on a business card, a taxi receipt, all excited him with the possibility of a double life and yet on their own meant nothing. Even so he made a note of the phone numbers just in case he could catch her out later.

Her mobile phone he was wary of. These things could leave traces of espionage. But she never attempted to hide it and as it clanged with arriving mail he would look at the missive before it went back into sleep mode. None of them made any sense, sentences disembodied from context, like his mother's, and everyone signed off with a kiss, kiss, that was just part of mobile culture.

While she was out he would also root through her wardrobe, checking through piles of heels, sniffing the instep, going through her knicker drawers licking gussets. And as punishment for leaving him behind he turned her sexier dresses inside out and rubbed himself over them. He pulled the tresses through his crutch, gently tugging them over his genitalia and backside, before returning them, right way round, on their hangers.

As he toyed with her clothes their sensuality aroused him and it wasn't long before the changeover took place. Hervey's nondrinking, boxer's training life had kept him fit and slim and he could get Lucy's French knickers on and also at least one pair of her stockings. They were wool hold-ups in blue and white hoops and he rolled and slid them up his tight legs. There was a Proms dress – larger than the others – peacock blue, which his boxer's waist could fit into. His deep chest suited the hang of the off shoulder number. He liked the feel of her clothes, but he didn't use Lucy's full length wardrobe door mirror to look at the whole. He liked to see his legs in the hooped stockings, he was excited by seeing his manhood folded and veiled under gossamer lace. But he did not want to see the whole picture, scared the fantasy would evaporate. By seeing himself in parts the clothing suited him. He actually looked good in them. From the parts, he was aroused by what he imagined was the whole image. Dressed in Lucy's clothes, dressed as Lucy he waited in bed for her return. Lucy the dirty stop-out. He fought not to ejaculate. Who was chatting her up? His penis probed out through the French knickers. He pulled up the silk ruffs of the proms dress, rubbed his hands over his crutch – both hands as a woman would – and tucked his erection back in. 'You dirty cunt.'

It was gone three in the morning by the time Lucy got in. She was only dimly aware of Hervey, now wide-awake from the latch closing and ready to be Lucy's lesbian. She kicked off her shoes, which disappointed him, and climbed into bed otherwise fully clothed and started drifting under the warm covers. Hervey was rampant and pulled her face towards his by her hair. She was snoring already.

'Wake up baby, look who's here'

She stirred, 'I am,' she slurred. Hervey ignored her fetid wine breath and pushed his tongue into her mouth. He loved it when she sucked his tongue, but she was gone. Too tired, too warm, she slept.

Hervey pulled up her skirt, lifted her prone body off the mattress and tugged down her knickers. He got out of bed and went to the bathroom. There under the light he checked her underwear. The gusset was wet to the touch. 'You filthy fuck. You gorgeous slut . Let me lick your cunt come.' His engorged cock pushed the proms dress out like a tent. And as he came he sucked the knickers. It was urine.

Hervey's new found penchant for being Lucy was let down only by the shoelessness: none of hers fitted.

Shoe shops were out of bounds. He did not have the front to buy oversized erotic female footwear from a youthful assistant. He felt more comfortable with an old granny, one of the invisible people, whose judgment, if it were made at all, counted for nothing in his eyes. Sexually spent they were already the departed as far as Hervey was concerned. So he was soon scouring charity shops for size 9 stilettos. He found a pair of black patent leather, strap-on, platforms, with lacing which criss-crossed up around the ankle, in the local Mencap shop. 'Some old tranny gone and got dementia,' he laughed solicitously at the elderly manageress.

'What dear?'

'These shoes, I need them for a fancy dress. Sad – must've belonged to an old transvestite, what do you think?' he said with false cheer.

'No dear, they was a man's,' she winked, 'he's one of our best donors. He likes to dress up as a woman, and just like us ladies he's always changing his shoe style. I've got a rack load out the back. Would you like to see them?'

'No, you're all right. It's only for a party. Just a one-off. It's just for a laugh.'

'Yes, dear well they'll fit you I should think. Mrs Laidlaw always brings in shoes which can open up, you know, so's he can get his feet in. Men have got broader feet than us. It's not just the Adam's apple you know.'

'Mrs Laidlaw?'

'Yes, dear. You can always tell by their hands, can't you?…or their feet.'

'Mrs Laidlaw, you say?'

'Yes dear he's quite open about it. He once came in with another one, Heidi, his name was, tall and a great shock of grey hair and she had such beautiful legs, what I wouldn't have given for a set of pins like that when I was a girl. But he's usually on his own, is Mrs Laidlaw, always has a laugh and a joke with us. Used to be in the army as well. It's a different world now, isn't it? Mind you it's always gone on. That'll be three pound and forty-five pence. Bargain really. Mrs Laidlaw only wears them once or twice – look at the soles they're still glossy.'

'Perhaps I will just take a quick look at the other shoes. There might be something even more outrageous.'

'Of course dear, help yourself, just in the store-room through there. You don't mind if you do help yourself, do you? Only I can't leave the counter til my relief gets here at mid-day.'

'No that's fine, thanks very much.'

Hervey pushed in through shelf loads of celebrity biographies, bin bags of old clothes, rack loads of smelly coats and shirts all with the hum of the last sweat. Terminal perspiration. The last living trace of a human being is one of decay, he thought grimly as he waded through cardboard boxes filled with obsolete conduits of music: vinyl, cassette tapes, and videos. 'These, too will have a grave soon. As landfill,' he muttered.

And then at the back of the store-room was a vast rack-load of footwear from ceiling to floor.

Peep-toe heels with worn insteps, ankle boots with gold studs missing, semi-collapsed kinky boots, all for small feet. Ladies' feet. Then, at the far right side, the shoes got longer. Funny how stilettos, once over-sized, stopped looking sexy, became a parody of sexiness. Butch-looking, brutal pointed toes, too wide, too long, too cumbersome to serve erotica effectively. The need to hold heavy calves five inches off the ground at a 45 degree angle dictated a build which was close to civil engineering. Not so much Jimmy Choo as Isambard Kingdom Brunel.

They were there in a more garish variety of colour than the authentic women's section: diamante turquoise, patent canary and lime green. At the end of the giant ladies' footwear section the rack held several pairs of old boxing boots.

'Does he come in often? Mrs Laidlaw?'

'On and off dear, on and off. In fact he's coming in on Saturday he wants to clear his wardrobe. So he's bringing Mrs Laidlaw's dresses this time.'

'Oh, right.'

'It's only cheap stuff, dear, you know from the market. It's not designer, nothing like that. That way he can keep up with the fashions.'

'Oh that could be useful.'

'What? For your party, dear?'

'Yes. I know some of the other lads from the rugby club bash – that's for charity, too, by the way, a charity fancy dress, will need stuff.'

'Oh I'm sure Mrs Laidlaw will have plenty. He always comes first thing usually just as we're opening..'

'Brilliant.'

'Do you want me to put his things by?'

'I'm sorry?'

'The clothes. Do you want me to put them to one side, dear?'

'Yes, yes, please let me have first refusal.'

'Not that with Mrs Laidlaw's sizes they exactly fly off the shelf, but you never know these days.'

On that Saturday morning before Lucy got up, Hervey was out of bed, showered, shaved and talcum powdered around the anus. Then he slid on the French knickers, rolled on the hooped stockings, pulled the proms dress over his head and set it down on his shoulders. He laced on the strappy shoes. And stood close to six foot off the ground. This time he did look at his complete transformation as he needed to get the blonde-pink-tinged wig, he'd bought from a novelty shop, adjusted properly, then after applying Lucy's pink lipstick. He took stock. He looked stunning. And immediately became aroused. Then he spotted Lucy in the mirror. She was fingering herself.

'That really does turn me on,' she said.

'But it's not for you.'

'Oh, please. Let me have you.' she advanced then knelt down in front of him and pushed her head up his skirt.

But Hervey pushed her away.

'It's not for you...maybe later. I'll see how I feel.'

'You're going out? In my clothes? You wear those for me no-one else OK?' Lucy was getting angry, 'I want sex, now, fuck you.'

'Hey, hey, calm down. I'm on a mission. I have to go undercover. I will tell you all about it later on.'

'Undercover as a fucking tranny? Are you fucking meeting some fucking queer?' she was getting hysterical.

'Hey come on, I let you go out dressed up.'

'Oh fuck off. You poof. you're not touching me.'

'I don't think you mean that.'

Hervey was right. Once the door slammed Lucy scrabbled for her vibrator, lay back and fantasised about her macho woman.

On the early morning tube station Hervey experienced a quiet sanctity. It was like being in an underground cathedral. A few

94

worshippers were half asleep and there was the occasional echoed mumble. Then came a breeze, which lifted the frills of Hervey's proms dress. 'Perhaps like the first train, the Messiah's arrival will be presaged by a breath of wind,' he said to himself.

He looked at his reflection in the rattling tube train window. The wig sat well on his shaved cranium. His fitness from years in the boxing gym had kept his face taut and with the rouge and Lucy's lipstick he appeared sexually desirable in a way that a woman might be described as handsome. There was clearly a question over his sexuality, which added a frisson to it. If you were that way inclined, you would be staring inquisitively and having solved the puzzle you would be even more strongly attracted to this person for being so overtly sexual. If you were that way inclined.

Hervey crossed his stockinged legs. Sheer, and with their shapely length exaggerated by the patent ankle bindings they led the eye irresistibly to an imagined conclusion. That journey's end might be a giant cock flattened up hard under a truss of black hosiery was what you hoped if you were that way inclined.

He recognised Jim Laidlaw immediately. She looked good. Older, certainly, and with a certain gauntness which emphasised the impressive jaw-line. But she wore a hairpiece which framed her face well. A titian bob. Her throat was skinny. She had clearly kept up the workouts which had prevented the neck piping protruding. She'd always had good arms and they were bared under a black velveteen dress with a PVC panel across the chest. The hands weren't so good:

fingers coarsened and buckled but she'd made the best of even these with glued on black talons.

As Jim Laidlaw carted in her clothing from her Mazda sports car, boot open on yellow lines, Hervey entered the shop and snatched a pair of aluminium steps, 'I'm just going to look at those on the top there, don't worry I can help myself,' he said as the elderly shop assistant came over to help. He climbed to the top to inspect some books on a high shelf and hitched up Lucy's ball-gown hoping his black French knickers could be seen.

Mrs Laidlaw came through with armfuls of clothing and laid it on the glass-topped counter.

"Morning Mrs Laidlaw. How are you keeping?'

'I'm well, Mrs P., I'm well,' and noticing the striking pink-blonde with underwear showing, added, 'and all the better for seeing your wonderful display.'

Mrs P gave a faux-shocked grin. 'Can I have your post-code again, love, for the tax-free gifting.'

'Of course, my dear,' said Mrs Laidlaw still looking up Hervey's skirt, 'you can have MY POST CODE. And I don't just hand it out to anybody,' she winked and pursed her lips, nodding towards Hervey, 'It's N 90 BG,' she said out loud, 'but keep it to yourself. I don't want the plebs in Edmonton to find out. I've got a flipping leisure centre at the top of my road, EDMONTON LANE, and who wants to smell the sweat of the great unwashed, not me. I don't want to see my great taste in glamorous couture being enjoyed by locals and as you know I always come here because you're so charming, Mrs P.'

'Oh you do make me laugh, Mrs Laidlaw. You know how to enjoy yourself, love. The thing is you're always happy. I suppose it's because you trans-dressers come out of yourself. Now what did you give me. Three skirts, four tops and a full length gown… your legs are too good to hide under that…oh and another pair of shoes. OK now I'll put your post code on all those items. N 90 BG.'

Hervey had taken the hint but did not need to follow his target to her home. Instead outside the shop he offered her a trip on the Thames.

'How romantic, I'd love that. But can you park there?'

'No problem, not for a hairdresser's car like yours,' grinned Hervey.

'Don't be bitchy sailor boy. Are we over-nighting?'

'Of course. We're going cruising. By the way can we be on first name terms? Mrs Laidlaw is very formal.'

Mrs Laidlaw grinned, 'I'm Jasmine and if we are over-nighting I must get a change of clothes and my over-nighting bag. And of course something for the boudoir. Is it en suite?'

'The master cabin is.'

'Oooh, the master cabin, I like the sound of that.'

Hervey explained he would need to get the boat fuelled up and would meet Mrs Laidlaw later at the dock. He passed on details of how to get to Limehouse Basin, where to park and the berth number.

'Your ETA at Carpe Diem will be 18.30. That will give us half an hour before the lock opens.'

'ETA, well you are the real deal, sailorman. But Carpe Diem ? How gauche!' Mrs Laidlaw laughed with delight, 'Why did you Christen your ship with the name of a beach hut?'

'I didn't,' said Hervey, 'that was her name when I bought her.'

'Her? Oh yes of course ships are she's aren't they, like me,' giggled Mrs Laidlaw, 'but surely you can change the name? Much as I admire the sentiment, it is rather a cliché don't you think?'

'It's bad luck to change a vessel's name.'

'Oh well Carpe Diem it is then, darling. I'll see you in the master cabin, at, what is the ETA in old money?'

'Six thirty.'

'Yes captain,' saluted Mrs Laidlaw.

It was low water when Hervey arrived at Limehouse Basin. He'd returned to Lucy's of course and changed while she was at work. Putting her proms dress back in the wardrobe, but stuffing the knickers, shoes, stockings and wig in a holdall which he put aboard Carpe Diem.

He climbed down one of the worn sets of 'stairs' to the river-bed. They'd been used by ferrymen rowing people across the river since the 18th century, but were now forgotten steps which disappeared mysteriously into the tide and were lost between high-sided warehouses, once packed with all the good things milked from the colonies of the east, but now decked out as fashionable apartments for those currently benefiting from London's atavistic rapaciousness. He walked along the little beach which ran beside the towering flats and which was studded with smooth and worn red bricks: legacy of the Blitz when the bombers of another European power fought for its own set of colonies and sent London's dock buildings tumbling into the river.

He skimmed a stone out across the now flooding river. It pattered over the water until buried by the wash of a high-speed catamaran carrying City dwellers down river to more high rise, but ersatz 'warehouse' style flats at Canary Wharf, South Dock and Woolwich Arsenal. From their digital work stations to their gated communities these well paid, high flyers robotically moved from screen to screen via portable screens.

Hervey watched them tapping at their phones as the ferry whisked them by. They sensed that living beside the river was cool, desirable, but they knew not the great tide's pulse. Whether it was coming in, going out, spring or neap, stilled by the raising of the Thames Barrier to prevent their homes flooding, or racing to let the flood waters above bridges escape to the sea, mattered not. The catamaran went at the same speed whatever the tide was doing. The river was just another road.

Since meeting Lucy, Hervey often walked along the river at low water. He liked it here. Nothing stopped the river, it came in with plastic fish boxes on its back, maybe they'd drifted all the way from Holland, but anyway marine flotsam. It went out with bobbing tree limbs swirling down the reaches, maybe all the way from Gloucestershire, but anyway the jetsam of terra firma. This muscular conveyor could carry you anywhere, could drown you in a trice, could shine a reflected sun in your face. It glittered under the moon.

It was reflected a thousand times in the Babylonic towers of Canary Wharf. And yet it was ignored. It never stopped, it would go on forever. Atoms of its might washed against the footings of the Golden Gate Bridge, the fangs of Cape Horn, the mangrove roots of New Guinea.

Hervey's reverie was broken at Wapping. The tide had crept over the worn bricks and denied him further strolling. He watched the tide streaming around a weedy pile. Watched it climb the greenheart finger, close over the hanging mooring rings, lift a ragged rope gasket. Here it was that Captain Kidd had spent three tides lashed to a gibbet after his capital punishment.

Hervey rubbed a hand over the weedy pile and lifted the rope gasket, pulled it taut then let it drop, the metal made a dull clang and sent up a herring gull at the water's edge.

He walked up the narrow beach to the brickwork embankment and spotted a capsized and half buried shopping trolley: a forgotten reveller's joy at the sound of a splash. He wrenched it free of the sand and looked at the length of chain used to tether it to its fellows. He pulled out his Leatherman and used a blade to force open the link fastening it to the handle and packed the chain snorter in his jacket pocket. He climbed the next set of stairs beside the Old Town of Ramsgate pub and emerged into the street. A Porsche squealed by over the cobbles. He walked back to Limehouse through valley-ways of converted warehouses.

Back aboard Carpe Diem, Hervey placed the length of trolley chain on the saloon shelving and rummaged through his toolbox to pull out two snap shackles. He unscrewed the pins at each end and fitted them to the chain. Then he slipped into the French knickers, rolled up the stockings over his firm legs and laced up the platform shoes and set the wig neatly over his shaved head. Over his naked torso he draped a black lace throw and sat on a saloon berth thinking about late night Lucy discovering Mrs Laidlaw in her bed instead of Hervey. He would watch, he would encourage, he would tease them until like baby thrushes they'd be fighting for his worm.

'Hello? Sailor? Is anyone there?'

'Come aboard,' shouted Hervey.

'I fully intend to,' giggled Mrs Laidlaw, and placed a five inch heeled, gold leather boot on the deck of Carpe Diem. She hauled herself into the cockpit and Hervey could see up through the companionway, that she was wearing a gossamer pink bikini beneath a black PVC skirt, fishnet stockings and the knee length boots. Hervey's knickers stretched with lust and were thrust aside by his cock which clearly liked what it saw.

'Come below,' he said, 'you must come down backwards that's the seamanlike way.'

He watched as Mrs Laidlaw's long booted legs found a footing on the steps from the cockpit into the cabin and her convex PVC posterior lowered into the saloon.

Mrs Laidlaw turned round.

'Able seaman Jasmine reporting for duty. I say do you greet all the crew to that?' her eyes glistened with heat.

101

'I'm just piping you aboard. All new members of crew have to sign the articles,' said Hervey waving his erect meat.

'And there was I trying to remember whether Gregory Peck tied sheepshanks when there's no need for knots as you've already landed Moby Dick,' said Mrs Laidlaw, her eyes dilating.

'Like all women I know how to spoil a man,' she said coupling a buckled hand around Hervey's penis.

Hervey watched the black glue-on nails wrap around his manhood.

'I lived with a he-man for many years who really loved me. He used to make love to me on black silk sheets. He used to stroke me with an ocelot fur glove. He adored me for what I could do to make him feel like a real man. But I grew older and he wanted a younger model – all girls face that. But I've still got it,' she said her face filled with the joy of seeing what she had produced in Hervey, 'haven't I?'

'I'm still so very sexy, aren't I? Do you think I'm really very sexy?'

Mrs Laidlaw watched the lustful hatred fill in Hervey's eyes.

She knew he was gagging for her and loathing himself for that. And it turned her on. She was a woman. This is what women experience. The one and only hold they have over the dominant sex. Sexuality.

'I know the angel of resentment is battling with the demon of lust. That's girl power,' she giggled kneeling down and sliding Hervey's bell end into her salivating mouth.

Hervey pulled her by her wig and her head went willingly down fully onto his cock. She was happy with the huge meat deep into her buccal cavity, sucking until she was gagging but not with Hervey's semen – although that was plentiful – but with a restricter around her neck. She could hardly breath as the chain snorter was shackled around her neck and she pulled up , unable to swallow. The spawn spilled from her mouth, not part of life-making biology, just a sleazy fluid.

Mrs Laidlaw's buckled hands went up to her neck trying to loosen the chain.

'Fock, fock, get it off,' she croaked looking at the de-wigged Hervey and in a momentary terror of recognition bolted for the companionway. But Hervey had also shackled a length of rope to the necklace, which was lashed to an eyebolt for the cabin table. Mrs Laidlaw was yanked up short and fell over backwards, snapping off a five- inch heel as she fell. She could not reach the companionway ladder without choking herself. She was obliged to crawl back into the cabin to take the load off the chain.

Hervey helped her up onto a saloon berth. Mrs Laidlaw realised she would have to sit quietly or strangle herself.

Hervey pulled off Mrs Laidlaw's wig. The ageing head of Jim Laidlaw was bald and peppered with brown speckles: the freckles of youth which had expanded into darker blotches between tramlines of wrinkles which had the aesthetic misfortune of running fore and aft across his pate instead of across it. They looked odd. His hair was white around the ears which themselves had grown long and fleshy with bristly lobes.

Hervey looked and was repelled. He quickly stripped off his ladies' wear and put on a lumberjack shirt, boiler suit and toecap boots. As though a working-man's garb put him back on the right side of sexual inclination.

He looked at Jim's hands, bent, arthritic, coarsened, with too thick fingers for the badly glued on black nails.

'You're gonna need to keep warm,' said Hervey, 'tuck this around you,' he threw a grubby sleeping bag at Mr Laidlaw.

'Arvee, why?' Jim said.

'Don't talk now Mr Laidlaw, just get under the rug.'

'But why?'

'Just cover that tat. NOW,' shouted Hervey yanking the tether, 'Do what I fucking say. All right?'

'All rye,' said Jim and slowly, to avoid putting tension round his necklace, tucked the bag around his chest and legs.

Hervey approved. 'You'll need gloves too,' he said, 'it's cold out on the water.' He handed Jim a pair of orange boxing gloves. 'I'll help you lace them on.'

Mr Laidlaw was now bound and gagged and tied to the leg on the saloon central table. His hands in the boxing gloves had no way of trying to untie the bindings. Now Hervey could unshackle the chain snorter.

Carpe Diem nosed out from the lock into a surreal green lawn of algae floating on the surface of Limehouse Basin entrance. Hervey watched dispassionately as his boat mowed a black wake through the lime-coloured bloom, which broke up from the ferry wash out in the Lower Pool.

He turned seaward and started motoring down through Limehouse Reach with the glass towers of Canary Wharf smoking at their summits as air was conditioned for the storeys of brokers on the other side of the panes.

Moneymen rattled by on the overhead toy-like railway, which weaved around the towers which have sprouted up in the seed beds of the old West India and Millwall Docks where all sense of tangible commerce has disappeared. The smells of spice, tea and tar which once spilt from lifted sacks, now a commodity icon on a computer screen. Unseen, untouched, invisible. Physically dealt with somewhere else, by someone else, compartmentalised, containerised.

Carpe Diem rolled around the edge of the Millennium Dome and steered for the Thames Barrier's glinting silver knight's visors. On the Woolwich side of the river Hervey was given a green light to pass through and the boat's engines echoed briefly against the barrier's vast battlements.

Below the real estate protected from rising sea levels by the great dam, lay a wasteland of obsolete industry and marsh. The silted gates of the Royal Docks crumbled beneath the City Airport, the capped off red piles of the partly-demolished Becton gas works stood like the Terra Cotta Warriors on the side of the river, too much work required in their removal. Ford's abandoned car plant, a brown field site awaiting investment. A pair of listing lighters hung in the tide their cargo battens rattling, and their half empty hulls banging as they rode to the fast ferry wash.

Police car sirens sounded far away somewhere over Thamesmead.

Hervey had read how when excavating the footings of a new housing estate in Plumstead, developers had found skeletons in chains. They had died aboard the old prison hulks and been buried in their manacles.

'What a bastard place,' Hervey muttered, 'this great world city seen as a bastion of liberalism was as rotten as any fledgling metropolis in its day. Its civil advantage built on the corpses of thousands just like the pyramids.'

Perfidious Albion could as readily be applied to domestic affairs as international, Hervey thought.

A muffled complaint broke Hervey's reverie.

Mr Laidlaw was trying to speak.

Hervey switched the helm to autopilot, made a sweep of the river to make sure all was clear and went below. Mr Laidlaw's gag was dark from saliva as he tried to talk. Hervey thought it odd his eyes were not registering alarm.

'I'm happy to take the gag off,' said Hervey, 'but you need to understand that it will go straight back on if you start yelling. Not that it would do you much good. We're in the middle of the river and the engines will drown your shouts anyway,' Hervey knew this to be a lie. Engine noise on a boat muffles talk between sailors, but away from the boat itself conversation can be heard quite clearly as crew speak up to make themselves heard over the propulsion.

Mr Laidlaw shook his head to confirm he would not be shouting.

Hervey removed the gag.

'Look I know what this is all about,' gasped Mr Laidlaw, 'all those years ago…at school.. the boxing match. I know I gave you a pasting, but I actually saved you from exclusion. The other teachers wanted you out…' Mr Laidlaw gasped for a drink.

Hervey handed him a tin mug full of water.

'By giving you a good hiding I won them over to your case. They felt pity for you. Said I'd gone too far. You were rehabilitated.'

Hervey looked out of the companionway, Mr Laidlaw could tell he was mulling his response.

'So you think that Mr Batchelor, who also gave me a good hiding, would not have been suspended on the spot had he assaulted another boy? Another boy who'd reported the attack to his parents? To parents who gave a shit?'

'I can sympathise with that. Both my parents are dead,' said Mr Laidlaw, 'but they were dead to me when they were still around. Having a child was a hindrance to them. A resented expense.'

'So you took it out on another child?'

Mr Laidlaw ignored Hervey and continued his stream of consciousness.

'I can remember my father's face when on a rare occasion he spent time with me. Utter boredom. He'd sit in the park while I played on the swings, look at me go so high, or down the slide, look at me going face first, or on the roundabout, look at me doing a hand-stand. He just read the paper. I'd go to the far end of the park and watch him from behind a bush to see if he was concerned, like other kids' dads. He'd just look round shake his paper and start on the

107

crossword. I'd watched other parents go crazy if their kids were out of sight. With him I could sense he hoped I'd gone forever.'

Hervey watched a tipper lorry's unsteady climb 300ft up a road of rubbish which wound up a landfill site on Rainham Marshes. At the summit it shed its load. The crash of the drop reached him a good 20 seconds after witnessing the discharge. Seagulls swirled over the litter as a bulldozer cranked into place to level the trash.

'So you want to beat kids up to get your own back?'

'No, Hervey, no. I was, am, skewed certainly. My mother was no more interested than Dad. She just did whatever was required to please him, which included isolating me.'

'So you're taking it out on society. They fuck you up your mum and dad and all that.'

'Hervey. I just had to get away from home as soon as possible. The only job on offer for a sporty type was the Army. Men living in close company discover each other's weaknesses quickly. Mine was my emotional inadequacy. I cried easily. I was bullied mercilessly, but because there was no mum and dad to run to, I got used to it. Even started enjoying it. It seemed I belonged. It seemed people cared enough to notice me at least. I learned to love men there. I had partners. Real ones. I had a family at last.'

'You are just an old man dressed as a woman,' said Hervey.

'There is something very real about heels and hosiery,' said Mr Laidlaw, 'they are accessories for sex. It doesn't matter who wears them. Their function is simply to excite, to be obvious, to make a raw statement…'

'Like dressing to kill?' smiled Hervey.

'Yes, like dressing to make a killing. Many women like seeing men in such accessories, for all the same reasons. The only women who object are those who feel their sovereignty's been breached. Men who aren't afraid to explore understand this, too. It's just clothing.'

Lorries glittered nose to tail as they chugged across the great span of Dartford Bridge. Carpe Diem's engines echoed beneath the soaring arch. 'A sailor's eye view of the M25,' said Hervey looking up at the concrete spans passing overhead.

'Look Hervey, I think I can read your mind. You want a re-match, yes? You want a fair fight, this time? I can see you are as fit as a butcher's dog, while I'm, as you say, an old man now. You can get even. I know a gym we can use.'

'Did you think the fight unfair then?'

'Well it could be seen that way. I mean, you have me here for a reason. But, you're right, the fight wasn't exactly unfair I had trained you up after all. But I wouldn't blame you if you *thought* it was.'

'But why do YOU think it was?'

'Well, as I say, I'm not saying I do, but it could have been perceived as being unfair...you might have felt it was unfair...'

Hervey turned the wheel to avoid the Gravesend foot ferry, which appeared to be ranging across his bow.

The steel white sides of the ferry rolled close.

'HELP,' yelled Mr Laidlaw.

Hervey flicked the boat onto auto-helm, leapt below and nutted Mr Laidlaw, spreading his nose across his face and knocking him onto the saloon floor. Before he could move he shackled the chain snorter around his neck again. And went back to the wheel.

The ferry rolled away across the river towards the Tilbury landing stage. People stood on the deck staring at their phones, a young couple were hugging each other, a youth stood one foot on the guardrail, holding his bicycle steady. All ignored the swelling river. It was as though they were on a bus.

To mask Mr Laidlaw's continued muffled grunting, Hervey turned on his cockpit CD system playing For Those In Peril On The Sea and steamed down Gravesend Reach. Past the old tavern with its name painted on the roof: The World's End, past the abandoned power station still black with coal dust: its turbine nemesis twirling away ineffectively further down river, past the lighter roads at Denton, where the great steel boxes swung booming against each other on the wash of a passing tug and turned north into the Lower Hope, a reach named after the tangible as opposed to the spiritual, and therefore, base feeling of medieval sailors: if they could fetch this far up Old Father Thames they were guaranteed deliverance from the sea's perils. Further down there was still a chance of being ensnared on one of the great river's shoals. Here the river started to widen out and Carpe Diem sailed on into a great flatness of sea and sky where giant cloud forms dominated the estuary filtering sunlight down to the far horizon. Moses himself would not have looked out of place sliding down the great sunbeams which pierced through the ballooning cumulus.

'The natural world order. God's world order...' muttered Hervey as the boat steamed ever eastward into a space defined each mile by less of man's structures. It was as though he was sailing into a giant painting, rather than a journey to the centre of the self.

The tide was now running against Carpe Diem. The mudflats of the Blyth Sand glistened in the low sun, awaiting to be covered once more by the new flood. Tiny birds strutted across the banks drilling their beaks into the surface for worms. On the opposite bank strange metal giraffe-shaped cranes dropped grabs into the holds of container ships the size of toppled Manhattan tower blocks. Hervey kept the boat running over on the Kent shore out of the tide. Not that his powerful engines could fail to push the boat easily over it, but there was no point in burning extra fuel.

The Black Widow beacon passed by far away on the marshy shoreline at Yantlet Creek, scene of Hervey's youth, this isolated creek had been where he had camped as a lad. The black steel beacon had a wide triangular 'skirt' topped by a sphere which looked like a giant head. Years of neglect had seen the 'head' drop down over the neck of the marker leaving it resting on the top of the 'skirt, The Black Widow was now a scrofulous old hag.

For Hervey the carefree days of youth were about not being held responsible for his actions. He started huge beach fires on the marsh burning driftwood, old rope and then topped off with plastics: bottles, fenders even discarded trainers, Hervey's blazes sent up black boiling clouds of smoke and once invited attention from a Coastguard helicopter which hovered overhead as Hervey hid in the long grass behind the sea wall. Here it was that an old piebald pony had been tethered to a marshland fence and Hervey had practiced trying to knock it out with a right hander, managing only to break a finger on the nag's jaw. Those happy times came to an abrupt end after a few summers when he read in the local paper of a youth being jailed for a serious traffic offence. He was 19. Hervey read the news column in horror: he was now 19 himself: old enough for prison.

He smiled at the memory as Carpe Diem motored on down the estuary and he nosed across towards the Maplin Sand.

By the time he passed the Blacktail Spit buoy there was no land in sight. Just a few tall chimneys on the far horizon astern and ahead the dark Swin Channel which winked at him as night fell and the lights of the navigation buoys showed the route down along the sands.

A small boat at sea at night is a bleak place and one where sailors climb into themselves. Hervey was no different and he started to consider his childhood. He reached the conclusion that it was empty, ideologically. He had never been cherished, taught how to behave, or what to believe in. His parents themselves were immature and without ideas. Survival day-to-day from bills, by cutting corners, gaining temporary advantage mendaciously. That was the language they understood. But Hervey sensed this was low. Surely human kind amounted to more than scale-free creatures which ducked and dived like the lowest form of life? It was why he had drilled down into the Bible, to find a voice he could believe in. The book's role models were extreme but well-defined.

And bibles were freely available in prison. He had served two sentences in young offenders' institutes for affray and ABH during his teenage years, but he had spent the time usefully in building up his boxing skills, and dedicating time every day to grapple with the repetitive family trees, the hatred directed toward murderers and thieves, but equally to liars, and adulterers and the harsh punishments meted out which he found in the bible.

In this book bad people didn't get away with it. However smart they might be at covering their tracks God was always looking.

The crucifixion, Hervey learned, was not just a punishment reserved for Jesus, it was a common method of dealing with all criminals in ancient Rome. 'There will be judgment,' Hervey muttered to himself.

The charts depict Dengie Flat and the neighbouring great sands of the Thames Estuary as cow brown and when they are dried by a hot summer sun they do take on such a warm colour. But under grey skies, they, too, are grey. And dawn saw Carpe Diem dried out in a grey desert. The only perpendicular feature was a tall post sticking from a sunken barge which was at an exaggerated angle in the shifting sand.

Shackled to the post was Mr Laidlaw. Hervey had led him off the stern of the boat and across the sand by his chain snorter necklace and lashed him to the post. Mr Laidlaw's ankles were lashed to the foot of the post, his neck shackled at head height. Mr Laidlaw had to keep his head tilted upward to breath. But his hands were left hanging loosely at his side, but they were useless, tightly laced as they were in the boxing gloves.

Once he was trussed to the post, Hervey knelt down and re-tied the laces of Mr Laidlaw's boots.

'Your predilection for kinky boots will give you extra time,' Hervey said, the blackness in his soul creeping up through him like earth through the multiple skins of a leek.

Mr Laidlaw shouted over and over again as Hervey watched dispassionately. But he realised his situation was hopeless. The cries could not be heard ashore on the lonely sea wall over a mile away against the westerly wind, assuming there was anyone there to hear them.

And so his yells carried away on the wind, over the Buxey Sand, over the Barrow Sand, over the Little Sunk Sand over the Long Sand where only seals roamed. From there the fretting North Sea ran eastwards for almost 100 miles to the coast of Holland.

Mr Laidlaw watched the dried sand take on a moist appearance. The tide was returning and the Raysand Channel was starting to fill, bringing the water table up beneath the vast shoals and spreading in a damp arc across the sand. When the water itself arrived Mr Laidlaw watched it creeping speedily over the rilled sand, halting momentarily as it formed little puddles here and there, before spilling over onto the next stretch of ribbed mud and moving forward relentlessly, a creamy scum of cockle spawn riding its back. The tide, when it swirled around his calves, was momentarily a relief: like the support experienced from a warm bath. But soon a chill crept through him as the tide rose. By the time it reached his groin the water was too deep for the affect of the warming sand to make any difference to its temperature and Mr Laidlaw drew a sharp breath as the cold water covered his scrotum.

The rising tide slapped Carp Diem's bottom – like some grotesque applause – before lifting her clear of the sand. Mr Laidlaw watched Hervey sitting on the stern of the boat dispassionately. Hervey wondered if it was true that drowning was peaceful. He was impressed with Mr Laidlaw's manner. He was dignified. A soldier to the end.

'HELP. I BEG YOU HERVEY.' Mr Laidlaw suddenly shouted and Hervey watched fascinated as the tide slapped Mr Laidlaw's chin.

'FOR GOD'S SAKE'

Mr Laidlaw stretched an inch or two higher as the ball of his left foot worked its way backwards through his remaining unbroken boot and stood on the heel of his stiletto giving him a momentary gain in height.

His boxing gloves waved in a futile way at the sea level climbing towards his mouth. Momentarily he was able to punch the tide away from his face.

'HARBLEY,' he gurgled as the rising tide covered his mouth.

Hervey watched the water cover Mr Laidlaw's head, lifting his dyed wig hair like some grotesque weed. His gloved fists threshed at his throat momentarily then dropped.

Hervey started the engines, hauled up the anchor and headed south-west into the breeze. All that could be seen astern was an old post sticking from the sea like Excalibur's sword. And the tide kept rising.

What started as a dust-swirling, willo-the-wisp over the great plains of the Mid-West, became turbo-charged, by the heat rising from sun-baked deserts of corn destined for burger buns, and convected eastward as a tempest given top spin by the Coriolis effect. This swirling, invisible cone of air roughed up vast acreages of the Atlantic Ocean before arriving to disturb the Billy Fury-like quiff of Gascoigne's fringe as he tried to impress the girls of Galway. How he hated the always windy Galway, the first recipient of weather, in Europe.

'In Galway the weather's so rubbish it takes the rest of Ireland to drain and tame it,' he said, 'but by the time it gets to Turkey it's nothing but a welcome breeze on a hot afternoon.'

As Gascoigne grew up his wanderings around the craggy coastline of Connemara had begun to pall. When he was a lad the next bend in the coastal path had kept him going as he hoped-for buried treasure, then, more realistically, a dropped coin, finally the fantasy of a sexual encounter. But every corner provided just a change in wind direction, or a blast of rain. The great outdoors was no place to hang out looking sexy.

Galway with its bloody black beer and bar ballads was a nightmare of parochialism for an egocentric young man who found the pale skin and coarse dark hair of Irish girls to be retarded evolution: 'The historic and contemporary relentless barrage of weather has held them back as cave women,' he once said to a friend, 'and look at their mothers: prematurely grey lard bags with broad feet. Ugh.'

Gascoigne had noticed that the thicker and blacker a girl's locks were, the quicker they became greyed and the more bristly as they aged. 'Who wants a woman with grey cactii for ear lobes and nostrils like bog brushes with alopecia?' he said.

Gascoigne wanted to be walking among lissom young blondes which a great capital promised. A capital far from the battering Atlantic weather fronts which produced – on both sides of the English Channel – hag-like Celts in oversized jumpers, and horrid flat, trendy leather sandals who smoked too much in an effort to keep warm. No one wore high heels in Galway. And so he travelled to London, rented a room in a shared flat in Earl's Court, and got a job as a barman in the nearby Gloucester Hotel.

In London he soon realised that his mother was wrong. His 'gift of the gab', which she told him gave him an advantage, was more than matched by the eloquence and wit of others. Even his ethnicity left him with no advantage. There were hundreds of Irish in London. Many of them with just as nice hair, many taller, and many better looking. Gascoigne's 'edge' was left behind on the windy shores of Galway Bay. He was just another employee in the catering trade with a white shirt and waistcoat owned by the hotel.

His days off were in the week and he spent them wandering the streets of South Kensington with its multitude of distractions: pubs, coffee houses, and beautiful women by the yard. Back home a nice pair of legs would have him double-taking perhaps once every couple of days. Now he did not even need to sight up the same girl twice, another would be along before he had time to turn round.

And it was so easy to window shop. Gascoigne could gawp all he liked as almost without exception these sirens were locked to mobile phones as they walked.

His chance arrived with Beth, the new receptionist at the hotel. She was from some forgotten backwater in the Fens equally as dull as Galway.

'If you like gormless Poles with dirty fingernails who smell of sugar-beet, it's great place for a lass,' she told Gascoigne in the staff canteen.

'If you like women with hairy armpits who smell of black pudding then Galway's a great place for a lad,' said Gascoigne impressed with this woman's confidence and uncomfortably realising that even his 'gift' could be topped.

Beth was unlike her Fenland neighbours. They were stocky and heavy limbed from lard fried chips, marrow fat peas and saveloy sausages, a diet designed to counter the dreariness of their surroundings and to make up for the constant disappointment that it did not match the lives of those they watched on TV, then read about the following day on the websites of popular newspapers. These unprepossessing blimps had to paint on beauty via the tattooing salons which glowed with cheap promise in most shuttered Fenland towns. To parade their allure meant baring shins and arms and even feet all year round. Like corpulent peacocks they waddled around in cut-away polyester clothing, happy at least to belong.

Beth was reared on the same food but was blessed with a metabolic rate like a human blast furnace: carbs were atomised instantaneously and nothing was laid down to spoil her length with width.

Her slimness, tallness and subtle blondeness was a kind of ideal. The kind that the needle men created on the limbs of the peasant stock. Her natural beauty caused her no problems with her contemporaries, she had grown up with them and they were, once, all the same height. All with the same bodies. Although she grew beyond the stunted forms of her brethren she was one of them and they were pleased to be exposed to glamour at first hand, glamour that was theirs.

But Beth was not going to hang around in the peaty swamps where cabbages, carrots and leeks were encouraged by sluices, which held back the toppling seas of the Wash, to fight for life. The straight lines of man-made dykes which, even in a fast-moving car, you could never outrun, were utterly depressing, a geometry of agriculture, whose symmetry was so quickly familiar she despised it. There was nothing random about 'going for a walk' in this terrain. All spontaneity, such topography could once have offered, was combed into submission by fat-tyred tractor rakes for the battalions of root vegetables.

'People talk about battery hens,' she said to Gascoigne, 'but what about battery potatoes. Row upon row upon row of bloody veges all reared skywards year in year out with nothing taller than a McCain's Chips sign pegged in the dirt. Imagine that as a landscape. You can see for miles and there's nothing to look at.'

At night jerking lights flashed in the distance as giant machines crawled like drunken wasps across the muddy fields. 'They never stop working, shift after shift, cudgelling, probing, turning Mother Nature's face, coaxing yield from the loam. And there's mud everywhere, mud tracks on the roads, mud on the pavements, mud splattered up the fronts of the houses.'

Beth loved the metropolis where boulder clay was put in its place: beneath the footings of London. Her heels no longer sank into the ground they clicked on paving.

To earn extra money she took a waitress job in a nightclub three times a week. It was upmarket, that's to say the sort of men who went there had the wealth to make up for any inadequacies. The punters of Mayfair were uglier, older and far richer than their counterparts in Soho. Along Old Compton Street the venues nestled alongside gay bars and were plastered in garish sinage, with touts shouting you in. It felt safe from its overt ribaldry. Mayfair was very different. Posh, understated. You had to know where to go. It produced aficionados of sleaze. If Soho was for the package holidaymaker, Mayfair was for the international traveller and most of them were from the Middle East.

Beth soon discovered that her duties included using her natural charms to entrap men into purchasing more alcohol than was good for them. Although she didn't drink she was obliged to simper coquettishly for champagne on which the mark up was astronomical. The idea was to dangle the promise of intimate liaison behind a set of moving Moet goalposts.

Most of the punters were benign. Many were ersatz princes of the desert. Back home their regal robes and headgear held the common Bedouin in thrall. In London their corpulent bodies were stuffed less ceremoniously into Savile Row suits. Here they could drink alcohol, fornicate with men or women, and leave the prayer mat rolled up in the cupboard. But here only money gave them authority. The divine right of cash.

The Oasis Club was membership only for licensing reasons, but members 'joined' every night with a fee of £50 half of which was refunded upon exit, if the punter could be bothered to ask for it. Usually the members were aroused to such a degree that they forgot about it. The club rule was that no hostess could be touched on the premises and that any arrangement between a member and a hostess was a private affair to be consolidated outside the club. However no girl could leave the club until one am or after and any member who wished to take a hostess onwards from the club had to get a 'release form' from the night manager signed by both parties.

Beth wasn't interested in taking matters further and always got a cab home alone when her shift finished until the night she met Farzi, tall and lean and dark and for the Oasis, young.

'What is your gas doing under our sand, eh?' he said with a wide smile.

'Sorry?' said Beth.

'Your gas. The UK's gas. The energy upon which your society relies. You want it so bad.'

'Do we?'

'You do. It's inconvenient that it just happens to be under our sand.'

'Why's that?'

'Because you have to overlook the way we live. Did you know that if you wore a skirt that short, in my country, you would be arrested?'

'Would you like some champagne?'

'I might like some champagne. I can certainly afford champagne even at these prices because you buy my country's gas.'

'And if you drank champagne in your country would you be arrested?'

Farzi beckoned Beth to sit at his table. She did so and thought his brown eyes kindly.

'I should be, but I won't be.'

'That sounds fair.'

'Yes, it's not fair, but that's the way it is. Alcohol is forbidden in my country, but in exclusive places, expensive places you can drink it secretly. And no-one gets arrested because it would undermine the law.'

'But that's bonkers. Surely drinkers undermine the law by NOT getting arrested?'

'No the point is that nobody drinks alcohol in my country. If there were arrests it would mean they did. And if they did then we might encourage radicals and they would stop us providing you with your gas.'

'I will remember that next time I fry an egg.'

'YOU will remember it but your Government choose to ignore it.'

'That's governments for you.'

Farzi smiled and Beth warmed to him. His was not the forced charm of so many contemporary Englishmen she'd met with their exaggerated guffawing over nothing very funny, their theatricality about prosaic daily details as though they lived the most fascinating lives and their loud insistence it be shared in public in a pathetic bid to seem interesting.

She shrank away from people who drew attention to themselves. Farzi was quietly spoken, with those friendly brown eyes and that easy smile, his was not the leering gargoyle of cynicism, the crude mask of FUN worn by a show-off, or the goon-ish upturned mouth of some metro clown. Farzi's smile made him appear as though he was watching the antics of a child and genuinely delighted by it. It made him seem happy!

It was very attractive.

'So if I order champagne you have to drink it with me, is that how it works?'

'I don't drink, well not alcohol, although I'm not supposed to tell you that.'

'Well thank-you for revealing the secrets of your little empire. What can I get you to share this oasis with me?'

'I don't need a drink as long as you buy champagne for yourself.'

'I cannot sit drinking alone. Selfishly supping in front of a guest.'

'OK a lemonade. It's almost as much as the champagne anyway.'

'Ah, yes, humour the great English secret weapon. With this you once ruled the world, until Bismarck came along with his blood and iron.'

'Which we countered with bloody-mindedness and irony?' it was Beth's turn to smile.

'Very good!' exclaimed Farzi, 'you are wasted in here.'

'No you're wasted in here, or you're supposed to be.'

'Ha, the Germans fire mustard shells and you kick a football at them.'

'Soccer - another of our secret weapons.'

'And even when you lose you win, look at Dunkirk.'

'Little ships for little shop-keepers.'

'And the bombing of London?'

'Donna versus blitzkrieg,' they both laughed.

'If there's one thing that defines the British it's the V-sign,' said Beth.

'Ah, of course Churchill's famous cigar-holder.'

'No, no he adapted the V-sign by turning it palm forwards to make it palatable for the press. The real one is the other way round and was used by medieval archers to show the French they still had the digits required to rain arrows down on them. Those fingers were cut off by the enemy to render such artillery useless. So when we used it it was a taunt.'

'I see, that's brilliant.'

'Yes and it's still used today, still very powerful even now, it means go away in street terms, although over the last few years just one finger means eff off, which is even more dismissive.'

'And only one finger is required to pull a trigger,' said Farzi who had hardly touched his champagne, 'but dismemberment in the west's latest conflict involves the removal of heads. A little more difficult to deal with.'

Apart from a large nodule on his left cheekbone, over which Beth suppressed a desire to squeeze, Farzi had a fine-boned almost aristocratic face. She could imagine his wise gaze scanning the sandy horizon where all perpendiculars zig-zagged in a heat haze.

His suit was woollen, dark-blue with a large-squared feint check. Expensive but modest unlike the shiny silver-grey mohair suits worn by the older men in the club who were trying to look younger.

Nor were his shoes ostentatious, just straight Oxfords, not the chisel-toed Chelsea boots or buckle-sided loafers preferred by the older Arabs.

'But why do you show yourself like this?,' said Farzi.

'Like what?'

'Such beauty should not be displayed. It should be honoured. It is from God.'

'I'm not on display, as you put it, it's just fashion. What is wrong with enjoying your beauty?'

'It is holy. It should be kept for respectful eyes. The eyes of a husband.'

'You're not my husband and you are enjoying it.'

'You are right, Beth, and I am not comfortable with such voyeurism. It reveals I am unworthy of sight.'

'Leave off! Or perhaps you just don't like others seeing your appetite. Maybe why you come out at night?' she teased, 'but why should you feel so guilty about being red-blooded? British men don't.'

'But British men do not respect women. There is a cultural chasm between us, it is true. In my country women are covered because we respect them.'

'Do they have a say in the matter?'

'It is the law, that is true, but they are happy. Happy in modesty and in the fact they can go about their daily lives without being treated as "objects" which your feminists say here.'

'But these poor women are forced by the laws made by men to be *their* objects. To be disrobed when it suits men: like a troupe of dancing girls when the theatre curtains are pulled back.'

'No, no. Not at all. Women are free in the home. Only in public will they wear the hijab.'

'But I'm sorry, that would make a western woman feel even more like an object: that she could only disrobe when in her partner's realm, an exclusivity for his eyes only.'

'But the home is safe. It is where people share themselves respectfully,' said Farzi.

'In the west it would be seen as possessiveness, that men-folk don't trust women to be themselves without being "on display" as you put it. If a man in this country kept his wife like some bloody parrot – under wraps until he wanted to admire her plumage – it would smack of insane jealousy.'

'Beth you are a funny woman and it is your humour which should be on display. That is the real you.'

Beth was flattered. She hadn't realised she could talk like this and to a prince.

'Goats dressed up as kid,' the night manager would sneer to Beth as the older, playboy customers rolled away in the early hours, 'fucking fossil fuel Pharoahs.'

And in the early hours of the morning that she left the Oasis with Farzi, the night manager held his tongue but pulled a face at Beth behind Farzi's back as if to say 'Are you sure?'

She gave him another very British signal, a thumbs up and they left in Farzi's chauffeur-driven Bentley. She had made it clear she would take a lift home from him, that she would not be going anywhere else.

When the car stopped halfway along the road, which cuts through Kensington Gardens, Beth was not unduly worried. The car had a driver. But when Farzi put his arm around her shoulders she shrugged it off.

'No thanks.'

He tried to kiss her she pushed him away, and tried the door. It was locked.

127

'Let me out. Now.'

The seat she was on had been slowly going down she realised. It had become a bed and Farzi was on top of her. She fought him but was soon pinned down by the driver. Farzi ripped off her dress and started licking her shoulders. She managed to knee him in the groin and he started punching her in the ribs. Furiously, frenziedly he went from beating her with his fists to caressing her with his tongue which he plunged into every orifice while her arms and head were pinioned by the driver. She screamed and the driver sat on her face while Farzi punched her again using serious blows.

The driver suddenly yelled in pain and leapt off Beth. She had bitten through his trousers and deep into his buttocks. Suddenly headlights lit up the road. Beth was thrown from the car and her dress thrown after her. She watched the Bentley roar off. A half dressed Farzi looked through the back window at a lone figure holding up two fingers.

Shoeless Beth calmly walked home through the park.

It took two days before the bruising came through. But when it did it was shocking. Beth's whole torso was dark blue.

'God,' said Gascoigne when she told him the story. 'Jesus Christ,' he said when she, with modesty, showed him the bruising.

'So what are the police going to do?'

'I haven't been to the police.'

'You're joking?'

'No. What am I going to say? That some bloke called Farzi from the Middle East beat me up? He didn't actually rape me. There won't be any DNA. He's got a witness to say he dropped me off safely...'

'There's DNA in saliva,' said Gascoigne gently.

'I bathed him away as soon as I could. The cops don't take rape seriously, they'll take attempted rape as a joke.'

'But Beth they will take ABH seriously. You really have to report it. You need to log it. Even if they don't get him this time...he's clearly a beast, he'll do it again to someone else and how do you know he won't come back for you?'

It did not surprise Beth that Farzi did come back. She knew he was smitten, knew, too, that Farzi was the sort that treated women in this way. That the women from his desert kingdom expected to be covered over in dust-sheets until the prince was ready for love. Knew that he wanted her to be hidden away from the lusting world. That he could not bear the thought of her beauty revealed. And on the same Thursday night the following week he turned up at the Oasis. Beth had not gone to the police, nor had she told the club manager what had happened.

But as he came in she slipped out and made a note of the Bentley's registration. It had diplomatic plates from Qatar.

She then phoned in sick on her mobile and walked straight back to the Gloucester Hotel.

'Give me a double vodka,' she said to an astonished Gascoigne.

'You don't drink.'

'I do tonight. He's back'

'Farzi?'

'Correct'

'So, go to the police.'

'Too late for that and in any case they certainly won't take me seriously now. A vege picker's daughter's word against that of royalty. In any case I want him hurt, not given the chance to bribe his way out of responsibility. He's a diplomat.'

'Really? Well you're laughing then. The cops hate diplomats. They never pay their parking fines, they never get convicted, they never even appear in court. They get away with murder, literally. Shame he's not Libyan.'

'Won't Qatar do then?'

'Better if he was Libyan. There was a WPC shot dead by a gunman in the Libyan Embassy. He was bagged up and flown out. No one could touch him.'

'Well there you are then.'

'Yeah but the cops have their ways. They could plant something on him. Humiliate him.'

'I don't want him humiliated I want him beaten up.'

Gascoigne's chance of having a beautiful, sexy girlfriend had arrived. But he was no fighter.

Over the years growing up at his mother's side Gascoigne had been told about his father. She had painted a picture of a strong, independent individual. Joe was a bit wild, a bit of a 'wrong 'un', as she put it, but no-one ever crossed him or his boxing son, Hervey who was a serious handful. And Gascoigne had been fascinated by the folks back in England. He was proud to boast that he was half English and convinced himself it was this that kept him one step beyond the bog. He knew that one day he would make contact. That day had arrived.

'Well don't look at me,' he said.

'I thought all you Irish were street brawlers,' laughed Beth.

'I'm half English remember, we always get someone else to do the dirty work.'

Beth laughed again.

'No I'm serious. I think I know who to call upon.'

———————

Gunfleet Boatyard was not an easy place to reach via public transport especially at the weekend. Gascoigne had to take the London Underground from Gloucester Road to Tower Hill. He was glad Beth was working and couldn't accompany him as the gleam of his shining armour might have dulled a touch if she had witnessed his enthusiasm for a little sight-seeing: he could not resist a quick stroll around the boundary of the Tower of London and the footings of Tower Bridge before catching his train.

At Fenchurch Street the pace of his journey started to drag. There appeared to be little urgency in carrying passengers eastward. The destination boards were switched off. There was no announcer. Even the trains – not required to bring thousands of workers into the capital on a Sunday - were shorter. Gascoigne emerged through a hole in the platform and found he had to walk 100 yards back towards the buffers before he reached the truncated train. He sat in the silent front coach, listening for sounds of mechanical life. The minutes ticked by until he heard a door slam and some scuffling from behind the forward bulkhead. The driver had arrived. But it still seemed an age before he activated the train which seemed to stand at stations en route for a painfully long time. A bell rang once, twice, three times and even then the train didn't pull away straight off. Although when it did it picked up speed quickly. His window passed crooked rooftops at gutter height as it whirred through Limehouse and beetled above dark, shining canals and deserted football pitches behind tall wire cages. Eventually beyond West Ham, beyond Barking, beyond Upminster the rows of terraced houses with their assorted extensions, or back gardens, chock-a-block with rusting barbeque pods, discarded bicycles and collapsing sheds of personal empire, gave up the ghost and became scruffy flat fields where horses in canvas covers grazed beneath the pylons of the National Grid.

It dropped him at a place called Pitsea. 'Armpitsea,' said Gascoigne to himself as he surveyed a huge litter-blown, out-of-town Tesco store behind a line of pollarded willows. Here he had to get on a connecting bus. Maintenance work took place on the over-used tracks at the weekend, ready to rush commuters back to their office blocks on Monday morning. The connecting bus stopped at four more railway stations before he finally arrived at Southend-on-Sea from where he got a local bus to the small Essex town of Rochford, where many of the houses were made of planks and leaned over. Here he had to change buses for a third time. There was an hour's wait before the next one. Eventually a grubby single-decker rolled into the bus station, and parked up. Gascoigne's eagerness to be on the move again was tempered by the driver as he switched the engines off and sat staring at nobody and munching sandwiches, a bolshy look of lunchtime defiance on his face.

Gascoigne tapped on the closed door.

The driver tapped on his watch and raised a hand displaying five fingers then turned away.

'Pleb' said a crestfallen Gascoigne under his breath, as a moment of homesickness overcame him. In Galway you could sit on the bus until it was time to leave. Here in the heartland of the South-East power-house it was taking forever to cross country. And public transport was timetabled to get you from A to B and to accommodate you only during that timetable.

As the bus left Rochford the countryside at least improved. The fields were intimate and attractive, dotted with the odd, distant copse and the empty road which wound through them was so deserted that crows flew up from carrion only at the last minute.

Finally the bus reached the end of the route. The doors hissed open to let off the sole passenger. The driver turned off his engine again and poured himself a tea from a flask on the dashboard.

'Do you know where Gunfleet Boatyard is?' asked Gascoigne.

133

'No idea, mate. Ask in the pub.'

A white, ship-lapped tavern bore the sign Plough & Sail. It was closed. Miles of muddy fields, hedgerows and a distant barn suggested the pub had got it only half right, for of the sea there was no suggestion. Not a gull, a rattling halyard, not even the smell of brine invaded the rural peace. But a rutted lane lined with dusty poplars led eastward beside the pub and a wooden finger post bore the legend: Public bridleway.

It was a good half mile over a dried earth track its potholes ill-fitted with half bricks and hearth ash before Gascoigne came across a five-barred, steel farm-gate which was padlocked. But then he noticed another Public bridleway post which led the footpath further on beside a hedge to one side of the fenced off and gated area.

The path ran between the hedge and a row of laid up boats. Their appearance suggested that had there once been water here it had long since dried up. Some were sat on beer barrels, others propped up on logs. One had a small tree growing through its bottom. Another was burned out. You could still smell the charred wood. As the path led clear of the hulks it disappeared into shingle and Gascoigne was now crunching across what appeared to be a cross between a car park and a boatyard. There was a boat hoist with hanging lift chains swaying gently in the breeze, a mobile crane with its door open, and beside a corrugated iron shed sat up on concrete mushroom-shaped legs were three jacked-up cars with panels and wheels missing. Suddenly a huge black dog bounded towards him. Gascoigne froze. The hound nosed its broad, damp muzzle into Gascoigne's crutch. He could feel it lifting his manhood on its bony snout.

But it wasn't biting and gingerly Gascoigne lowered a hand and let the beast sniff it before walking on. The hound appeared to lose interest and it wandered off towards the gate its huge scrotum swinging from side to side.

At the far end of the yard the ground sloped up to a wall and disappeared over it between two, low, heavy duty, steel flood barrier doors which were open. Gascoigne walked through and there in front of him sparkled a wide, flat river. A wooden boardwalk led out into its salty embrace and beside it a slipway was awash with skins of foam-speckled tide. On the far side of the slipway stood a ramshackle shed alone on the marsh.

The black-planked sides had not seen a tar brush for decades. Gravity was re-shaping the russet corrugated iron roofing and a badly installed window had dropped on one side, like a stroke victim's face. Halfway along a wooden door was ajar, held in position with a shiny hook. Gascoigne lifted the hook and entered.

Immediately his nostrils contracted with a mixed aroma of tarred hemp, paraffin and red lead. In the gloom the skeletal frames of a huge boat fanned out over his head. Hanging from the roof trusses were coils of dust-covered ropes, old ships' riding lights and above them on boards, were sat mounds of ancient flaked down canvas sails.

On the hard earth floor were scattered tins of paint, stacks of wooden planking still with the bark on the edges and stripped down engine parts, covered in oil. On a bench beneath the crooked window sat a giant mechanical drill and next to that grinned the swarf of peeled steel from a lathe.

As Gascoigne's eyeballs became used to the dimly lit interior he noticed that the seaward end of the shed was partitioned off with a hanging tarpaulin.

The smell now changed. It was sweeter, but not an appetising sweetness. This was no apple pie. It was wrong: something which instinctively repelled should not smell sweet.

He pulled an edge of the tarpaulin to one side. It was heavy and fell back into place as soon as he passed through. Gascoigne found himself in a make-shift chapel. There were old school desks each side of the shed with a row of car seats between them. There was a lectern holding a giant book – presumably a bible – and then shockingly against the far gable end of the shed a huge cross. As he walked up under it he noticed there were crude rusty nails every foot or so along the horizontal beam on the cross.

And beneath them a black crusty substance. Around the foot of the cross were puddles of thick, scabrous gore.

His heart thumping, Gascoigne, could see there were some bony remains behind the cross. He bent down to have a closer look and to his immense relief recognised the skull and vertebra of a sheep. Of several sheep.

The borrow dykes of Essex, so-named because in mediaeval times the earth was 'borrowed' from meadows to build sea defences, had a saline content which produced lamb peculiar to the wetlands. For centuries sheep farmers had let their flocks graze beyond the sea wall. Salt-marsh reared lamb had become a City delicacy with the money men who lusted for red meat after a hard day on the bourse. Allowing nature's most dim-witted beasts access to the succulent grazing below the high tide line was not without risk, however and the occasional sheep, especially when pregnant lost its footing on the springy marsh islets and toppled into the muddy rills between them. Stuck in the ooze they panicked, dug themselves in further and were left bleating as the tide made until their fleeces became soaked, they capsized and were left flailing until the farmer could make a rescue. When the odd sheep went missing completely, it was put down to the swift running tide which ebbed and flowed throughout the marshy delta of the Thames Estuary twice a day. Rustling was ruled out as, unlike the sheep thieves who operated on inland farms, no vans could be driven close enough to the creek-side for successful abduction. When Hervey went walkabout on the marsh and stumbled across a stranded sheep before the shepherd did, he was strong enough to carry the beast back to his shed. Here he strung them up by their back legs and watched them jerking in a bid to get upright. He was interested to note this went on for the best part of a day before they became exhausted and their bleating faded to a pitiful squeak. As he slit their throats he watched their brown eyes turn towards him almost, he felt, thankfully. It was more humane than any slaughterhouse, Hervey told himself. He enjoyed the knife work and the meat was excellent.

'Having a good nose are you?' a voice in the gloom made Gascoigne jump. He turned round to see a gaunt, disembodied face half lit from a dusty roof light.

'Good day, sir and forgive me. I'm looking for Joe Lamb'

The head's mouth opened beneath deep-set eyes which Gascoigne couldn't read as they were covered in shadow.

'Who said you'd find him here?'

Gascoigne was relieved to construct through the gloaming that the hovering head was in fact attached to a body. He could see the tarpaulin shake as the figure moved. Hervey was looking at him through an opening flap cut at head height in the heavy sheet.

'Well nobody actually. I've had this address for him, er, for years.'

'It's out of date.'

The face offered no explanation.

'So he's no longer involved with the yard?'

No answer came but instead a long shining tube poked out of the opening where the face had been and Gascoigne gasped as he recognised the barrel of a gun. He ducked under the cross, knocking over a tin of paint as he scrabbled to find an opening in the back of the shed.

He heard a loud guffaw. 'Don't panic I'm out of ammo.' He stared at the screen, but the face had disappeared. The flap had dropped over the opening.

Gascoigne could see the tarpaulin bulging as a figure moved along its length before pulling it aside to enter the chapel.

'I've used it all up downing these,' said a bizarre-looking figure waving two steaming geese above his head their wings dropped askew like broken fans. Under his right arm was the long shining tube. A shotgun. He propped the gun against one of the school desks and bound some twine around the birds' legs before hanging them on the nails of the cross.

The strange figure was wearing thigh-length rubber waders and over his clothes were pulled a pair of muddy white pyjamas.

From the suddenly mute visitor Hervey could sense Gascoigne's mixture of anxiety and curiosity.

'What people wear in the sanctity of their own realm is up to them,' he said as he pulled off his waders, 'and from your silence I take it you are feeling a tad guilty about trespassing on mine?'

'I'm very sorry. I had no idea this was in any way a private residence. I thought it was a workplace.'

'And now you find a gunman dressed in pyjamas it's difficult to decide whether it's private or public,' snorted Hervey with laughter.

'Well that's true but it's none of my business.'

'Unless it was business you were calling about. Then not unreasonably you would seek a shipwright in a shipyard, a boat-builder in a boat-building shed. But Joe Lamb hasn't picked up a caulking iron or mixed a tin of resin for years, and this is a Sunday so I'm thinking this is not a business call.'

'Well it's maybe as singular a business call as your mode of hunting,' said Gascoigne, relieved he was no longer the next target for the somnambulist gunman and getting back into his cocky stride, 'but it's business mixed with pleasure.'

'From a bird's eye view the pyjamas blur my profile. I can get up close to wildfowl when I'm wearing them,' said Hervey, 'you got up close too, but you have no camouflage and you've been spotted. Let's start with the pleasure. What are you doing with your leisure time rooting around in a boatshed? '

'I'm looking for Mr Joe Lamb. He is my long-lost father,' said Gascoigne, 'and after all these years I thought I would pay him a visit.'

Hervey stopped pulling off his boots and stared at Gascoigne.

'Mr Lamb only had one son. And it ain't you.'

'You must be Hervey. I've heard about you. We're step-brothers. How-do-you-do?' Gascoigne thrust out a hand.

Hervey grabbed it twisted it around behind Gascoigne's back and lifted him in a half Nelson across the shed until his nose was flattened against the crucifix pale.

'Mr Lamb only had one son.'

'Listen I'm sorry,' pleaded Gascoigne, 'very clumsy of me. Perhaps you don't know about me. I mean, well obviously you don't and it must come as a shock me blundering in like this. But perhaps I could explain?'

'There's nothing to explain. I'm Joe Lamb's son. I've got no brothers. My life has been brother-less and that's the way I like it and that's the way it's going to stay.'

'Well I'm sorry to spring this on you. I was taken away to Ireland by my mother. She met Joe many years ago in Crays Hill.'

'There is nothing to explain,' said Hervey forcing Gascoigne's face against the cross, ' you are NOT my brother.'

'OK, OK, sorry, sorry. Please let me go.'

Hervey relaxed his grip and Gascoigne slumped to the dirt floor. Hervey looked down at the quiffed head. The hair like Billy Fury's. The hair like his father once wore it.

'So much for the pleasure, what business is it you want the services of Gunfleet Boatyard for?'

'Well that's difficult, now.'

'Meaning?'

'Difficult to explain out of context. But I will try. I was told there is a Mr Joe Lamb who runs a boatyard in Essex who is not to be messed with. This Mr Lamb can look after himself, er, physically and he has a son, called Hervey, who can, too.'

Hervey smiled.

'So you want my permission to start a fan club?'

'I was hoping to enlist some muscle.'

An easterly wind had started to rattle a loose sheet of corrugated iron over their heads. The breeze was coming up with the flood. Freed from the friction of the vast mud-banks, as the tide covered them, the wind was picking up speed.

Hervey listened to the intruder's story of his violated workmate and his bizarre request for sub-contracted retribution.

'You see the thing is, Hervey, may I call you Hervey?'

Hervey nodded.

'The thing is Hervey, you say we are not half-brothers and I wlll have to accept your word on that. But put yourself in my shoes: I'm only going on what I've been told. And you know what I've been told – and I accept I may be wrong and if so I'm sorry – but you are asking what am I doing here and I am here because of what I've been told. My mother, Glenda, used to meet a Mr Joe Lamb, maybe it's another Mr Lamb. Maybe she's confused. But even after she left Essex for Ireland she still met once a month with a Mr Joe Lamb in Dublin who came over from England to see her. This is only what I've been told. So sorry, it's not my fault.'

Hervey looked impassively at Gascoigne. He remained unmoved. But his anger seemed to have subsided. He remembered his father going to Ireland on business.

Once again Gascoigne probed forward.

'She has an old shoebox of letters from this man which I've seen, so at least that's something I've not just been told about.'

Hervey's eyes flashed.

'So, Hervey, I have no-one else to turn to and – only because of the way things have been explained to me –that's why I am here because – as anyone would – you turn to, when you need help, at least what you assume is, your family.'

Rain started pattering on the tin roof. It was unusual for rain to come in from the east, but when it did it turned the coast into a bleak, cold, inhospitable weather shore. No sea ever ran in the Thames Estuary, white horses were rare. Except when it blew from the east. Then the calm, coffee-brown delta seascape turned a vivid green flecked with white scars. They were only small waves, but they all broke into spume. It was good for business though. Strong easterly wind drove the fish into the rivers from the North Sea and cloud cover meant they couldn't see the shadows of the men and their angling paraphernalia set to snare them.

'My father died three years ago,' said Hervey, 'so you'll need to find another father figure.'

'Oh dear, I'm sorry. And he never said anything? I mean he never mentioned...?'

Hervey stared coldly at Gascoigne.

'Well I've told my story to you and thank-you for hearing me out. I have no wish to repeat it to anyone else and so would you be interested in the job of teaching this Arab a lesson?'

Hervey was doing all right. His father in his grave, his mother in a care home the tab for which was being picked up by the NHS because her dementia was no longer a care issue but a health one. He was sitting on seven acres of marshland. The boatyard was worth close to £2 million double that with planning permission. He was collecting rent from 22 live-aboards grateful for a chance to exist on a motley group of old barges, converted Thames lighters and rotting cabin cruisers which would not get a berth anywhere else along a coastline continually under threat of gentrification and development. It suited Hervey too. He did not have to worry about upgrading the strawboard lavatories or plumbing them into the main sewage system rather than let them flush into the river. These people were grateful to live in their own shit rather than pay more for modern facilities. Hervey also had his angling trips. It was all cash and no-one dared not pay up on time. The future looked good. It was all his. Now this Gascoigne had turned up. This 'son of Joe' this half-brother.

From outside the shed a distant howling noise was blended with the rising wind. Then it stopped. Then it came again much closer. A baying hound. Hervey knew it was close to High Water. Moose was barking. The geese must have come up river for shelter.

'I'm a businessman. A legitimate businessman. One day I find a trespasser, a complete stranger, rooting around in my boatshed. This stranger then tells me he's my half-brother and asks me to give someone a good hiding. It's a nonsense.'

'Well, again, I have to apologise. I sincerely believed I'd be "coming home" as it were. I mean I thought you might KNOW about me. About my existence anyway. I hadn't realised – assuming your father is the same man my mother's told me about –that I was a secret. It is perhaps a delicate subject.'

'Well he's not here to ask anymore is he?' said Hervey

Gascoigne's hopes were raised, Hervey seemed less aggressive, ready to at least consider their links.

'Look Hervey I don't blame you for your assessment of me. It does seem crazy on the face of it. But I came here in good faith. I didn't know you didn't know about me. I am dreadfully sorry to hear of your loss…but it's, er, my loss too. If I get my mother to send me the letters would you at least take a look? They are hand-written.'

Outside the shed the wind was blowing hard. Half-rotted blue plastic sheets were flogging against the sides of ancient dried out boats. Rigging slatted against masts, wire stays under tension whined. The tide was high, slapping at the underside of the jetty planking, boats rocked high on their moorings, much of the marsh was under water making the river look wider.

Yes, Hervey would like to see the letters. Yes Hervey, would like the letters in his possession. Of course Hervey would. Once in his possession they would stay in his possession.

'I don't see why not.'

Gascoigne felt like a general. He returned to the Gloucester Hotel full of confidence and promised Beth, long, sexy Beth, that the matter of Farzi's come-uppance was in hand. And she was soon in his hands, in his bed, in his life. He had his London blonde.

Farzi still turned up at the Oasis, once a week, Beth ignored his appeal for a drink and served others. She made sure she spent time with older clients. And Farzi would not approach in front of his peers. His diplomat's psyche was so deeply installed that the rule of law – never a concept to have plagued his homeland – registered not at all in his daily life. Nothing had happened following his assault on

Beth. These bloody Brits were such hypocrites, for all their Parliamentary even-handedness on the surface, they were the same as anyone else underneath. Women who were showing out, who were asking for it, got it whether they meant it or not and London society knew it.

'Look at Jimmy Savile,' Farzi said to his driver, 'he was having sex with fans of all ages – hundreds of them – at the BBC, in all the top hospitals around the country, in jail. Her Majesty's Prisons, huh!

All these women were dressed improperly, dressed to advertise their desires. Many cried rape. And absolutely nothing whatsoever happened to him. That's because MPs, police officers and judges are all doing the same thing.

'The only thing that's black and white in this decadent western world is an opinion.'

One Thursday night Farzi's driver drove to collect his boss and parked the Bentley as usual in the street behind the club a half hour before he was needed. With engine running, the sidelights on and a CD of his favourite Arabian flautist playing, it took a while for Beth to attract his attention. When he eventually saw the long, lean body holding her coat apart dressed only in knickers he threw open the driver's door and leapt out. What a dream, could he taste his master's choice before he emerged?

The iron marlin spike Joe Lamb once used for wire splicing was an effective cosh even sewn up in chamois leather and the driver dropped to the ground like a marionette with its strings cut. Hervey, dressed in a black jogging suit complete with hood and balaclava, rolled his victim over onto his stomach, the jacket of his Savile Row suit spread out and started soaking up the leakage of the club's air conditioning system. Hervey dragged the suit off his victim and then used cable ties to cuff the Arab. Beth pulled off her knickers, stuffed them into the semi-conscious driver's mouth. Then pulled them out again.

She then stamped on his nose which crunched.

'Hey, steady,' said Hervey, directing Gascoigne to pull on the driver's suit before bundling the man into the boot of the Bentley and gagging him.

Beth wiped her knickers over the driver's bloody nose and sealed them in a plastic bag.

When the slightly groggy Farzi emerged, some 10 minutes later he was excited to see Beth there dressed in a raincoat which she flashed open.

'Dirty bitch,' he muttered with a smile, 'she loves me.'

'Could you give me a lift home?' she said coquettishly.

'Of course, Beth,' get in. The aroused Farzi had eyes only for Beth's long limbs as she climbed into the car, he did not notice that his chauffeur had not got out to open the door as would be normal.

But once he was in he did notice, as the car pulled away at speed, that Beth was not the only passenger sharing the interior.

'Ali, Ali. Stop the car, look,' shouted Farzi. Gascoigne turned and gave the Arab a friendly wave as he sped towards the quiet road in Hyde Park. He did not shout again as Hervey's chain snorter choked off any further complaint.

Once they were in the park the car's headlights picked out a tunnel of oaks framing the lonely road which bisected the West End arcadia.

'Stop here,' said Beth and Gascoigne pulled over.

'The perfect place for dogging, Farzi, wouldn't you say?' said Beth who took the ends of the chain from Hervey and gave them a twist. Farzi choked.

'No don't worry I'm not going to strangle you. You'll need all the breath you can get, now, but I am going to restrain you. So be a good boy.'

Hervey slammed his fists into Farzi's abdomen as though it was his boat yard punch bag.

'OK. That will do,' said Beth, and then she loosened the chain snorter completely.

'This is the way you like sex, isn't it? A bit rough? Now you can feel me.'

Beth took off her coat and Farzi stared at her naked body dressed only in purple satin knickers. He stared at her long white legs held wide apart and anchored in red, patent, sling back stilettos which she hooked on each door handle. He watched the long fingers of her right hand slide inside the bulging triangle of purple satin which started to dampen.

'No Beth, I love you Beth' said Farzi.

'I know you do and now you can show me.'

'But not here, Beth. Let me take you home.'

'But here was good enough last time. And this is the way I want it.'

'Beth, no'

'OK more foreplay required. Would you oblige Mr Smith?'

Hervey smashed both fists into Farzi's stomach leaving him gasping for breath.

'Beth, please?' he pleaded.

'He's still not getting turned on. Again Mr Smith.'

This time Hervey produced his Green River knife, the six inch blade glistening with oil from the sharpening stone. The back side of it pressed into Farzi's neck.

'OK. OK, Beth . I promise to love you. Now.'

Beth undid his fly and started massaging. Farzi was quickly aroused the fear added an erotic touch to his libido. As the big member climbed out of his trousers, Beth put her mouth over the end. Farzi watched her glossy hair fall forward. He felt her tongue seeking out the opening. He started to gasp.

Quickly Beth retracted her head and caught the spurting fluid in what looked like a glove.

'OK look at this you bastard.' She held open the glove it was a pair of black knickers now covered in warm semen. She put them in a plastic bag and sealed it.

'And now look at this.' She pulled another packet from her bag, 'These have got your lovely driver's blood and saliva on them. It's not very diplomatic, but it's my immunity. Now fuck off back to your tent.'

149

Hervey and Gascoigne opened the boot and hauled out the driver. He was released from his cable ties and placed still semi-conscious back into the driving seat.

Beth opened a bottle of whisky and drenched both men.

All three walked away across the grass and under the dark trees towards Kensington High Street.

———————

Gascoigne made the same mistake with Hervey as he had done with the 'tough eggs' at school. He became over-familiar. Always the class clown he had used his lip as opposed to his fists to raise a rebel profile towards the teachers. And although for most of the time this was accepted by the more physical of his peers as entertaining, he did not have the credentials required for being a name and he was never accepted as one of 'them'. Gascoigne resented his inability to actually fight and sensed that his appeasement of those toughs as a survival tactic would be seen as 'arse-licking' by others at school. So to counter the humiliation he kidded himself the hard-nuts were actually friends.

Hervey was unconcerned, at the peculiar chumminess proffered by his 'half-brother' all he wanted was sight of the proof that the man was who he said he was. Hervey had recalled enough of his past to believe Gascoigne, but continued to deny to the strange fellow from Ireland any filial consideration to his face until he saw the letters which were, Gascoigne promised, being sorted by his mother who would post them.

Gascoigne revelled in his new links with England. He wanted to organise dinners, weekend visits, nights out at the pub to strengthen his relationship with the tough guy from Essex. Hervey mostly held him at arm's length, but eventually, at Lucy's bidding, they met up, as a foursome, in the non-resident's bar of The Gloucester Hotel.

Gascoigne was on top form showing off, throwing his arm around Hervey's broad shoulders and flirting innocently with Lucy who enjoyed the attentions of the dark-haired Irish boy and also the chance to shine against Beth, the country girl.

'Hervey, my son, you are the business,' Gascoigne said after his third pint, 'no-one messes with Herv.'

'He scares me, too,' said Lucy, 'and I love it.'

'He's a great guy, and I'm proud to know him,' said Gascoigne.

'And I understand you are related?' said Lucy.

'That's up to Herv,' said Gascoigne, smiling.

'They say you can't choose your family. But if you're now telling me you can,' said Beth, ' I wish I'd known earlier. I'd have picked someone, anyone as long as they weren't from the Fens!'

Lucy was impressed with the bumpkin. 'Well I think you should be bloods,' she said, 'Hervey's too much of a loner. He could do with some rellys.'

Hervey sipped his soda and lime and smiled.

'He can be my relative anytime he wants,' said Gascoigne feeling much more confidant with Hervey in front of the girls.

'You certainly don't look alike,' said Lucy, 'you with your lovely Irish hair and Hervey with his battered bonce. But then I'm not keen on beauty in men. Makes them vainer than us.'

'Beauty can be bestial, too,' said Beth, 'and a beast is more likely to provide a girl with a sense of security. We like the look of that.'

'So beauty or the beast? Or maybe beastliness is beautiful. Show them your phone, Hervey,' laughed Lucy, 'he's got Mike Tyson as a screen saver.'

'Hey, whose saying Herv's been hit with the ugly stick? Certainly not I, Mr Smith!' said Gascoigne draining off his fourth beer.

'I would rather deal with Mike Tyson than Hervey when it comes to cancelling a mobile contract,' continued Lucy, ' "Where are you?" he asked the poor fella when he eventually got through. "No, WHERE are you? Where are you sitting now? What can you see? What I'm saying is: Which country are you in?" You should have heard him when he found out it was Mumbai. "Mumbai, eh? Forgive me but this is a mobile phone right? And T-Mobile is in the business of communications, yes? And it's taken me 13 minutes to get through, OK? That's 13 minutes of listening to the Pineapple Waltz interspersed with a repeated message of how valued my call is to you. If I'm going to have to wait that long at least play The Who, yes?"'

Everyone was laughing including Hervey very proud of his girlfriend's recall. He had no sense of feedback and found accurate observation of himself flattering.

'It gets better,' said Lucy getting into her stride, 'this guy then tells him he's going to have to put him through to another department. Bugger me if this time it's another foreign-sounding voice and Hervey's off again with his where-are–you-sitting-now routine. This time it's a she and she's in Cape Town! At which point he rings off in disgust. What does he do? Goes back onto their website and instead of pressing Customer Care he goes straight to purchases. A woman answers the call straight away, no recorded rigmarole. "Ah, a human being. Where are you?" he asks, "South Wales" she says. "Bingo" he says and within minutes has his two-yearly contract reduced to a rolling monthly job.'

'Brilliant,' said Beth.

'Not just a pretty face then,' said Gascoigne to a giggling Lucy.

It was always difficult for Hervey in company. A teetotaller he despised drunks but envied the fraternity of tipplers. He could never know how false that was and how those who drank knew this only too well: the brotherhood ended as the party died.

'Do you fancy some live music?' asked Lucy, 'come on there must be somewhere round here. I want to boogie.'

'No problem, madam,' said the still-drinking Gascoigne, 'there's The Troubadour just round the corner. Hendrix played there once although he won't be there tonight, ha, ha.'

The party shuffled out of the bar and onto the street. Gascoigne linked arms with Beth and Lucy as Hervey followed up astern.

He was getting that erotic surge once more, that arousal which burned upwards from his crutch whenever he got jealous. And Lucy for all her put downs of vain men was all eyes at Gascoigne. Hervey lusted after her slatternly demeanour. He would made her talk about Gascoigne, later, in bed.

The cool air went to Gascoigne's head, the beer to his legs.

'Hold him up, Beth,' Lucy laughed as he stumbled forward and she lost her footing as a heel keeled over.

'I've got him,' said Beth, but they both spilled over into a potted bay tree outside an Italian restaurant knocking it over.

Screeching with laughter Lucy helped haul Gascoigne back onto his feet and put her arm around his waist to hold him upright. Beth became a biped once more and propped him up on the other side. Hervey rescued the bay tree as a waiter behind a steamy window pretended not to notice.

'I can't let him in, love. Sorry,' said the club doorman, dressed in a black overcoat with a wired microphone in his ear, 'not in that state.'

'In what state?' roared Gascoigne.

'Shut up, Gaz,' said Beth, 'He'll be all right I promise. He's with us. He's no trouble.'

'I said in what STATE? We're in a UNITED STATE,' shouted Gascoigne.

'I don't think so, darling,' said the doorman.

'Look at the STATE of you,' yelled Gascoigne, 'wearing a deaf aid are you? Want me to speak up do you?'

'I think you'd better take him home.'

'Home? That's what you'll need, mate, a CARE home, mate.'

'Gascoigne do be quiet,' said Beth, 'I'm very sorry about this. He's been celebrating.'

'Better go and celebrate somewhere else. He's not coming in here,' said the doorman.

'Hey, don't talk to her. Talk to me. Oi, deafhead talk to me if you've got something to say.'

'OK, sir. I will. Go away before the police have your guts for garters.'

Gascoigne pulled away from the girls.

'See this gorilla here?' he pointed at Hervey, 'Yes, mate the ugly one. He's my brother. Never mind fucking garters, he'll take your spleen out and use it as a rain hat.'

The doorman pulled out a handset from his chest pocket, pushed a button and said: 'I need back-up.'

'You'll need more than back up. You'll need an army against Rambo-man. He'll use your intestines for sausage skins,' he yelled dancing round the doorman.

'SHUT UP Gascoigne,' yelled Beth, but Lucy was laughing.

There was no stopping the Irishman now. 'Pancreas? He'll toast that. Liver? – with bacon please,' Lucy was crying with laughter, 'Kidneys? In with his lamb casserole.'

Gascoigne pushed his face up to the doorman's nose.

'My brother, he knows Mike Tyson and your guts aren't good enough for his garters. You lay a hand on me and he'll whack you so hard you might even get your hearing back.'

155

Hervey rushed forward, gripped Gascoigne in a bear hug and lifted him off his feet.

'See? See how strong he is,' yelled Gascoigne as he was carried away, 'all I've got to do is say the WORD. OK? I've just got to say the word and the only door you'll be guarding is the Pearly Gates, pal. Yes, mate, the Pearly Gates. Yeah, mate you'll meet Jimi Hendrix. He'll love seeing you again.'

The party entered the Gloucester Hotel through a staff only door and via a narrow corridor, made narrower by the temporary storage of cardboard boxes, and in single file sidled along to Beth's basement one-bed studio flat where they gathered around a low table. Beth produced vodka from the fridge, for herself and Lucy. 'There's brandy, too. On the table,' she said pointing to a glass decanter. Gascoigne poured himself a tumbler.

Hervey drank coffee.

'He was bang out of order,' said Gascoigne trying to effect a Cockney toughness for Hervey's sake, 'for Christ's sake I didn't do anything,' he added more plaintively.

'You couldn't do anything, not even stand. He could see we were holding you up, at least to begin with. Then, unfortunately you got your second wind,' said Beth.

'Just his bolshy attitude I didn't like. Typical doorman think they can give you the evils and you're just gonna swallow it. Bloody poseur with his secret service ear-phones. "Look at me I can get back up". Ponce. He'd have bloody needed it if it had kicked off. He had no idea who he was dealing with, eh Herv?'

How could my father be responsible for such a gobby prat, Hervey thought. 'Yes, but there's no point in inviting trouble,' he said.

'But I wasn't Herv. For Christ's sake I'd had a drink, yes, but I didn't DO anything. Did I?'

'You look very sexy when you're angry, Gascoigne,' said Lucy, 'don't you think so, Beth?'

'Well he certainly talks a good punch,' Beth said, 'but I'm glad Hervey was there to carry him back to his corner.'

Everyone laughed.

'Listen,' said Gascoigne, Herv's my brother. That's what you do for family. Look after each other. I'd do the same for Hervey. I mean I'd be there for him.'

'I think Hervey would rather you weren't,' said Beth laughing.

'No seriously I would do anything for my bro.'

'If you could,' said Beth.

'What are you saying? Are you saying I couldn't handle that doorman?' Gascoigne raised his voice.

'Come on, let's go back there now,' he shouted, 'I'll show you. I'll tear his head off and shit down his throat.'

'I don't think Hervey'd be interested in a bouncer as offal after that.' Everyone laughed. 'Now be quiet Gascoigne or you'll have the hotel's security on your case next.'

'Your eyes really light up when you are that roused,' said Lucy, 'all that brotherly love. How come you've never mentioned you had a pin-up for a brother, Hervey?' asked Lucy.

'A month ago I didn't know I did. If indeed I do,' said Hervey calmly.

'But you do Herv, you do,' said Gascoigne, 'you see ladies, Herv, understandably is confused. He was never told about me. His dad – our dad – was a bit of a shagger,' Hervey froze, 'and my mum isn't Hervey's mum.'

'Skeletons, skeletons , eh Hervey?' said Lucy, 'my family's full of them, too. Like a fricking ossuary our cupboards. It's nothing you can do anything about. Who cares?'

'But Herv still doubts our bloodline. Don't you Herv? Eh? You can't believe this boozy bugger from the bogs has turned up out of the blue?'

'You're not wrong.'

'But what's not to like? Eh? We're a team, now. Isn't it great to discover you've a brother. A Bruvver in crime,eh?'

Hervey's tight-skinned face was hard put to hide his distaste. There are not enough folds of flesh on an athlete's countenance in which to conceal expression.

'The advantages have yet to reveal themselves,' said Hervey.

Beth laughed.

'Yeah, like everyone wants a little brother to have to be responsible for. What could you possibly have to offer Hervey?'

'I could be his partner. I could come and work for him. I could help run the boatyard. It'd be great he'd have someone to trust. Someone who was family.'

'But he seems to have been doing fine without you,' said Beth.

'He does have the right looks anyway for being front of house,' added Lucy.

Gascoigne slugged another tumbler of brandy: 'Well there must be something I can do, eh Herv? I mean that's surely too big an operation you've got there out in Essex, to have to run on your own.'

'It keeps me busy.'

Gascoigne poured another brandy.

'Come on Herv. There must be something. Don't be greedy. You could say half of it's mine anyway.'

Hervey stiffened, but kept cool and laughed.

'You're something else.'

'Something else, maybe but I'm not someone else. Joe's my dad, too. And I think he would have wanted to see me all right. Gunfleet Boatyard has my name on it, too. For Christ's sake Herv, we're already blood brothers in deed if nothing else.'

Already a month had passed and still no letters had arrived from Ireland. Gascoigne had never requested them because he knew his mother would never send them. She did not know that Joe was dead, but even if she did the letters would remain locked in her little safe. They were part of her union with the man she had once loved. Like Gascoigne they were all she had from her only carnal relationship. Hervey was feeling duped. There would be judgment.

———

Carpe Diem was not a good boat in a seaway. Once the waves were a metre high she slammed into them. As a performance hull the motor-boat could not be driven slowly: she would just wallow in the seas if throttled down below six knots. To keep steerage way on she had to be driven at speed and when it was rough she bounced up into the air and slammed back down into the sea all the more.

Seated at the swivelled steering position on the flying bridge the ride was exhilarating and Hervey squatted on the leatherette, pump-action, chair peering through the spray-spattered windscreen as the wipers worked at top speed to give him a semi-circle of visibility. Astern a distant mauve smear marked the disappearing marshland of Essex. The vast sky over it was spreading with dense black cloud which tripped over the horizon in angled sheets. Rain was chasing them. Each side of the bilious green channel the water turned brown and was flecked with breaking sea horses. Even an hour from High Water the great estuary banks were never far from the surface.

Down below it seemed as though Carpe Diem would break up at every impact as she pitched over the watery hillocks.

A prone figure in a nylon sleeping bag was curled into a banana shape bouncing on the port side bunk. Gascoigne was trying to sleep off a hangover while bracing himself with back against the hull and feet against the bunk side as he involuntarily pummelled the vinyl mattress.

Through the crashing noise of the hull and the high-pitched whine of the engines Gascoigne became aware of another sound. Was it music? He pulled the sleeping bag over his throbbing head as the boat slammed onwards. But, yes, there was definitely something composed weaving through the cacophony of marine travel. Something that wasn't just noise.

It reminded Gascoigne of school assembly. It was a hymn.

Wasn't there some bloody religious music playing last night, too?

He'd come out to Essex the night before, on a Friday after work, invited by Hervey for a boat trip. At last Hervey was coming round, he thought. Hervey had said they must make an early start so it was best he didn't drink too much the night before, but that there was no reason he couldn't sink a couple in the Plough and Sail. Such was the pub's isolation that the locals enjoyed regular 'lock ins' and Gascoigne was thrilled when he heard Hervey describe him as 'One of ours' to the landlord.

When they eventually emerged Gascoigne's skin was full and he carried a bottle of brandy with him. Locals could purchase off sales at anytime. The lane was an obstacle course in the dark and Gascoigne stumbled slowly forward under a lemon yellow moon close to its waxing gibbous phase. A large yolky circle surrounded it and cloud flew across its face.

'Rain on the way,' said Hervey authoritatively. Gascoigne was swaying, his flies open as he relieved himself in the hedgerow.

'Stay here I'll get the van.'

Gascoigne sat on a low brick wall and opened the brandy. This was grand. He was bonding with his bro. He'd soon be working with him. He would soon prove his worth. He could expand the business. Get some investment. Get this bloody rutted lane metalled for a start.

He'd bring in custom from The Gloucester. Half those fool Americans had no idea about the real England. Hervey's bloody shed was held up with timbers from Darwin's ship HMS Beagle which had been broken up here. Think of that! The Yanks would go crazy for it. He could do historic tours. Bright lights bounced up the lane towards him, blinding him, throwing the lane's pot-holes into relief.

'In you get old son,' said Hervey almost affectionately.

Some dirge was playing on the van's radio.

'Christ, Herv, you going to a funeral. What IS this?'

'I like to play it when I'm driving.'

'OK, no problem. Hang on, I know it. All things Bright and Beautiful,' he started to sing, but the rolling organ music of Martin Luther kept curving back into itself. It did not develop as Gascoigne had anticipated.

'Hang on, no I don't. Oh well, each to his own. Listen Herv, I've got some great ideas. You know for Gunfleet Boatyard. This place is dripping with history.'

'I'm all ears.'

'Good man. But I'll tell you what you won't be able to play this shite. It'll depress the hell out of 'em'

'Of who?'

'The tourists. Yank tourists. I could bus 'em in.'

Once aboard and in his sleeping bag Gascoigne had quickly passed out.

Now as the boat smashed over the waves he could no longer sleep or even nurse his hangover. He rolled out of the warm sleeping bag and pulled on his trousers in intermittent stages between slams.

'This bloody mattress is showing signs of memory loss,' he shouted up at Hervey, 'it's as hard as nails.'

If he heard him Hervey said nothing and instead pulled the wheel over to starboard and eased the throttle back, the boat immediately stopped slamming and instead rolled from side to side.

Gascoigne climbed out onto the aft deck, holding onto a stainless steel grab rail. All he could see across a grey-brown plane of jumping water were the blades of distant wind turbines turning in slow, mesmerising symmetry like jugglers' clubs. Then alongside the boat a black post appeared to be stabbing out of a floating pontoon which rose and fell on the sea as Carpe Diem ranged alongside.

'Ah, you're up. Quick take this line and get a turn,' said Hervey throwing Gascoigne a rope.

'Do what?'

'Jump on the pontoon and tie this line onto it'

Gascoigne timed his leap imperfectly and fell heavily onto the pontoon, but quickly stood up, hauled in the rope and wound it around a cleat on the edge of the floating box.

Carpe Diem plunged up and down with the pontoon as Hervey threw Gascoigne a second line this time from the bows of the boat.

'Make that fast, too,' he said.

'What?'

'Tie it up like the other one.'

Gascoigne started winding the spare end of the rope around another weedy cleat as Hervey dropped fat, blue, plastic fenders over the side and pushed them between the boat's plastic hull and the steel pontoon with his feet. He then knotted their tail lines to the guard rail.

'I suppose this is how you park a boat, is it. In the middle of the bloody ocean. I've often wondered where you stop at night in a boat. Bit bloody bleak though, isn't it?'

'I need to check the pots. Here put this on,' said Hervey climbing onto the pontoon.

'What's that bondage gear? Didn't know you cared Herv.'

'It's a safety harness. It's to stop you joining the crabs. See, like mine?'

Gascoigne noticed Hervey was wearing a belted ensemble over his torso.

'Here I'll help you,' Hervey said as he slipped a webbing strap over each of Gascoigne's shoulders and fastened a belt around his waist. He then pulled a crutch strap between his legs and clipped it onto the belt.

From the belt dangled a five foot long rope cable with a safety catch on the end.

'Now clip on, like me', Gascoigne watched as Hervey wound the rope cable around the post and clipped it back on itself. He then did the same.

164

'There must be an easier way to catch crabs,' said Gascoigne who was turning green on the pitching pontoon, 'I think I'm going to be sick.'

'Here hold your head up, this'll help,' said Hervey throwing on the chain snorter and clamping Gascoigne's neck to the post as a projectile of liquid vomit splashed over Hervey's jacket, momentarily warming him.

'Shit,' said Hervey dropping to his knees and cupping salt water to wash himself clean.

'Hey Hervey let me go, mate. This isn't working,' Gascoigne choked as he threw another jet of regurgitated alcohol across the pontoon deck.

'It will you'll see,' said Hervey.

'Now come on, Hervey. Joke over. I need a drink, mate.'

Hervey slid across the greasy pontoon and went back aboard the rocking Carpe Diem. He reappeared with a bucket on a rope and retrieved enough sea water to sluice the pontoon clean. Then he pulled the bottle of brandy from a pocket.

'Here you are.'

'No, water. I need water,' Gascoigne held the necklace clear of his neck as the pontoon rose and fell. He spread his feet to balance.

'It's all we've got. Unless you want sea water. I forgot to fill up the fresh water tank last night. Too busy looking after you,' Hervey dipped the bucket and splashed another pail–load over the swaying deck.

'OK. Anyway I don't need this on anymore, bro.'

'You are not my brother.'

Hervey dropped to one knee and started unbuttoning Gascoigne's trouser belt. He pulled the tops of his trousers down and lifted up his shirt tucking it behind the harness straps.

Gascoigne tried to reach Hervey's head but the chain necklace bit in. He had no choice but to hold the snorter off his windpipe in order to breath.

'Herv? What's going on? What ARE you doing?'

Hervey stood up and produced the bottle of brandy again.

'You will need this now. As an anaesthetic.'

Hervey forced the bottle into Gascoigne's mouth and pushed his head back. Brandy gurgled down his throat. He swallowed until he felt he was drowning then wrenched his head away.

'OK. OK. I'm not your brother. I've made it all up. Let me go Hervey. What are you doing?'

Hervey ignored him and forced the bottle back between his teeth. Gascoigne was forced to swallow repeatedly until the bottle was empty.

Gascoigne had a surprisingly taut lower belly for a hard drinking man, but then he was still young.

'For Christ's sake, Hervey. No , no do not....'

'Don't worry. I've Googled it,' said Hervey grinning, a jocular Satan at his work.

Hervey's grass sharp blade drew across the white belly and the skin peeled back allowing the intestine to herniate and fall out in glistening coils, steaming into the chill salt air. The redness came as

166

an obscene shock in the monotone greyness. Gascoigne passed out and Hervey lashed a bowline on the bight under his victim's armpits and around the pole to hold him up and prevent him asphyxiating.

He then pulled enough of the intestine out of the gory slot to enable it to be led behind Gascoigne's back and gaffer taped to the pole.

Hervey then climbed back aboard Carpe Diem and sat on the fly bridge with a flask of sweet tea. He scanned the horizon through 360 degrees. There was nothing apart from the white sticks of the lonely turbine field still tumbling their juggler's blades.

He watched as the waves started to flatten out. The tide had turned and was now running with the wind instead of buffing up against it. He cast off as the pontoon started to drop. Today it had a 16 foot range, but then the lower intestine was 20 ft long. According to Google.

———————

Memory Lodge was a huge red brick, double-fronted 1930's house with high pitched roofs and extensive outbuildings. It had once been the villa of a Jewish lawyer and his family who had left Hannover in 1933 shortly after Adolf Hitler came to power. It was surrounded by other large houses which were built in the early 1930s by a Jewish diaspora which chose suburbia over London. The houses had long since been carved up into one-bed flats. Each time the voluminous buildings were sub-divided into smaller living spaces, the area went further down market. First time buyers could now afford to live in the once exclusive manor, but avoided it because it had become blighted by drug dealers. It was rent land where discarded mattresses, old cookers and fridge freezers were left on the crumbling crazy paving of the shared frontage. Once proudly carved barge boards artistically fitted beneath eaves now sprouted the ears of satellite dishes.

Memory Lodge had been sub-divided, too, after being bought by the nationwide chain of old folks' homes. It was perfect for the job it was now required to do. The original 12 bedrooms had been expanded to 25 by converting lounges, recreation rooms and mezzanine areas. All of them were now filled with old people mostly over 80 and predominantly women. By night they slept in their beds next to wardrobes stuffed with too many clothes, and stacks of CDs which, as a new experience each time for dementia sufferers, were inserted into their TVs over and over again by staff, who also dusted off photographs of families who no longer visited. By day they slept in the lounge area - those who could still walk shuffled on sticks - those who could not were craned into bath chairs and wheeled there by staff. The large wall-hung, flat screen TV, was largely ignored and the residents sat out their days either calling for tea, or being woken up to be fed.

Memory Lodge was set in a plot with a back garden which nudged near to the back gardens of the road behind: another street of 1930s houses. Between the two gardens ran an alleyway into which had been tossed more discarded white goods, lawn cuttings and unwanted bicycles. But you could still pick your way through and Hervey did so one evening around the time his mother was due to be fed her dinner.

A back gate was padlocked but easily scaled by Hervey in his boxing shoes. He padded across the garden towards the yellow squares of windows each showing the blue glow of a TV screen.

He skirted around the south side of the building where, in the conservatory, his mother spent her waking life perched in her adjustable chair.

From another large flat screen TV, tuned to a radio station, he could hear the tune: 'I could have danced all night,' playing to the dozing residents.

Then he came up to the window directly behind his mother's chair. Although the curtains were drawn he could see the pale blue uniform of a carer, between the drapes, bending over his mother whose white hair was sticking above the back of the chair.

Suddenly her hair appeared to jump up and he heard her yelp.

He quickly skirted around to the side of the bay window where he could see his mother's profile below a window blind only half pulled down.

Her upturned head showed the left eye was blazing in fury her mouth resolutely shut tight in crumpled flesh. Above her hovered a spoon of liquidised food held by the hand of the carer whose face was obscured by the blind. Hervey looked down at the grubby carpeted floor and to his horror could see the carer was standing on his mother's feet.

'Now come on Betty, EAT,' she suddenly shouted and lifted her heels of her black lace-up pumps off the ground putting her full weight on Betty's socked feet.

'Open your mouth, Betty. NOW.'

Hervey bashed his fist on the window then ran around to the front of the building and twisted the door handle. The security lock was on. He pressed the buzzer, but it took a good three minutes before one of the overworked care staff turned up to let him in.

'Hello Hervey, how are you?' she said, but Hervey pushed past and rushed into the conservatory.

His mother sat glowering, her eyes like that of a confused tiger, not sure on what to focus and who or what was the enemy. But unlike a tiger her mouth was firmly snapped shut.

Down a large towelling bib was a stream of regurgitated food. She was alone.

'Mum, mum. It's me Hervey. Are you OK?'

'Get away you bastard,' she suddenly shrieked.

'It's me, Hervey. Your son.'

'Murderer,' she shouted.

'Ssshh, mum. It's me, Herv. Look in my eyes, mum.'

Hervey backed away a few feet and tried to get his mother's gaze to lock on to him. She was staring beyond him.

'Are you trying to kill me? Like all the other poor bastards here?' Betty ranted, 'because if you are you won't get away with it. You hear? I'll call the police.'

'Mum, don't worry I saw what happened. I'm your son and I'm going to deal with it.'

'Don't you start, I don't have a son.'

'You do, mum, you do. It's me. Don't you recognise me?'

'LIAR,' shouted Betty,'I want to go home. Where's mummy?'

'Look mum. You've been assaulted. I know I witnessed it. Are you in any pain?'

But Betty fell silent. She sat there mouth clamped tight, eyes still blazing and scouring the room for the enemy.

Hervey knelt down and gently removed her socks. 'Jesus,' he muttered. Her feet were purple and black.

'Get off me, killer,' Betty screamed.

There were five Filipino staff on that night and Bunty the Ghanian Born Again Christian. He knew it wasn't Bunty, but he did not know which of the Filipinos had been feeding his mother. They closed ranks and professed ignorance of any maltreatment. He looked down. All of them were wearing black, lace-up pumps.

'Betty have poor circulation. This make her hands and feet go dark skin,' said the duty manager.

'We all try to feed Betty. She no want eat. We try liquids. But she not swallow. She spit out,' she added, 'But we all try. Have to get her take liquids. She dehydrate otherwise. Have to call doctor.'

In Hervey's experience the Filipinos were excellent carers. They were patient. Loving. But clearly there was a bad apple in their midst. He controlled his anger. He did not berate them. He had no choice but to leave his mother in their care, he had no desire to make things worse for her when he was gone.

He returned to his mother's side. She had calmed down and this time recognised her son. He squatted beside her, held her hand and whispered a lengthy monologue.

He brought the pristine Gideon's bible from her room. He put her hand upon it and his upon hers.

There would be a judgment.

Hervey's face held the strange beauty of the boxer's, at once brutalised and yet benign. It had been moulded by blows, which had left his an almost baby-faced, rounded, undulating countenance. Like a Great War battlefield it had been landscaped by violence, but now the fighting had stopped, time had softened it. It was, he knew, the wrong sort of face to be sporting in the vicinity of a city bank late at night and yet he could hardly sit in his white van wearing a ski mask. So he had spent the evening lying on his stomach on a mattress in the back of his Ford Transit van. It was the high roof model with an offside sliding door, which Hervey had left just cracked open to let in much needed air in the fetid heat. It also let in sound. The only security camera in Old Jewry was mounted about 18 feet up on the façade of the building at the north-west corner. With his van parked facing south and bumper to bumper with Adele's Mercedes sports, the offside door was not in recordable view. He had already retrieved the magnetic GPS tracker from the underside of the Mercedes' rear bumper.

It was Adele's clicking heels he heard first, then the whirr of her central locking. Before she had time to open the door he was on her like a cat. One hand over her mouth, his free arm wrapped around her, he lifted her bodily off the ground and bundled her through the side door into the back of the van. Then, knees pinning her shoulders down he gaffer-taped her mouth, turned her over and tied her hands and with the fall of the Dyneema rope bound her ankles, arcing her body in a bow, hands behind her back down towards her feet.

Once he had immobilised her he was gentle. He made sure she was comfortable. He positioned her so she was lying like a reverse foetus with two steadying ropes to her bondage lashed to the framework on each side of the van to keep her central and prevent her from sliding around on the mattress. He then lifted her head and placed a cushion beneath it and covered her with an old sleeping bag.

Adele could feel the warmth in the mattress from where Hervey had been lying. It smelled of fish.

As the street lights picked out the moving van's interior all Adele could see, under a corner of the sleeping bag was the odd glistening streak of scarlet tissue smeared over the panelling. They were lugworm, the bait which Hervey dug from the Dengie's great sands for his fishing parties and which had crystallised in the summer heat.

173

Someone who had never seen a lugworm might wonder where the dried gore had come from. Adele had never seen a lugworm.

The city streets were clear of traffic until the white van emerged on the Mile End Road where the whole of London's youth appeared to be partying. Mini-cabs, black cabs, night buses all shunted nose to tail through throngs of lads in T-shirts and jeans and girls flashing flesh, as they tottered along in and out of open market stalls, and steaming fast food stands.

Denied passage, Hervey's heart felt like it was expanding in his chest. Tension built as he willed the cars to move. His destination burned in his brain. He was computing the routes, turning left and right in his head, yet he was going nowhere. The traffic would go no faster.

Suddenly someone banged on the side of his van. Hervey started. 'Whoop, whoop, whoop' yelled a stumbling girl as she walked past waving at Hervey with a bleary smile.

He turned on the dashboard CD player. The plodding bars of A Mighty Fortress Is Our God calmed him, made him stoic. Made him take things philosophically. Put him back in control, at least the sort of control that denial of your circumstances brings.

His mother had taken him to Sunday School as a child. Religion then had been hubristic, too. Sticking stamps of images from the bible in a book in a dusty wooden hall normally used for secular activities, sitting cross-legged on the floorboards while the teacher read aloud, and singing hymns. The hymns had enabled him to feel there was an authority greater than his drunken father. For an hour at least.

Adele, desperately trying to hang on to normality, strained her ears to pick out the sounds of revellers almost but not quite drowned out by the Lutheran hymn.

A blue light flashed around the van's interior and Adele started with hope. Hervey tensed: his battered Everlast boxing boots hovered and fell over the pedals as he nosed through the traffic. They were the wrong kind of boots for fighting outside the ring. The wrong kind of boots for putting the boot in. The wrong kind of boots for resisting arrest.

The car with the blue light overtook Hervey's van. It was a paramedic.

It took 40 minutes to clear the tentacles of the metropolis, but then at last, as the stalls fell away from a highway no longer filled with customers, he had a clear road and the white van hurtled through the warm night towards the coast.

Adele was aware the van was unimpeded and moving at speed. For an hour the drive was smooth then the van slowed, turned left off the arterial road and was swallowed in the rural lanes of backwoods' Essex. She could smell the hedgerows and realised the journey must soon be at an end.

No matter how much ash and clinker was bedded down by residents of the few wooden houses which ran beside the boatyard lane, it was still rutted and in the dry heat-wave the muddy track was as hard as rock. Hervey swayed back and forth in the driver's seat as the van bounced slowly down the lane with Eternal Father now the hymn of choice.

The van pulled up and was parked at an angle: the bonnet higher than the rest of the vehicle. Hervey had driven up the flood protection ramp built over a sea wall.

He pulled back the sliding side door and Adele could smell the sea and feel the first delicious coolness for days as a light breeze played over the dark river.

She heard the driver's door slam and the crunching of pebbles as her abductor came round to the sliding door. He then lifted off the sleeping bag, untied her lashings and held her down while he gently removed the gaffer tape.

Adele spat in his face: 'You fucking beast.'

To her horror Hervey calmly wiped the phlegm off his face and licked it off his fingers.

'You've had too much to drink, not a bad vintage, though from the taste of it.'

Adele screamed until her throat hurt.

Hervey was completely unfazed.

'You are in the middle of nowhere, the only human ears for miles around are mine and you need to save your energy.'

'You fucking nutter, get off me,' she yelled.

And then the glistening eyes of some monstrous creature stared in through the van's door.

'It's OK, Moose. She's a lady really.'

Adele kicked him between the legs and then watched in disbelief as Hervey pinned her down with one powerful arm and with the other produced a knife. A fleshy roll of her stomach bulged around the blade then burst open issuing tissue like a wet, red rose.

'Now be quiet Adele, stop kicking and calm down.'

'I will. I will. I'm sorry. I'm sorry.'

Moose's huge head pushed in through the door and the hound growled at the blood Hervey pulled a bait-smeared plastic box towards him. It was a First Aid kit. He gently pushed back the tissue and lovingly applied some anti-septic cream to the wound, then covered it with gauze, cotton wool and held the dressing in place with more gaffer tape.

He then pulled off her shoes and sniffed the instep. He was momentarily aroused, but then threw them to one side concentrating instead on the job in hand ordering Adele to dress in a zip-up wool body liner, and woolly slippers.

With her body now completely enclosed in wool, Adele started to overheat, in turn the pain from the stomach wound made her feel faint. But Hervey was ready with hot, sweet tea, poured from a flask. She drank the sickly brew, Adele did not take sugar in her tea, but it made her rally.

'Is there anything I can do for you? Can I help you?' she asked politely, 'Clearly something is very wrong, but my husband is a man of means, a man who can get things done. If ....' she was cut short.

'You will be the redeemer. You will be the saviour,' he said, helping her out of the van and with an arm around her waist, steadied her over the noisy pebbles - deliberately laid around the old boatyard to discourage stealth in potential trespassers - and up over the sea wall.

177

Here on the seaward side of the flood barrier stood the old shed. The years of defying gravity had caused its planking to sag, its corrugated iron roof to bow, and its cracked windows to distort. The fact that the flood barrier had not been constructed to include it within its protective concrete battlements suggested it had been abandoned and indeed on big tides the river crept over its floor at the far end. Adele saw only a dilapidated store. The makeshift chapel which Hervey had erected within the far gable end was not obvious. But it had pleased him making the crucifix with wooden knees salvaged from the Beagle. Hervey had taken great delight in breaking up part of Darwin's old hull, which had been abandoned in the creek years before. Hervey had turned the vessel used to discredit creationism, into a place of worship. He had re-used the still sound former Royal Navy Dockyard timbers, to prop up his marsh-side church.

As the pupils of Adele's eyes opened wide and focused with the available light she became aware of a line of seats, rather like the stalls in a cinema. They were upholstered leather seats, but lower to the ground than a normal chair. She realized they were car seats.

'Here,' said Hervey, 'Row A, seat 5,' his voice had a mocking tone as he led her along the row to the centre seat.

'Now please take your pew.'

He gently pushed Adele down into the middle seat and used adjustable belts to clip her in, one across her waist, another over her shoulder.

She then felt him from behind her, shackling chains around her ankles. Next he looped a spliced rope around each of her wrists and shuffled it up her arm until it was at the elbow. Then he tightened the lashings.

'Now then I know you are sitting comfortably, and I know you are warm enough. So welcome to Gunfleet Lodge.'

Moonlight pierced the gaps in the shack's roof and slowly Adele made out a human-sized Christian cross at the back of the shed.

'Nobody should be a prisoner in a house of God,' Adele said. There was no reply.

'Hello? Are you there?' but all was quiet except for an occasional cracking noise above her head as the rafters cooled and shrank after the heat of the day.

It was worse being alone. With a large dose of denial Adele could use her captor's charm, cynical though it undoubtedly was, to lift her spirits. She knew that to survive she would need to rationalize her situation.

But being alone in that place was demoralizing and she could not afford to lose morale.

'And did those feet in ancient time, Walk upon England's mountains green? ,' she started to sing loudly. Then she stopped to listen, but there was nothing. Just the noise of shrinking rafters.

'And was the Holy Lamb of God, On England's pleasant pastures seen?' she continued determined to consecrate the DIY church. To turn its silence into supplication. Determined to make it a place of deliverance.

179

Jerusalem had been drilled into her at private school. She knew it off by heart, the hymn for those who believed England should have been the rightful setting for the Holy Land.

But the hymn was never designed to be sung solo, the timber shed would not even offer up an echo to alleviate the solitude and Adele's voice was simply absorbed in the darkness, a vacuum which did nothing more than amplify her loneliness. So she stopped.

Adele had never considered whether she believed in God. Now she realized that was because there had been no need to. Her life had been sweet, she might have been a tad selfish, true, but she reckoned she could handle Judgment Day as long as the bench were prepared to listen to her side of the story. But now seemed a good time to offer up a silent prayer, it could do no harm and there were no witnesses. Almost immediately she felt cheap. Why should she feel embarrassed? It was bad enough asking for the Almighty's assistance now she was helpless and there was nothing to lose. Surely she could summon the decency to make her appeal voluble? Surely she could set aside her metropolitan sophistication for the baseness of a plea?

'Our father which art in heaven hallowed be thy name... Will you please, dear God help me?' she said aloud.

'You've got a good singing voice, wasted in here, I'm afraid.' her captor had returned, 'the acoustic properties of pitch pine are virtually non-existent. But don't let that put you off, a good hymn is always uplifting.'

'Why don't you take me somewhere where the acoustics are good ?, I could sing for you. Or we could sing together. Any hymn you like,' said Adele startled, but almost relieved she was no longer alone.

'I prefer to seek salvation in the safety of my own home. Gunfleet Lodge. Which is your home, too, now you've been admitted.'

Hervey removed Adele's bandage, washed her wound with warm water and soap, then applied butterfly stitches and re-dressed it.

'There, you'll be fine. I've lost count of the cuts I've had to tend,' said Hervey mysteriously. He gently tucked a large, grubby duvet around Adele, 'Our night staff will keep an eye on you and I'm back on duty in the morning to serve breakfast.'

The reasonable tone, the bedding, the offer of food all helped Adele rationalize her predicament, but was all the more unsettling. She was the victim here, she was the one who needed to create a make-believe world to survive, not this maniac. If he was going to pretend this was normal then she would have to shake him out of it.

'Please, what is going on? I have not been "admitted" as you put it. I have been brought here against my will. You have kidnapped me, do you understand? You have assaulted me, you have stabbed me, I am wounded, do you understand?'

Hervey stood behind her in the darkness. 'Many guests wonder what is happening to them. They are confused, scared sometimes. That's understandable. It's all new to them.'

'I'm not a guest. I'm not confused. I know what has happened to me. What should be happening to me is not this.'

'Guests often suffer cognitive idiosyncracies. They forget what happened yesterday and go back to more vivid memories: the sort of mind pictures formed when their brains were new.'

'I am TALKING about yesterday and what happened to me then and even what's happening to me NOW. That could hardly be more vivid.'

'You can relax secure in the knowledge that Gunfleet Lodge is run by professionals. Now try to get some sleep.'

'How can I sleep sitting up?'

'Oh I am sorry. Please excuse me I almost forgot...'

Adele suddenly felt herself tipping backwards.

'All our chairs are recliners with headrests, they double as profiling beds. Now you should feel much more comfortable.'

A foot stool lifted up and supported Adele's feet as the chair back reclined and Hervey pulled out a headrest from the top of the chair. He puffed up a feather pillow which had the ubiquitous smell of sprats about it and wedged it beneath Adele's bob.

'There you are. Night, night.'

Adele could do nothing except submit to the angle of the chair. Apart from the restrictive bondage it was a tolerable bed. The warmth from her body lifted the shrimpy smell from the duvet and pillow but she soon got used to that. She dozed then snapped awake: a faint rattling noise was coming from outside as the land cooled and a light breeze blew offshore thrumming the halyards of the yacht masts. Although a stranger to the ways of the sea and ships, Adele identified the rattling as a background noise peculiar to the maritime world interspersed with the fluting of some marsh bird. The slits of light through the badly fitted corrugated iron roof disappeared as the moon dipped down to the north-west and she dozed off.

Early sunlight beamed in through a window and cut a widening ray through suspended dust. A metallic bang woke Adele from her blissful escape. She sat up and could now see the cross quite clearly. Incongruously it had ropes coiled around the bar piece and there were stains running down the stipe. Another tinny detonation shattered the morning silence as the hot, fast, rising June sunshine quickly warmed up the oil drums used to prop up hulls at Gunfleet Boatyard. The expanding air inside blew their tops from concave to convex lids emitting a loud bang as they did so.

'I will make your breakfast now, Adele,' said a soft voice, 'but would you like to use the ablutions first?'. A strange word, ablutions, not the sort of word she expected her captor to use, but Hervey was trying to be posh. He respected his charge's perceived class.

'Yes, please,' she heard herself say and she watched Hervey pull a trolley towards her on top of which was erected what looked like the supports of a wigwam.

'A sheer-leg lift. All part of the Gunfleet service, Adele.'

He manoeuvred the trolley until the sheer-legs were over Adele's chair then she heard a ratchet noise as a large steel hook was lowered towards her on the end of a chain. Once it was just a few feet off her prone body he unclipped Adele's fastenings.

'Now lean forward, Adele', she did so and he looped a rope around her back, under her arms and brought the two ends together in front of her chest. She noticed they had spliced loops in each end. These Hervey then impaled on the hook.

'Right. OK. Are you ready?'

She nodded.

The ratchet noise sounded again as Hervey pulled on the continuous chain hoist and effortlessly Adele was lifted from her recliner and up into thin air. Once clear of the chair Hervey then pulled the trolley to the side of the car seat 'stalls' and trundled a swaying Adele down the shed's eastward side, through a hanging tarpaulin, around one side of the great cross towards the seaward end of the shed until he stopped at a set of large doors.

They were padlocked with an ancient hasp. Hervey unlocked and unfolded them and brilliant sunshine poured into the shed making Adele blink.

A rusty steel girder ran out from the roof beams and hung over the river. It had been used once to haul boats in and out of the shed, but now Hervey, transferred Adele's looped strop from the sheer-legs to another hook which ran out along the steel beam. She now discovered the strop had a kind of open bucket seat sewn into it in which she was supported. It was a bosun's chair used by sailors hauled aloft to work on mast repairs.

Once she was hanging from her new perch Hervey yanked on an outhaul which pulled the bank CEO's wife , Lady Moulding, out of the shed and left her suspended over the river fifteen feet or so clear of her prison.

'We believe in maintaining the dignity of our guests,' Hervey said squinting into the rising sun against which Adele was silhouetted, 'when you are ready pull the light blue line connected to your chair and I will retrieve you.'

Adele looked back at the shed. She saw her captor clearly for the first time. A well built, athletic man with a bony skull-like head. The wide cheekbones, and high forehead though battered and scarred was quite beautiful in an ascetic way. In the past she had wished Sir Keith's own visage was more heroic and less weak as she scanned images of film stars, sportsmen even tribal warriors in the Sunday supplements.   Hervey wore a tank top T-shirt and a pair of tight shorts showed bulging muscular thighs. His stocky, hairy legs were thrust into grubby trainers. His right fist was raised against the sun to help him focus on his prisoner. She noticed the fingers were exceptionally long, but the middle one was kinked. He turned away to allow her some modesty and she could not help but compare the width of his perfect v-shaped back with the narrow-shouldered, pear-shaped torso Sir Keith attempted to bulk out with shoulder pads.

Hervey disappeared from the shed opening into the shadows of the interior.

Adele drew in deep breaths of fresh air. It was already very warm and the river sparkled with summer sunlight. She pulled her woollen leggings down and removed Sam's knickers. Then in the bottomless bucket seat relieved herself.

She looked down at the resulting cascade and noticed the water was shallow. She could see the bottom. Long black timbers ran out from

185

the shed and were submerged by the river. Weedy fronds waved up from them. They appeared to be some sort of ramp for launching boats. Little rotted mooring posts stuck up at their sides like black teeth. It was obvious they hadn't been used for years and that when the tide was down they would be uncovered.

With effort she stopped relieving herself, screwed Sam's knickers into a ball and then urinated on them. Once they were sodden she threw the lump directly down towards the little mooring stakes. A small air pocket kept the knickers afloat and they started to drift upriver. Adele's heart sank, but then so did the panties: as the tide snagged them against one of the mooring stakes they rolled over and were submerged.

She pulled up her leggings, dried her hand on the material and pulled the blue rope. A little bell tinkled, Hervey had attached an angler's bell on a clothes peg to the shed end of the line.

He re-appeared in the doorway and cupped his hand over the domed brow. He said nothing and appeared to be scanning the river. Adele's heart pounded.

'All done?' said Hervey, satisfied.

She nodded and he hauled her back into the gloom of the shed.

Adele's reclining chair was back in the upright position as she was lowered and strapped down again.

'You must be ready for breakfast now you've been toileted?'

'I would be grateful for some tea.'

Adele had successfully ignored the nagging dry fear, had swallowed it back like a dose of indigestion, and she was more thirsty than hungry not to mention a little dehydrated.

'Coming up,' said Hervey pleasantly and Adele heard him scuffling about in the back of the shed. Heard a kettle boil, heard some fat frying, then smelled bacon.

It was the odour of normality: not that Adele ever ate bacon herself, but she served it to Sir Keith every weekend and was repulsed by the little slivers of white fat which invariably jammed between his teeth.

Hervey brought her tea in a beaker as though serving a baby.

'Not exactly the bone China you are probably used to, but all our guests are treated the same,' said Hervey holding a plastic beaker to her lips.

Ignoring the humility of being hand-fed she drank the tea greedily. It was sugared, but again Adele did not complain. She knew she needed the energy.

'I'm glad you're enjoying it,' said Hervey watching Adele's throat jerking down the brew, 'you will get another cup at lunchtime. It's not sugared by the way. It's just that we use tinned milk: a necessity in the summertime.'

Her thirst slaked she was surprised at just how hungry the smell of the cooked bacon had made her.

However it was porridge, not bacon, that Hervey produced. He offered up a spoon of the steaming oats.

'I thought I could smell bacon?' Adele said.

'You can, but that's for the staff. Porridge is much healthier for you anyway. Here, eat up I've made it with honey.'

Adele obediently opened her mouth blew over the spoon and allowed Hervey to feed her.

'Strange thing about porridge is the thought of it seems boring but as soon as you taste it you can't get enough of it,' Hervey said, 'it's very popular with our guests.'

Adele nodded as she chewed, 'How many guests do you have at present?'

'You have the lodge to yourself at the moment.'

'And how long will I enjoy such a privileged existence?'

'It's good you recognize it as such. Here, at Gunfleet Lodge, care is our main priority.'

'That comes as welcome news, although my care was something I thought I'd managed quite well.'

Hervey said nothing and moved away to the back of the shed. He returned carrying a television which he set down on a table in front of Adele before running the lead to an electric cable extension.

Now Adele was transported to a brightly coloured studio with primary coloured images of giant petals painted over the walls and a black male TV presenter aged about 19 and a white female presenter about the same age both dressed as bananas.

She would discover that the only respite from daytime children's TV came at lunchtime when Hervey returned with cheese and tomato sandwiches.

'It's very kind of you to provide me with TV, but I'd rather be without it,' said Adele.

'Many of our guests like children's TV as it's undemanding. It doesn't challenge their fading minds. They are not left bewildered.'

'I'm sure. But there is nothing wrong with my mind.'

'Do you like sport?'

'I don't.'

'What films do you enjoy? I'm afraid we don't have pay TV here at Gunfleet Lodge but I'm sure we can find some old classics.'

'I'm sure you have a waiting list for such services as Gunfleet Lodge offers,' said Adele, 'and I can assure you I don't need care, not yet anyway. When I do I will make Gunfleet Lodge my first port of call. But right now I am just er, a bed-blocker. I really don't need to be here, I really don't,' said Adele fighting back tears.

'Well that's most considerate, but we have to get the timing right before I can sign your release forms.'

Adele did not allow herself to hope, and tried not to show too much enthusiasm for when the fantasy turned positive.

'The timing?'

'Yes, the tide timing. For your voyage to freedom.'

'Tide timing? voyage? I'm not very good on boats, you know.'

But Hervey had disappeared in the back of the shed. She could hear him opening a squeaky chest of drawers. Then there was a shuffling of papers.

He returned holding what looked like a large sheet of folded cartridge paper.

'X marks the spot,' he said jovially, ' not so much of buried treasure, but of revelation.'

'I'm not sure if you heard me,' said Adele as respectfully as she could, 'but boats and me don't mix.'

'Well it's the only way out of here, now,' said Hervey almost to himself, 'for both of us. And the tide will serve us tonight.'

The precision clunk of a mortice bolt woke Adele as Hervey unlocked the boatyard doors. At the end of the shed moonlight flooded in. There bobbing gently at the end of a wooden slipway was moored a candy white power craft with flying bridge and sinister-looking, black tinted windows. It looked incongruous in the ramshackle boatyard, like white goods scattered on a rubbish dump. Up closer Adele could see the boat's bathing platform and aft deck were covered in the congealed intestines she'd seen earlier in the back of the van.

'Would you like me to clean your boat?' she said trying hard to keep her nerve.

Hervey did not reply but helped Adele onto the bathing platform and then up into the boat's aft deck and sat her on a swivel fishing chair.

'You must wear a lifejacket,' he said and clipped the inflatable tube around her shoulders.

'Thank-you,' said Adele helplessly, her hope rising at the display of concern her abductor was showing for her continued existence. He then tied a bowline on the bight around her waist and made the bitter end fast to a grab rail next to the steering wheel. She was like a tethered dog.

Hervey pulled the garage doors closed and padlocked them.

He turned the keys in the boat's console and the twin engines started immediately and bubbled as cooling water ran up through their shiny black shafts spurting out under the engines' heads like steam from a hot water tap.

Hervey cast off the mooring warps, engaged the silver handles of the throttle and turned the wheel to starboard heading the boat out into mid-stream. Adele watched a black water road disappear behind her as the boat sped down river carving two glowing green lines of phosphorescence in its wake as its high revolution propellers liquidised plankton and jellyfish which had – in the continued heat – turned the river to a loosely-formed terrine.

Both sides of the river were bordered by a dark sea wall which channelled the waterway loyally for every turn it made on its way to the North Sea and with the exception of a silhouette of a lone donkey, the world was indifferent to Adele's passing. There were no perpendiculars in the flat, monotonous world which was now at least given a horizon as the sky, streaked with the first light of dawn, broke free from the sea.

The walls drew further apart as the river widened, but kept up their slavish, snaking border, deviating only to encompass a blind wartime pill box, until they finally gave up as the sea took over. Adele watched the flat shoreline disappear astern as it merged with sky once more. Only the faintest tracery of two radio masts anchored the horizon. And the boat sped on.

By now the dawn was throwing the open sea into relief: little black diamond-shaped shadows were speckled with silver, harlequin-shaped mirrors as the low light gave the little wavelets shape. And it was still warm.

The boat now slowed and turned to port, apparently in the open sea and soon a black pole stood up isolated, surrounded by water. As they got nearer Adele could see its base was a black, sunken barge its decks awash with the lazy wavelets.

'Is that a shipwreck?' she asked as the slower revving engines allowed her to strike up what she hoped would be a line of diplomacy once more.

'Yeah, a deliberate one. It was put there in the 1930s as a practice target for aerial bombing. It's handy as a marker as there's deep water the other side of it across these sands,' Hervey was back in his world and just being with him out there whether voluntarily or not, you were included.

As they closed with the wreck the boat's engines echoed off its structure and then Adele noticed a lumpen shape at the base of the pole, slumped on a pedestal-like pontoon which in turn sat on the barnacle encrusted deck of the barge. To her horror it appeared to be human. She saw a white-ish shape at the top of the sack, where the head should be. They closed right in and Hervey stopped the engines. Adele could see it was a head. A man stood there, composed and looking towards them. But there was something too-focused about his gaze. Why wasn't the sentinel of this mysterious wreck acknowledging their presence? Then one of his eyes appeared to crawl out of its socket and scurried away into his shock of lank hair. It was a tiny crab.

'Holy fucking shit, what the fuck is this?' Adele screamed.

'It's good fishing,' smiled Hervey.

'Listen, for God's sake, whatever it is, let's for God's sake talk.'

But Hervey turned to the corpse.

'Couldn't stop yourself, Gaz, could you? No matter how many times we warned you, you had to keep taking the piss.'

Adele stared in horror.

'Got nothing to say then, Gaz? Gone stum on me? Well there's nothing you can say now is there mate? It's all been said hasn't it?

'Anyway meet Adele. She's not a liberty taker. She's not at it. She's not some low life, Gaz, not the sort of woman you've ever met. She plays by the rules, she does. Adele's class, she is. She's going to save your soul, Gaz. And mine.

'But before that have another beer, it'll make you feel better. That's what you always did, Gaz, wasn't it? Drowning your sorrows.'

Hervey lobbed a bottle of lager at the effigy-like corpse.

'Does it make you feel better Gaz, now I've drowned your

sorrows for you?' Hervey laughed and started the engines.

The open sea was mirror flat, and Hervey headed his boat northwards across it wrinkling the surface under the rising sun, which although temporarily veiled by a thin, static, milky sky, was already producing an intense glare. Hervey donned a pair of fashionable wrap around sunglasses as he drove into the featureless shining.

'Where are we going?' Adele asked trying to mask her terror with matter-of-fact delivery. Are we nearly there yet had taken on an appalling aspect in her mind.

'To the highest point,' said Hervey mysteriously.

The Ray Sand Channel was a featureless stretch of water surrounded by coastline so low it could only be visualised by use of a chart. In plan it appeared as an inverted cone-shaped delta of shallow sea which divided the brown, amoeba-like shapes of the Dengie Flats from the Buxey Sand. These vast, flat sandbanks had once been part of mediaeval East Anglia, the Buxey was so named because it once supported deer- inhabited woodland, until the slowly sinking south-east corner of England and the wash from the timeless pulse of the tides erased the earthworks thrown up against the North Sea which now claimed the land as sea-bed for three hours each side of High Water. The Ray Sand Channel's pointed southern end had silted up and muzzled any chance of vessels joining the deeper Whitaker Channel which ebbed in a south-west to north-east direction draining the treeless, flat farmland of Essex. The Ray Sand, or Rays'n, as it was known locally, was therefore no longer used by small coasters and fishing craft. Even yachtsmen avoided it. The northern end still held plenty of water at all states of the tide, but it was pointless navigating into it as the bottom end dried out at Low Water. All mariners knew that entry into the Rays'n meant sailing into a dead end, a submarine cul-de-sac.

The whole area was therefore completely abandoned. Only a few black, isolated posts stood in the middle of the 'sea' when the tide was in, marking long-forgotten targets for war games practice.

Hervey switched the helm to autopilot and disappeared below. Adele scanned the glittering sea, desperately hoping for signs of another vessel. She peered into the pearly dawn horizon and tried to construct objects within it, tracing lines of vapour and seeking perpendiculars, but as she focused, so her ship-building programme dissipated into nothing more than pre-conceptions of hope. They were completely alone and the warm, sparkling sea became terrifying in its limitlessness.

Suddenly a sharp and incongruous smell reached Adele's nostrils. Bacon.

Hervey came out of the saloon with a plate of plump sandwiches.

'Have some breakfast.'

Succumbing to terror was not going to assist Adele in surviving, she told herself. The last thing on her mind was food. Dread was no appetiser. But to not eat was an act of childish self indulgence: you've hurt me, you've bullied me, you've tied me up – I'm not eating, so there. Better that she suspend reality, encourage any act of kindness in this maniac in front of her. Will on Dr Jeckyll. Build a relationship. String it out. But at the same time dare not hope.

'Thank-you,' she said picking up a sandwich, warm from the bacon within, and taking a bite, 'even though this is all a complete mystery and I've no idea where we are going thank-you for taking care of me. For keeping me warm, for supplying a life-jacket and now,' she took another bite, 'for feeding me.'

Hervey looked down, he appeared a little embarrassed. He was not used to being spoken to in such a civil way. He liked being treated as an equal with someone he admired.

'I think you like me,' said Adele, ' you've a funny way of showing it admittedly. But I can tell you care for me. OK so you were violent, earlier on, but you've realised violence is wasted on me. That's because you've sensed at last that I might like you,' she paused.

Hervey looked at her. A woman as classy as this, as intelligent as this was way beyond his dreams. Perhaps that's what a real aristo was like: open, candid, uninhibited. Perhaps it was just he'd never met one before.

'OK so you're a beefcake. A macho man. Don't believe what the feminists say, women do like physically attractive men. Of course they do, but you've got a brain, too. You're a thinker. I'm surprised you're not married.'

'What makes you assume that?'

'You have integrity in spades, that's certainly evident. And a married man with integrity does not make off with another woman. You swallowed my spittle, I saw you lick my shoe. I know you are

196

fighting your libido over me. Trying to control your true feelings. Well don't. Get rid of this bondage nonsense and I will show you how I feel, too.'

Hervey smiled: 'Don't eat with your mouth full it doesn't become you.'

Adele's heart sank. She swallowed and added: 'You're quite right, my mother always admonished me for that. I do everything far too quickly that's the trouble. I'm impulsive.'

'Always chasing to the next thing to look forward to, eh?,' said Hervey.

'Well that's one way of looking at it, yes.'

'The next new car, the next holiday, the next outfit. The only clouds in your sunny life shower you with hailstones of Ferrero Rocher,' laughed Hervey.

'There are all of those things in my life, in many people's lives, but they don't come along like buses. They come along as required. I think you may have mistaken me for someone else. Though, it's true, like the rest of the world I'm partial to chocolate.'

'No mistake. You are Adele Moulding, lady wife of Sir Keith. You have a detached, five-bedroom Georgian pad in Richmond, and twice a year in the spring and again in the autumn you fly to your farm in Tuscany. At home you drive a Mercedes SL, two-door, soft-top, he drives a Bentley.'

'Well you are correct on all counts, but none of that is difficult to know. The question is WHY would anyone want to know it?'

197

'Because the columns of your empire are built upon foundations of misery.'

'It's true to say that in a capitalist society the divide between haves and have-nots is unfortunate. But Sir Keith's wealth is hard-earned not inherited. The glittering prizes were there for anyone else to accrue.'

'For every material advantage secured, someone, somewhere else has to lose out,' said Hervey.

'You are right, but which path do you choose? That of the winner or loser ? What is wrong with equipping yourself with learning, and, OK, if you happen to be born with a head start is that something to shun?'

'Privilege, eh? Ordinary people resent that, but they live with it. In the case of Sir Keith, though it's being abused. He's abusing the power he has over other people.'

'Please, for goodness sake explain. I can assure you I will be the first to sort it out. I may be his wife but I am also his harshest critic. What is it he's done?'

'He's exploiting the elderly. His gilded existence is funded by a 48 inch pipeline of state cash which pours at full flow, non-stop, into the Moulding coffers.'

Hervey was enjoying this. He was speaking well which made him feel noble. This was all he had needed, all his life, just being surrounded by the right people, not pond life. How different it all could have been. By suppressing the thought that she was humouring him in order to save her life, he could believe she was showing him respect. Adele noticed his face change. He was animated, his eyes grew bigger, he seemed befriend-able.

'Ah, you are referring to Memory Lodge Residences. They provide bed, board and care to old folks. They are regulated like all such homes, but unlike many, have a good name.'

'He's making serious money out of decrepitude.'

'Which means serious investment in the first place. To build or convert places into suitable care homes costs a fortune: a fortune the Government relies upon to house an ageing population.'

'And because of all the money Sir Keith has invested – doubtless with help from local grants – in capital projects which he owns and which he can in any event flog off or re-convert into private residences whenever it suits him, he cuts back on staffing.'

'All MLR homes are fully staffed… but wait a minute, why am I defending myself? Clearly you have some personal reason to be dissatisfied with Memory Lodge. Do you have a loved one with us?'

'"Loved one." What sort of greetings' card sentiment is that? Does the phrase not make you cringe?'

'I don't follow.'

'It's used by those whose "care" can be put in the post, about those who are forgotten or dumped. Your homes are littered with them. They are pinned up on message boards, they line the shelves, they gather dust on radiator covers. Happy this, Anniversary that, From your loving daughter, 90 Today badges, whoopee. A celebration of what? 90 years old. That should be celebrated at year one. Eighty-nine years later it's just pre-funeral. 90 Today as you are wheeled into the room, craned from your bath-chair into your recliner, craned from your wheelchair onto the loo, craned from your wheels into the bath, craned into bed, craned out again. The orifices encouraged to take a fork or an enema. And the point is? The point is no man is God. The living rely on the old to die and when they don't the living catch up. Their purpose overshadowed by decline. Science keeps people alive. If people just lived and died like a switch, God could be understood like a Bible story. But because death is not part of life, but yet dying is...we are left as predators. Dying can't be sentimentalised: Do have a happy cremation. But death can: we are so sorry for your loss, if there is anything we can do, please accept our condolences.'

In spite of herself Adele could not resist blurting out: 'Gaz must be a loved one to somebody.'

Returned to grubby reality Hervey also returned to type.

'Don't worry about him. He's bog Irish. Troublemaker. He couldn't stop mouthing off no matter how often I warned him. He'd get pissed up, start showing off, start assuming familiarity. He was trying to wind me up. He was trying to get back at dad, claimed he was my step-brother. He might have been dad's seed, but he did not share mother's egg. He was no brother of mine. I'm no Cain. I did warn him. I gave him a slap. Told him to behave. But he wouldn't have it. So now he's repaying me in eels.'

Rant over, Hervey fell silent. The glow which had opened his face had gone. It was once more hooded, craggy, defensive.

'I'm sorry I didn't mean to upset you,' Adele apologised again.

Hervey stood breathing in the summer sea air. How long would it last, summer? When would the sun start to sink south, the days shorten? He was the same ashore, in summer: always seeking evidence of change, of decline because he knew it would come. In winter the yellow dead leaves and spiky bare branches reassured him. He felt happy. In death itself he was comfortable. Assured. In summer, decay was always on the way, in the diary, threatening. In winter it was here.

The boat glided along on autopilot over the mirrored sea and appeared to be running parallel with the coast. Adele could just make out a low smear to the west, she couldn't be sure if it was cloud, but then a barn-like shape formed from the smear and as Hervey's boat came abreast of it, he switched from autopilot to standby, took the wheel and turned seawards again.

Soon another black, mast-like pole stood out of the sea, but unlike the first it had no base. It was just there, a post in the middle of flooded nowhere.

Hervey conned the boat within touching distance of the pole and then pushed the control levers to neutral. The wash of the stopped motor-boat ran outwards from its hull and slopped around the base of the blackened perch.

The wavelets slapped a weed-covered buoy tied at water level. But then Adele noticed the buoy appeared to be punctured. Wavelets rippled out from its inside. Why was it still inflated? She probed this strange object with her eyes much as she had tried to make sense of the dawn mist earlier. The weed covered crown of the buoy was also covered with something else. It was muddy cloth, like a cap. Like a beret. Like a …hairpiece. Then beneath the surface she could see two bobbing objects, one each side of the buoy.

'The tide's ebbing. You'll be able to say Hello soon,' said Hervey.

Below the beret the round cranium-like surface of the buoy was speckled with barnacles and below that, as the tide imperceptibly dropped, Adele found herself staring at eye-sockets.

'Oh my dear God,' she muttered.

The skull's jawbone chattered as the ebb swirled past the post.

'Here, shake hands with Adele,' said Hervey, using a boathook to lift one of the bobbing objects clear of the surface. It was a mud-soaked, slimy, leather boxing glove, it's lacing crawling with tiny shrimps.

'You need anti-fouling, Mrs Laidlaw,' said Hervey, retrieving the boathook and letting the gloved arm drop back into the tide.

When Adele's Mercedes was found and the CCTV footage from the camera in Old Jewry was checked, it showed her parking the car and leaving it to walk south, but not her return. A few other figures were recorded walking past the car, some of them late eating diners from Brown's Restaurant. Several black cabs drove north down the one-way street, a despatch rider on a motorbike, a white van, but that was all.

Rod McKay decided to walk the ground. He and Dippy parked up in the same bay used by Adele after her car had been taken off on a Met low loader.

The first thing they noticed was that Old Jewry was covered by just one CCTV camera which was focused facing north. South of Frederick's Place, which formed a T-junction with the street, there was no coverage.

CCTV coverage picked up City life again only at Poultry and on checking those tapes there was Adele, dutifully recorded, heading west towards the Old Jewry turning.

'So we know she got that far,' said Rod, 'but disappeared somewhere between here and her car.'

No staff at Brown's Restaurant recalled seeing a lone woman walking down Old Jewry.

Checks with City beat police threw nothing up: no affray, or unusual behaviour, just one elderly insurance broker given a verbal warning for urinating between some wheely bins. But in the course of her routine enquiries Dippy was told by a desk sergeant he'd taken a phone call from a congestion charge clerk who said she was worried about a man making threats down the phone to her.

'But they aren't on duty over the weekend surely?' said Rod.

'They're not. But this call was ABOUT the weekend. It came through on the Monday morning as soon as the office opened. The clerk said the phone was ringing when she got to her work station.'

'And?'

'Some guy had said he'd paid the congestion charge by mistake – that he rarely drove into town and hadn't realised you didn't have to pay the charge at the weekend - and wanted a refund. The clerk told him it was possible, but that an admin fee of £60 more than negated the £10 repayment.

'He then gave her a load of abuse and said he hoped she'd die soon before slamming the phone down. Nothing unusual in that you might say, but this clerk was astonished at the man's sheer rage, on a Monday morning, too, and not fuelled by alcohol.

'Then she discovered an entry had been made earlier online via email from a driver claiming he had paid by mistake. And the driver had left his vehicle registration number hoping for a refund. So she thought she'd report it as a matter of record.'

'What? In case she died!'

'Yeah, I know it sounds daft, but guess what?'

'Go on.'

'I've checked the registration and it doesn't exist.'

'Moody plates?'

'So it would seem.'

Det. Inspector Rod McKay and his deputy looked again at the CCTV footage. The white van was sporting the false plates.

'Bingo,' said Rod, 'but not House. There are tens of thousands of high roof Ford Transits in the UK. But it's a good start, well done Dips. Let's go back to Browns, see if anybody remembers a white van.'

'Sir, you go, I want to get the nearest image of the van digitally enhanced.'

'Good girl. You tackle that and call me if you get anything.'

Nobody at Brown's remembered any white vans or rather took care not to, but that was all in a day's work for Rod. Metroman never wanted to be involved in anything which would upset his comfortable bourgeois existence unless of course that existence itself was threatened or had been violated. Then he wanted every police officer in London working on the case. That night Rod McKay walked through the alleyway which led to his flat from the Co-op store laden with a plastic bag full of Old Speckled Hen. He felt his boot come down on the shell of a snail and halted half-step, stumbling, not wishing to crush the creature completely. The absurdity of his compassion made him laugh: he'd left the mollusc mortally wounded and stickily vulnerable to a passing blackbird and almost sprained his ankle at the same time in trying to preserve it.

'You're a good man, Rod,' he said aloud. A good man with a failed marriage, his sense of righting wrongs had not saved that. Why did he get so much pleasure from arresting wrong-doers? It was at the core of his work. He was not a time-server, not a man spinning out the days to get the fat pension, not a man who was no good at anything else. No it was vocational, catching the bad guy. But why? his more pragmatic colleagues asked. In a God-less world man was a barbarian, there was nothing to hold the line except the law and Rod McKay wanted the line held. There was something profound about that, something which made his life meaningful. He had realised long ago that the deeper qualities in a man were abstract and took time to germinate. He was trusted, he was respected, he was relied upon and he knew that by never cutting corners, never making stuff fit he had created his own integrity, created his own order, created around himself a fair world. That was where he wanted to live even though it cost him his marriage. His ex-wife Erica was a good woman, but with materialistic vice. She had wanted the extra holidays, the detached house, the new car every three years which so many of Rod's colleagues seemed to enjoy.

'Does it really matter if some scroat goes down for the one crime he DIDN'T do?', she'd asked, 'at least he's off the street and if you are never going to catch the bastard who DID do it then you might as well utilise the crime usefully.'

But she did not understand that even the most villainous opposition despised bent coppers, especially the ones in their pocket.

'There was an old lag once,' he told Erica, 'and he said to me "Rod, as you know we are professionals, we go out of our way to cover our tracks, so if we then get stitched up with someone else's job that's not fair is it? I mean that's anarchy. That's the Old Bill being unprofessional." You see the crims want law and order, too. They have wives, houses, cars, children, school fees. Lifestyles that cannot flourish without law and order. Also squealers won't squeal to a dishonest cop.

'Not to mention what a moody conviction is like from the victim's point of view.' And a wrongful conviction was, indirectly, a second crime committed, this time with the collusion of the law. That was a greater sin than the original crime in Rod McKay's book. That was society turning to barbarism. And he knew the officers who fitted up Erica's scroats felt inadequate. It wore them down, hobbled all their police work from then on, created their own world around them: one of cynicism at best, self-loathing at worst.

'It's corrosive,' he told Erica, 'they are like Gogol's Dead Souls.'

'Who?'

'Google him,' Rod laughed, 'Google Gogol,' he lay on the bed in his studio flat, drank his Old Speckled Hen and wondered who Erica was seeing.

His mobile purred into life.

'Dips. Don't tell me you want to join me for a drink?'

'Anytime, boss, but you might be interested to know that our white van was, or maybe is, owned by a Born-Again Christian.'

'Holy shit.'

'Precisely.'

'Boom boom, and what brings you, my inferior, to that conclusion?'

'The van once had a fish symbol on the nearside back lower panelling. The symbol's gone but there's a faint dirt mark where the glue was. It's in the shape of a fish.'

'A Fisher of Women?'

'Well it's definitely been removed. Either by someone who does not want to be associated with Christianity or who does not want their van identified.'

'Like someone who might fit false plates, you mean? Well done Dips it's something or nothing and I think it's something.'

The triangular sign bearing the legend New Scotland Yard which revolved on its stainless steel pole outside police headquarters, still gave Rod McKay a buzz. He'd posed next to it with his father, Roy, for his mother's camera when he'd passed out of police college. It always reminded him of the monolith surrounded by apes at the beginning of Stanley Kubrick's film 2001: A Space Odyssey because it, too, was an incongruous edifice, a talisman surrounded by a sea of savages.

He had the chance to admire it most recently when one of the assistant commissioners called him in. It had been explained to him that he was to make the search for Lady Adele Moulding a priority.

'Her husband is in the same lodge as the deputy commissioner.'

'Lodge?' said Rod.

'Masonic department.'

'I should have known Moulding was one of the funny hand-shake brigade,' Rod said candidly, dangerously, even, for he did not know if the assistant commissioner he was talking to was 'one' himself.

Rod had turned down several discreet offers to join the masons even though he knew it could lubricate the rails of his career path. He was proud of being a police officer, felt he was a natural dispenser of justice and saw the masons as a cheat's charter, a club for journeymen or worse.

'Yes, Inspector McKay, the funny hand-shake brigade indeed,' said the assistant commissioner, smiling, 'just find Lady Moulding.'

'I'm on the case, sir.'

'You can clear the slate of anything else, Inspector.'

'We've got one or two leads, sir.'

'Good, chase them up, drop everything else.'

Rod cleared security and walked back out into the heaving streets of Victoria. He'd never liked Victoria. It was a part of London which was an architectural mess and of all the capital's manors had no sense of being a village. It was a sprawl. Villages were easier to demarcate, both cops and robbers felt they had order. Cops had a known world to patrol, robbers a manor to control. Sprawls weren't conducive to good order: no man's land produced nervous tribes and uncertain tribalism blurred the focus of both crime and punishment.

He'd arranged to meet Dippy in a nearby Costa coffee bar. He sat in the window with a medium latte and watched the throng pass by on the other side of the glass just inches from his face.

Women, like human dolls, passed by, immaculately made up, fashionably dressed and phone-roboticised on the next happening. Men, like cloned tailor's dummies, passed by, soberly dressed, importantly strapped in briefcases, an endless procession of spread-sheet psyches. A scrofulous female in a grubby shell suit sat at the edge of the window on a square of cardboard. She was knitting. Beside her were examples of her wares: knitted Thomas the Tanks,

Super Marios and meercats. Mass media icons to stroke in the safety of your own home. They sold well, too. Instantly recognizable objects, but original at the same time. The knitting beggar was a shrewd marketeer, a lone pioneer with the sort of direct initiative great corporations sought, but rarely found, in the workforce which passed her by.

Rod sipped his latte and thought of Freddie coming into this world. Getting him away from Erica's material blinkers every other Saturday might not be enough to secure him a walk-by role instead of a cardboard cut-out.

'Detective Inspector McKay, drinking latte? And in this heat? I promise I won't tell your mates,' said Dippy as she joined him at a window stool.

'Dips. You got here fast. It cools me down, would you like a coffee?'

'Got one,' she held up a cardboard beaker, 'you're so absorbed in people watching, but you didn't spot me.'

'When you watch the anonymous pass, you create their narrative. When it's someone you know, the make-believe disappears.'

'Deep,' said Dippy.

'Look at them, the passing multitude. That's civilisation. Trouble is there's nothing left to discover. There's no astronomers out there measuring the angles between the planets, there are no philosophers inventing democracy, or lawyers discussing ethics. All that's left now is shopping!'

'Hey, Rod, I prefer you on Old Speckled Hen and there's nothing villainous about the fruitless chase of acquisition by the way.'

'Sorry, Dips. You're right these people are our charges. We are here to protect SHOPPERS!'

'And one in particular, I understand?'

'Yes it's all systems go on the search for Lady Adele Moulding. The gallant Sir Keith is in the same masonic lodge as the gaffer's number two.'

'That's one place we shoppers have yet to infiltrate.'

'Meaning?'

'The masons. They have yet to embrace universal suffrage,' Dippy was smiling.

'As you know a woman's place is in the home, a mason's home.'

'True, and I suppose the ironing must be piling up at Sir Keith's'

'If this mystery white van had anything to do with the good lady's disappearance then it was driven by somebody who knew she was going to be there,' said Rod, 'somebody who knew she was going to park in Old Jewry. Someone who was arsehole lucky, not.'

'So he was following her?'

'He or she has to have been and not tail-gating her either, not through London traffic.'

'So using some sort of tracking device?'

'Yeah. They're two-a-penny in any High Street electrical store. The more expensive versions come with software you download onto a computer. Maplins do one for around three hundred quid which works with a laptop.'

'So there's a remote unit and a mother station, a docking unit so-to-speak?'

'Correct.'

'And the remote unit, how would you fit that on the outside of the car?'

'A bloody great magnet welded onto the casing I suspect.'

'Which is a start. So much for a potential 'How', but what about motive? There didn't seem much evidence of that in the Moulding testimony,' said Dippy.

'We need to talk to him again. At home. Come on let's get out of Victoria. I'll drive you to Richmond. Mouldo's taken time out from work.'

Dippy noticed how grand West London was compared with the East End. Large, detached homes, with proper larch fencing, interspersed with well kept brick built high street areas with delicatessens, shops selling nothing but candles jostling with Lexus motor car showrooms.

'This is swanky. It must be heaven on earth for..' her voice was suddenly drowned out by the roar of a Boeing 747, its giant fuselage flashing in the bright sunlight as it dropped down over the rooftops.

As the air brakes stopped screaming, she added: 'I was going to say burglars. Hey no wonder they want the airport re-sited on the other side of London.'

'It's down to the bloody royals. They built their castles up wind of the chimney smoke. While those of us in the East End, the plebs, were left chewing on the soot of London's hearths blown over us on the prevailing south-westerlies,' said Rod, but now they've got Heathrow over their battlements they're getting a taste of our medicine, serves 'em right!'

He had grown up in the old East End. When railway arches were used to house car breakers and not wine bars. When quick-witted boys sold carrots off carts and not coffee beans in commodity markets. And when the streets were safe for women to walk down as criminals only ever 'done their own.' Or so those, who were nostalgic for the old East End, believed.

Rod was not nostalgic.

His first Saturday job was helping an old crone called Daphne Leovold run her pavement stall at the far end of Bethnal Green Road by the tube station. There was only just enough for the two of them in her little square tent from which she sold cigarettes, matches, and chewing-gum. When it rained she threw a plastic sheet over her wares and scattered pac-a-mac raincoats and plastic rain hats over the top. She spent all day in her tent, and only sat on her stool for lunch, drinking tea from a flask, her false teeth clicking on home-made sandwiches.

One day Rod watched as a bulbous hand reached into the tent and spread over a packet of 20 Embassy cigarettes. The cigarettes were kept right at the back of the stall. The fingers of the hand were covered in small cuts and over one a large clumsy gold ring bulged. Rod followed the hand upwards. It disappeared under a Prince of Wales check suit. He looked up and a thick-set man with black eyes behind heavy-rimmed glasses stared back scowling.

'Daphne?' he said. His voice was surprisingly squeaky.

Daphne looked up from her copy of the People's Friend and jumped. She hadn't spotted the hand's arrival.

'Just a minute,' she said and pulled open the worn wooden drawer where the petty cash was kept. She pulled out a ten pound note and gave it to the well-dressed man who then pocketed the cigarettes as well.

'Hey you haven't paid,' said Rod. 'It's all right Rodney,' said Daphne.

The man turned back to the tent, bent down and staring into the mirror, which Daphne kept for customers trying out the rain hats, combed his thick black hair back over his ears.

'But he took cigarettes,' said Rod. The man re-knotted his knitted silk tie and then pocketed another packet of cigarettes. 'Rodney it's OK. All right?' said Daphne waving her hands beneath the counter.

Rod said nothing. The man stared at him curiously. Then walked off.

'You don't mess with the Twins,' said Daphne.

'Who's the Twins?'

'Never you mind, Rodney. It's just life. You've gotta pay someone.'

'But why, Mrs Leovold? He didn't give you anything, he should've paid you for the cigarettes.'

'What he provides is protection,' she said opening her magazine again.

'Protection? From what?'

'From rivals, from threat, from the big, bad world.'

'But Mrs Leovold, you've got the police for that.'

The old crone smiled mirthlessly, her perfect even, white teeth a plastic incongruity in her shrivelled mouth, 'From them an' all,' she said.

A few months later just as Rod was in his last days at school his father, Percy, came home from the pub early one Friday and went straight to bed.

'He's not well, Rodney, leave him be,' said Rod's mother, Marjorie, but the next day Rod found out what had happened from a schoolmate, Charlie, who lived over a nearby pub, the Grave Maurice, now converted to an Asian grocery store.

Percy, worked in an insurance office, as a humble clerk and always knocked off early on Fridays for a few beers with his pals. They had gathered at the bar of the busy pub on the Mile End Road where, as the cigarette smoke curled round their trilbies, the story of an illegal bare-fisted boxing match between two dockers from the Royal Albert was recounted by one of Percy's cronies, a fork-lift-truck driver. Apparently the fight had been fixed: one of the combatants had been paid to lose. The trouble was once he was in the makeshift ring, set up behind the fences of a scrap-yard, it proved impossible to get a punch landed on himself in order to be able to fall over and go 'out for the count', because his opponent had also been paid to lose!

'When your dad heard that, he jerked backwards with laughter and knocked someone's drink over. The whole pub went silent. And you dad turned to apologise and asked the man what he was drinking. But the man said: "No, what are you drinking?" Nobody said anything. The pub was deadly quiet. So your dad realised he'd better do as he was told. You know what your dad drinks?'

'Yeah, gin and tonic,' said Rod.

'Yeah, well the man ordered him a gin – a triple – but without the tonic. Then he told him to down it in one. Then he ordered another. And another. Your dad had to drink four of those straight off and ended up puking up in the gutter outside. Then one of the man's friends came up to your dad and said: "Congratulations you've just had a drink with Ronnie Kray."'

It humiliated Rod more than his father. He developed a visceral hatred for the bully boys who 'ran' the East End. He watched in disbelief as showbiz and sporting stars hob-nobbed with them and was horrified when he discovered a contemporary of his from schooldays had been slashed across the buttocks with a sabre for a drunken tirade while inside the Twins' Double R club.

He was disappointed to find that even the old vicar Richard Hetherington of the church Rod went to each Sunday, St Matthews, on the Bethnal Green Road, spoke well of them.

Rod could see that fear was the vice keeping everyone in line.

'The butcher, baker and candlestick-maker are all turning the other cheek – not to receive punishment themselves but to be able to ignore it. They are all rationalising thuggery because they are not equipped to confront it,' he told himself at his bible class. And with a burning desire to end injustice he joined the police cadets.

The blazing sunshine glittered fiercely off the Thames as they drove over Richmond Bridge. The large leafed plane trees along the towpath were unmoving not even a cats-paw ruffled the water and the bank-side reeds stood as still as spears. Several Londoners had removed their skirts and trousers and sat in their underwear legs dangling in the river.

Dippy had removed her uniform jacket and for the first time Rod noticed she was wearing a T-shirt bearing a message. It read 'Make Bono history'. Rod laughed.

'I love it,'

'What?'

'Your T-shirt.'

'Oh that. Yeah, bit of teenage foolishness.'

'But you've got a point. He's a self-aggrandising little twat.'

'I'd forgive him that if only he could sing,' said Dippy, 'back home we actually export food anyway, well bananas. What we could do with are some decent live bands.'

They pulled up in a quiet residential road outside a detached Victorian villa with a large slate car park on which sat three new automobiles.

'There's still enough room to park a Mercedes sports,' said Rod, ' but forensics have still got Lady Moulding's car.'

Dippy pulled on her police jacket as she surveyed the Cypress trees in Grecian-style pots and a stone gazebo in the front garden complete with Corinthian columns.

'How tacky,' said Dippy, 'he's got a Caesar-complex.'

Sir Keith was waiting for them in the shade under the glass veranda, which was covered in vines, at the front of the house. The windows were all open. Sir Keith's cocky office demeanour had gone. Without the edifice of Canary Wharf and his underlings to impress he seemed suddenly vulnerable, easy to sum up. There was no mystery to Sir Keith he was just a small man who'd used a certain initiative to achieve material wealth. Physically and intellectually unprepossessing he carried the uncomfortable burden of knowing it was only the power of his wealth which gave him any appeal. On the other hand he had got used to that fact over the years and was never beyond using it to his advantage. Aware he therefore lacked integrity he tried to adopt a sort of laddish braggadocio, which being naturally cautious, he failed to pull off. But all that had gone now as he sat alone in his mansion.

'Something has definitely happened to her,' he said, from behind a pair of fashionable sunglasses, the type with wide black frames at the temple, 'no way would she play a game for this long.'

'Does she play games then?' asked Rod.

'As I say we had our silly set-tos but that was years ago.'

Sir Keith poured the police officers some iced lemonade from a jug. Rod gulped greedily, but Dippy declined a glass, 'No thanks,' she said.

'God how do you put up with this heat?' asked Sir Keith.

'I was born on the equator. So what happened the night she went missing? Who were you with? Any reason to think there was somebody there who would have designs on your wife?'

'I was flirting with a pretty young woman. But then so was Adele. It was just a bit of tom-foolery. We were exciting each other. Trying to make each other jealous.'

Sir Keith was not holding back. He was being candid. He was genuinely worried.

Dippy sensed this and for the first time felt sorry for the man.

'So who is this woman?'

'Samantha Shelly. But she's an innocent. Just a pretty young PR girl with her eye on the main chance.'

'That chance being you?'

'Correct.'

'So your wife would be a rival?'

'No, no it's not like that, believe me. We were just a pair of old fools letting our libido off the leash. And Sam played us both.'

Dippy raised an eyebrow.

'Adult games, eh?'

'Precisely.'

'I brought her back here when Adele didn't show at Ronnie Scott's. I'd thought Adele and Sam had been getting on like a house on fire. I was hoping, that, er, that well we might all end up as one happy family for the night.'

'I see, so what time did she leave?'

'I ran her to work the following morning before heading to the City myself.'

'Sir Keith,' said Rod who'd listened to the prattle play itself out, 'are you sure you can't think of anyone who might hold a grudge towards Adele?'

'No-one. No-one, that's the thing, she's just a bourgeois, middle class, housewife. In fact if anything she's quite caring and certainly less selfish than me. There's absolutely no reason I can think of why anyone should hold a grudge towards her. Is that the line of inquiry now, then? That someone's got it in for her?'

'I'm not assuming anything,' said Rod.

'But with respect, Sir Keith, you are clearly a lot more worried now than when we spoke to you earlier,' said Dippy, 'and that suggests to me that something unexpected has befallen your wife.'

Sir Keith's little chin almost folded into his neck as he nodded his head in agreement. The check shirt he was wearing was opened a button too low from the collar for a man his age. Perhaps it had been done for Sam's benefit, thought Dippy. Chest hair was a totem of virility, yes, but only in the years before it turned white.

It was the same with those close-cut jeans: the effect back-fired. Tight trousers on strong, youthful legs, yes, but on an older man skinny jeans simply displayed skinny legs. His tan Timberland boots gave him a much needed extra inch in height, but on a small man bulged disproportionately adding a cartoon-like quality to his overall profile.

'Aren't you hot in those?' Dippy couldn't resist asking as she pointed to the clumpy footwear, 'in this heat?'

'No, they're as cool in summer as they are warm in winter,' Sir Keith said self-consciously, aware suddenly that his Peter Pan dress sense was open to ridicule,

'They're pricey, but so comfortable. Another drink?'

Rod held out his glass, 'Thanks. So, while obviously we always keep an open mind, at the same time it could be the case that someone rather than something has interfered with Lady Moulding's plans. She did have plans, didn't she? She'd gone to get her coat from the car and was going to follow you on by cab to Ronnie Scott's? She stated that in front of you and Miss Shelly. She had already struck up a warm relationship with Miss Shelly, she was looking forward to the club...'

'She'd had a drink. What if she'd had an accident?' said Sir Keith.

'What sort of an accident?' Dippy asked.

'I don't know...knocked down by a car, tripped over and hurt herself...'

'She had ID on her?' asked Dippy again, wiping the sweat from beneath her afro-covered brow.

'She should have done. She always carried her driving licence, she had credit cards, store cards, and her mobile had her Facebook page as a screen saver,' Sir Keith said.

'Well we would know by now whether she had been admitted to a hospital. Who knew you were both going to the Mansion House that night?,' asked Rod.

'Apart from old friends sharing our table, nobody, why?'

'CCTV has picked up a suspicious white van in the same road where your wife's car was parked,' said Dippy.

'Suspicious in what way?'

'It had false number plates.'

Sir Keith looked appalled. His little chin receded further into his bristly neck as his mouth fell open, 'Good God, but we don't know anybody with a white van.'

More acceptable if it had been a Winnebago, thought Dippy, 'What about you Sir Keith, is there anybody – anybody – who might hold a grudge against you?'

'I'm shallow, foolish, vain, lecherous, but as CEO at the bank I have some 245 people under me and all are grateful for their jobs. Staff turnover is low. I also raise money for charity…'

'Like on the night Lady Moulding went missing,' said Rod, 'that was for an Alzheimer's charity was it not?'

'It was, it was,' Sir Keith, wiped the palms of his freckly white hands on his too-tight jeans, 'there you are, I'm a benefactor, not that I go around shouting about it. And the battle to combat Alzheimer's is not exactly going to line my pockets. In fact very much the opposite.'

A heat haze was rising from the ground. It gave a kink to the perspective of the garden and sunlight burned on the Italianate flagstones of the veranda, in dappled pools between the shade of the vine.

'Ah yes, your care home chain. I suppose many of your customers are sufferers?' said Rod.

'They are, although I prefer to call them clients.'

'So you're responsible for 245 workers at Metrobanc, but that's different to those at Memory Lodge PLC. They are employees, are they not? And there must be many more of those?' asked Rod, crunching the melting ice cubes from the last of his lemonade.

'We provide jobs for some 900 carers at our 60 homes throughout England & Wales,' said Sir Keith, 'on average we have around 15 carers per home, looking after on average 40 folks per lodge. That's a good proportion of carers per client. Some homes have only two or three carers for 50 or so residents.'

Rod looked out over Sir Keith's grounds. To one side of the house the pink, gravel surface of a tennis court was sectioned off behind a high wire fence. Around it a lawn piebald with earthy patches was suffering from the lack of rain.

Rod turned to look at Sir Keith: 'When people become numbers no-one investigates their disappearance.'

'Very profound,' Sir Keith, said, 'No, I'm sorry. You're right, forgive me. But I'm just giving you an overview of the business. There are many bosses of such care homes who would not have the figures at their fingertips.'

'That's OK. Forgive me, too, but could there not, within that small multitude, be someone with a grudge?'

'I don't see why. As I say Memory Lodge PLC employs more carers per home than most which means their duties are fewer. The carers themselves know this from the grapevine and the proof of that is

223

evident from the numbers we get each year who want to transfer from the homes they are working for to work for us.'

'Do you check their visas, before employing them?' asked Rod.

Sir Keith was silent for a minute and rubbed the grey bristles on his neck, 'We aren't obliged to, but on the whole we do make checks, where we can,' he said eventually.

'Tell me about the time you appeared at the High Court. Wasn't that to do with the employment of illegal immigrants ?'

For the first time during the interview Sir Keith took off his Raybans and squinting in the bright sunlight, said: 'You have done your homework, haven't you? Anybody'd think I was the villain of the piece.'

'He's simply casting his net wide,' said Dippy, 'over the ocean of the known. We have to try and find a lead.'

Sir Keith turned to look at Dippy his eyes, now used to the light, stopped squinting.

She noticed the irises, once brown, were tortoise-shelled with age and rimmed with white circles like half moons joined together.

No wonder he wears shades even in the shade, she thought.

'I do know this,' he said pompously, and turned his back on Dippy to address Rod.

'Three months ago it had come to the notice of the Department of Work and Pensions that a member of our staff had a visa which had run out.'

'Hardly worthy of the High Court's attention. Are you sure it was just one?' asked Rod.

Sir Keith pulled a lime yellow ball from a basket beneath his wicker chair and threw it over the fence and watched it bounce across the tennis court.

'No. There was a raid by the Immigration Agency on the south-eastern sector of our homes and it was found that 19 staff had out-of-date visas. But because I was able to show that we did endeavour to keep proper records, the case against Memory Lodge PLC was dropped, although the nineteen – all from the Philippines – were deported,' said Sir Keith unwittingly pouring himself a slug of Pimms while offering his guests lemonade.

'Do you know what it was that alerted immigration to your homes in the first place? I mean was it just a random sweep?' asked Rod.

'It wasn't. There had been one rogue carer whose visa had expired…and investigations subsequently threw up others,' Sir Keith slurped his Pimms, a little paper umbrella brushing his nose.

'Rogue carer?'

'Yes, Riza Santiago. She was, by all accounts, a good woman: six years working in the care industry, NVQ status of the right order, and popular with her peers. But things started going missing at the home she worked at.'

'Which one was that?'

'Memory Lodge in Dagenham, Essex.'

'What things went missing?'

'Well rings, necklaces, brooches. The difficulty we have with this sort of thing is that the resident often claims her property has been stolen when in fact she's either lost it, or never brought it to the home in the first place, or the family have taken it away for safe keeping, at least that's what they say. But with this lodge it happened too many times to be just another case of mental deterioration,' Sir Keith sighed, 'the trouble is families either come down on us like a ton of bricks thinking that heavy-handedness will make us quake in fear and treat their loved ones with kid gloves, or they under report for fear of their relatives facing repercussions.'

'So what did you do?'

'We asked a trusted staff member to keep an eye open,'

'To spy you mean?' said Dippy.

'I think you call it surveillance,' said Sir Keith cattily.

'Dips, please,' said Rod, 'Sir Keith you were saying,'

Sir Keith was mildly delighted that the attractive Dippy, a girl he could sense found him pathetic, had been put in her place.

'The trouble was all remaining jewellery had already been stashed away and for a good few months Ms Santiago was dormant, so to speak. Then we discovered someone had been physically abusing one of the more awkward residents – some of them can be very feisty and make false accusations or lash out verbally – but this one in particular lashed out with her fists.'

The desperate lost world of the unseen, thought Rod, thousands of dilapidated souls who simply cannot be tended by their hard-working families, are locked away in big old houses throughout the land, to get on with the business of dying. At least in the old East End of his grandparents' day they were kept at home until the bitter end. But then they didn't live so long. Smog and poor diet killed them off.

The Pimms and the heat loosened Sir Keith up. He relaxed back into the wicker chair and continued.

'Then one day our informer came to us and said she had witnessed Riza Santiago slapping this resident around the face. Once Santiago had left the room our source went to the resident and tried to feed her, but she was tarred with the same brush. The poor woman thought everyone in a light blue nylon uniform was there to torment her. The manageress was called and it was decided to wheel the resident to her room, to try and break the cycle and hope her dysfunctional memory would allow the incident to pass allowing her to be properly cared for once more.'

'So what action was taken to deal with Riza Santiago?'

'Our informer, who knew her well, indeed was a friend, acted very bravely and gave a statement to police. She actually went to court and gave evidence against her and she was deported. The publicity from the case alerted the Home Office who then ordered the check on our workers' residential legitimacy. Their investigations threw up the visa shortfall and we lost a lot of excellent carers over the incident.'

'What was the name of this resident?

'Betty Lamb.'

'And does she have family?'

'I don't think so. She's a widower. But I'm afraid it took her a long time to get over it,' said Sir Keith, 'we had to replace all the uniforms to dark blue before she'd let any of our staff near her again.'

'Would you mind if we spoke to your "informer"?' asked Rod.

'Of course, you need to ask for the manageress at Memory Lodge. Her name is Isabella Sanchia, but how a Dagenham-based Filipino care worker can help find Adele, I don't know.'

The oppressive midday sun glared off the white gravestone chippings which crunched under police issue boots as Rod and Dippy walked up the driveway of Memory Lodge. At the glass-fronted door, Rod stamped off the dust from his uppers and pressed a large ceramic button which set off a continuous buzzing sound. The entry hall beyond the door was empty until a tall, old man in a suit appeared, walked up to the door but looked straight through it and beyond Rod and Dippy, who smiled in anticipation. But instead of opening the door the old man turned round and walked back into the lobby and disappeared down a corridor. The buzzer, meanwhile, kept on buzzing. Rod looked up at the gloomy edifice of Memory Lodge.

Some of the hanging tiles cascading down the gable end over the entry door had slipped and been mortared back not quite into place. A discarded surgical glove had been used to tie back a rose briar in the flower beds around the ground floor and one of the windows on the flank wall was broken and had been shuttered over on the inside with a flattened cardboard box. The place had an air of mend and make-do about it, of budgets being kept tight. The buzzing sound stopped suddenly, the door swung open and a young Filipino woman ushered Rod and Dippy inside. She did not ask who they were or who they had come to see, the secured door was to stop people getting out not in. What possible malign interest could there be for an outsider in a house of the dying?

There was a slightly sweet pong in the air. Of something foul being masked by something out of an aerosol can. Like cheap deodorant it failed: the spray was simply polluted by something repellent and therefore succeeded only in flagging it up.

The dazzling sunshine was prevented from penetrating too far by rotting curtains, which also held in the day's heat.

Rod removed his jacket.

'Detective Inspector Rod McKay, and this is Detective Sergeant Dippy Daud,' said Rod flashing his ID card.

The oriental face of their host, was not designed to hide expressions of doubt. Round, open and with flawless skin the woman could have been aged anywhere from 19 to 40. The frown which suddenly dominated her previously smiling face suggested tears, like cloud before rain.

'You want see manageress?'

'Yes please.'

'Plea wait here,' she said and scurried off.

'I thought they're s'posed to be inscrutable?' said Rod.

'That's the Chinese,' said Dippy.

'Especially when they bring the bill,' he added.

Dippy laughed, 'Steady…remember I could take offence at such racial categorisation.'

A short, girl-like woman came along the corridor, in black wool tights, her feet in schoolgirl like strap-over pumps and wearing a more highly decorated uniform suggesting authority.

'Hello,' she smiled, through thick spectacles, 'you are here about Betty?' One of the reasons she'd been promoted to manageress was her standard of English.

'That's right. Detective Inspector Rod McKay,' he said thrusting out his hand, ' and you are?'

'Isabella Sanchia, I am the manageress of Memory Lodge. I presume this is about Betty's son?'

'Well, you know, about what happened,' said Rod craftily.

'He was very upset, which is understandable, although I'm surprised he's gone to the police.'

'Well just run us through it. From your standpoint.'

The tall, smartly-dressed old man they'd seen earlier, came walking down the hallway towards them. Although his pace was slow, it was marked, deliberate, though his bespectacled stare appeared to stare from within. As he passed Rod noticed the neatly-pressed expensive suit was incongruously matched with faux leather slippers.

'Careful, Tom,' said the manageress as he passed, but he said nothing and disappeared into one of the lounges.

'Betty can be difficult,' said the manageress, 'but we are trained to deal with that. It's part of the decline Alzheimer's sufferers face. Some deteriorate calmly becoming babies again without a fuss. Others fight. Betty fights. We had one carer here who lost patience with Betty – totally inexcusable – and as I'm sure Mr Lamb told you...' before she could say more the old man reappeared walking back the way he had come.

'Careful as you pass the kitchen, Tom,' said the manageress as he shuffled by.

This time Rod noticed patches of grey bristles on his neck which the razor had missed.

'Tom was a top barrister in his day,' said the manageress.

'Why does he keep walking up and down?' asked Dippy.

'He's looking for his wife. She doesn't visit much.'

'You were saying...about Mr Lamb,' said Rod.

'Yes, well he turned up one night when Betty was particularly disturbed. She would not eat, well that we can deal with. But she wouldn't drink either and that, as I'm sure you know, is more dangerous.'

'They can dehydrate – especially in this heat,' said Dippy.

'Yes, but we've dealt with the carer in question she's been sent home to Manila.'

'Yes, quite but take us back to the night in question.'

'Of course, and I'm glad you want our side of the story as well, as things can get misconstrued around care and goodness knows we've had enough bad publicity – I mean not this home in particular, but I'm sure you follow.'

'I do,' said Rod.

'Well this carer was trying to get Betty to drink – she hadn't had any liquids all day – we'd all tried to get her to take tea, juice, even rice pudding which she normally likes, but with no success. When it was Ms Santiago's shift, Betty refused to open her mouth. She just sat there with her lips snapped shut. Ms Santiago gently nudged the baby feeding bottle's beak between her lips and tried to tilt her head back when Betty punched her on the nose. I'm afraid that's when Ms Santiago lost control.'

'What did she do?'

'She slapped her around the face and all hell broke loose. Betty was screaming blue murder,'

'Were you there?'

'I don't work nights. But I have the full report in my office,' Mrs Sanchia showed them along the corridor as Tom came padding back towards them.

'Where's the bus stop?' he said.

'Just keep going Tom, down the end, be careful of the kitchen, Tom.'

Rod and Dippy turned to let the old man pass. Rod noticed this time that he was wearing a food-encrusted bib inside his jacket over his tie. Tom stared straight ahead and wandered down a threadbare Paisley carpet with a shiny, worn causeway in its centre, to a place locked in his dream.

Mrs Sanchia led them outside into the blazing sunshine. They skirted a well-kept lawn which had square wire frames implanted into it. All were draped with drying bed-sheets.

They arrived at a large log cabin style shed. The manageress turned the key in a padlock and opened a stable-type door.

'Come into my kingdom,' she said, 'there's no spare room in the lodge for administration.'

She pulled a large red file down from a shelf and thumbed back through the pages.

'Here we are. There were six staff on that night. Bunty Tieg, she's the night manager, and five junior carers, including Riza Santiago. "Ms Santiago is reported to Bunty Tieg as having assaulted Mrs Betty Lamb. Two carers to comfort Mrs Lamb, two remaining check on other residents who might be disturbed from Mrs Lambs' shouting. Son of Mrs Lamb called 8pm. Failed to placate Mrs Lamb. Son left 8.30 pm. Remained calm, but angry upon departure.'

'Well that's the bare bones,' said Rod, 'could we see Mrs Lamb. Is she OK now?'

'She's fine now. That was three months ago after all. She still has behavioural issues, but that is down to her condition.'

The manager led them back into the lodge. A meal was being served from stainless steel trollies to the residents who were seated around the walls of the three large lounges on adjustable armchairs with desk style tables in front of them.

'We don't want to distract her from eating,' said Dippy, 'should we wait?'

'She probably won't eat anything anyway,' said Mrs Sanchia, 'but we are managing to get her to eat porridge in the morning. She might have a drink, now, but not much more.'

Mrs Sanchia ushered them into a bright conservatory with blinds pulled across the glass roof to keep out the direct sunlight. A large steel fan was whirring away stirring up the fetid air.

In the corner bay beneath an open window sat a little monkey-faced woman. Her freshly-washed white hair was combed back behind her large ears and held in a clip over her scalp. She was dressed in a smart white blouse, open at the neck where a bulbous mock-pearl necklace sat. Her mottled legs thrust out of a navy blue nylon skirt and were raised up in front of her on an adjustable footrest. Her socks had been deliberately left off in the heat but she had a pair of red and blue, polka dot slippers on her feet.

'Bet ~Tee. How are you?' said the manageress loudly, 'look you have some visitors, come to see you Betty.'

Betty appeared to ignore her and stared straight ahead apparently focussing on the middle of the room. There were eight other residents sitting there all with their backs to the walls, plus the regular visit by Tom as he paced in and out. But none of the old folks were interacting with each other. They all sat independently ignoring one another with their personal demons, fading memories, or mind pictures. It was as though they were willing themselves out of the community. One old woman sat with her mouth permanently wide open, like some wretched iguana trying to cool down in the desert. Others were dozing, trying to sleep their way into oblivion.

Another woman bewigged and in a wheelchair suddenly said: 'Take me to bed.'

'No not yet Connie,' said the manageress, 'later.'

'What time?'

'At seven Connie after your dinner.'

'Get me my dinner.'

'Not yet Connie.'

'What time?'

'At five Connie, that's when we serve dinner.'

'Take me to bed.'

On the lounge door an adjustable calendar, with a wipe-off panel was hung. It read '8th June, hot and sunny all day'.

'At least they know what day it is,' said Rod with a smile.

'Very droll,' said Dippy.

The large flat screen television was tuned to a daytime children's programme. Two youthful presenters jumped around in rabbit suits singing: 'Hoppity, hop, we go. Hoppity hop. Will you go hoppity hop with us? Yes you go hoppity hop.'

'Bet Tee? Want a drink Bet TEE? Look some visitors for you Bet TEE.'

Rod smiled at Betty and introduced himself. But she looked straight through him. Dippy stepped backwards into the middle of the room where Betty appeared to be focusing. She looked directly into her gaze.

'Good morning Betty. How are you keeping?'

Betty suddenly connected. Her eyes opened wide. She locked onto Dippy's face.

'Go, now. Get out. Quick. They'll have you. You of all people.'

'Who will, Betty? Who'll have me?'

'The Germans. They'll take you. They'll gas you. They will. That's what's happening. The Jews, queers, brown people like you. And gipsies. Don't tell them I'm a Romany will you?'

'Of course, not Betty. In fact we're police officers and I'm here with Rod to help you.'

'Thank-you. Thanks so much. Get me out. You'll have to lift me and make sure they don't see you.'

'Betty I wanted to ask you about the night one of the Germans hurt you,' said Rod.

Mrs Sanchia shrugged her shoulders and left them to it.

'Do you remember it? When you were slapped?'

'Of course I remember it. How do you forget a thing like that?' she said, 'They were trying to drown me,'

'To drown you?'

'Yes. One of the uniforms, a woman, they're the worst you know. She was trying to force a pipe down me throat, it's one of their torture methods, no doubt. But I wasn't having any of it. And when that didn't work she tried sending me on one of them forced marches.'

'Forced march?'

'Yes. She was stamping on me feet, trying to get me to walk. But me legs have gone, more's the pity, otherwise I'd have kicked her where the sun don't shine. So then I got crafty. I pretended to go along with it. I opened me mouth just a tad and she leaned forward with the hose and wallop I gave a her a left hook straight on her conk,' Betty cackled.

'Well done Betty, an act of self defence if ever there was one,' said Dippy.

'You want cup of tea?' one of the carers came in to the conservatory. Rod had done his best to ignore the patented air fresheners which failed to mask the smell of communal evacuation, but the thought of consuming within the walls of Memory Lodge, was a step too far.

'Yes please,' said Dippy much to his surprise. 'No sugar, thanks, just milk.'

'Not for me thanks very much,' said Rod.

The carer wheeled her trolley away.

'You're taking your life in your hands aren't you?'

'Nonsense. The kitchens in this place will be cleaner than those of a luxury liner,' said Dippy, 'have you noticed how all the staff are wearing surgical gloves? In a place as vulnerable as this everyone's committed to germ warfare.'

'Good point. One bug could take them all out, I suppose.'

'They wear them gloves so's they won't get caught,' said Betty, 'I'm surprised you hadn't thought of that being Old Bill.'

'Aha Betty, I'm pleased to see nothing gets past you. And you are quite right there would be no fingerprints would there? After you managed to fight off the German what happened next?'

'Well then they all come in. Fussing about and trying to make out nothing had happened.'

'But you do know that the member of staff who assaulted you was prosecuted, don't you?'

'What does that mean these days? A slap on the wrist. I was told she was just sent home.'

'Well, yes deported, Betty, sent back home on the other side of the world. No doubt in disgrace and with little chance of visiting the UK again.'

'They should have sent her to the dark side of the moon. But she'll pay eventually, my cherub will see to that.'

The wall mounted TV was now showing an old black and white film. A heavily made-up Fred Astaire, was dancing cheek to cheek with Ginger Rogers and Betty started to hum along.

'I'm in Heaven, I'm in Heaven,' crooned the old stager as Betty wagged her head back and forth and a slippered foot slowly wagged out the tempo.

'He looks like a rent boy trying to pass himself off as a doorman at the Dorchester,' said Rod, ' but clock Ginger, what a beauty, makes Monroe look like an overfed chav. I think we're wasting our time here. Dear old Betty's in Dingley Dell.'

The smiling carer arrived with more tea on her trolley. She handed Dippy a gleaming mug on a saucer with two Custard Creams.

'Thanks very much,' she said, and turned back to Rod, 'You're being a little harsh on the screen goddess of all time. But I agree Ginger has an on-screen innocence that poor old Marilyn had bleached and dyed out of her. Where's Dingley Dell by the way?'

'Where the fairies live.'

'She's been lucid up until now, her account matches what we know already. Don't you want to pursue the cherub?'

'Be my guest.'

Dippy bent down and started singing along, very gently, to the TV.

Betty turned to her and gave her a huge smile. 'Isn't he lovely? People nowadays don't know what they're missing, yet even in your country they know about Fred Astaire.'

'How true Betty, they don't make them like that anymore. Did your son visit you that night when it happened?'

'He's an angel. He came in, he got them all out of the room. He knows the truth. He said she should be crucified for what she done.'

'He must have been very worried about you, having to leave you here.'

'We're all in this war together. But such evil won't triumph, one day Germany, and the Germans will pay. My angel will make them pay.'

'But what if they find out?'

'They don't know where to find him. He's hidden.'

'What you mean like the resistance?'

'Yeah that sort of thing, love. Look at him dance, what a mover.'

The women watched as Fred twirled Ginger gracefully around the floor.

'So Hervey's got a plan at least, to help?'

'How do you know his name?' said Betty suddenly suspicious.

'One of the Germans told her,' said Rod.

'Bastards.'

'Yes. He's got God on his side for starters, oh I do love him, look at that man. Where have they all gone, dancers like him?'

The heat of the day was forcing its way into the home. The fan moved turgidly, its large blades slicing, dicing and simply redistributing the stifling air.

'So when will Hervey come back to check you're all right?'

'When he's finished preparing.'

'Preparing? Preparing what?'

Betty's slippered feet, raised on the footstool tapped together as she followed Fred Astaire looping round the ballroom.

'Calvary, dear.'

————

Brilliant sunshine threw a long shadow of the beacon over the drying sand as Hervey, bare-footed and wearing only shorts and T-shirt marched Adele, now forcibly dressed in a rubber dry suit, across the ribbed mud towards the cage-like structure.

Behind them Carpe Diem was nosed up onto the bank, an anchor leading from her bow, lay over on its side on the flat surface, unburied, simply chucked out as a formality.

As they approached the beacon a large black bird sitting on the apex of its north Cardinal mark spread its wings in silhouette against the sun. The triangles of the topmark should have been black. Instead they were white with bird lime. The four great baulks of the beacon's timber legs sat in puddles on the sand. About six foot off the ground was a corroded cross beam. A ladder was fixed to the structure. It had once enabled access for Trinity House workmen to paint the top mark.

When they were within 50 yards of the beacon the bird took off and flapped crookedly away.

'A cormorant. He's been fishing. This is a good perch for him. As the tide makes he can see the dabs moving through the mud,' said Hervey.

'This suit is intolerably hot,' said Adele, 'is it really necessary?'

'It will protect you.'

'But you're not wearing one,' said Adele battling not to consider the implications of the difference.

'But I'm not staying out here.'

Adele broke free from Hervey's grip and ran across the sand towards the far sea.

Hervey did not give chase and Adele soon stopped running. She was overheated in the rubber suit, and fell to the sand panting.

'You can only run into the sea and what would be the point of that?' asked Hervey as he approached.

'For God's sake I have done nothing to you NOTHING,' shouted Adele.

'This is not so much for God's sake as for mankind's,' said Hervey, 'I accept you have done nothing but that is exactly your sin. You, your husband, your family, live like kings, live oblivious to the bedlams you run, out of the sight of the wretches who provide your wealth.'

'Well give me the chance to rectify this. How can I do that out here?'

'Your multitudes of broken people, badly housed, tended by poorly paid and unqualified foreigners are impossible to manage properly as long as profit is the motive. There will always be abuse.'

'The Quality Care Commission takes abuse very seriously indeed. If there is abuse homes get closed down. There's not much profit in that.'

'My mother was abused. She was beaten, she was bullied, she was force-fed. She lives in a state of terror. The home has not been closed down.'

'Which home? I will deal with it. I will see your mother gets the best care available. I will see to it that she gets full compensation.'

Hervey helped Adele to her feet and walked her back to the beacon.

'Compensation? You mean money? Money does not compensate for time lost, for time irretrievable, for hours, minutes, seconds gone never to come again. But it's good that you want to help. I want you to help. I want you to defeat the anti-Christ that walks among us and you will help by becoming the Messiah. It did not work the first time but this time there will be a female prophet.'

'This is wrong. I am not religious.'

'You pray. I've heard you. Atheists don't pray.'

'I'm not an atheist. Agnostic perhaps.'

'Now is the time to get off the fence,' said Hervey pointing at the foot of the beacon's north-western leg where a corroded bolt stuck out proud about a foot above the sand.

'There you are. Hop up on that,' said Hervey.

'This is insane. I'm telling you. I cannot bring the heavens down on Memory Lodge PLC out in this fucking wilderness. But I can if you take me back ashore…'

Hervey brandished his Green River knife and Adele did as she was told.

Perched on the bolt she felt a rope placed around her midriff.

Once she was secured, Hervey lifted each of her arms out parallel along the cross beam and fastened them around the wrist to the gnarled timber with cable ties. Adele was still perched on the protruding bolt, the rubber bootees of her dry suit, hung toe downwards from the rusty thread. Hervey gathered her feet together, crossed them and trussed those, too with a cable tie around the weedy, piled leg.

He then walked back to Carpe Diem and returned carrying a plastic jerrycan. He placed it on the sand at the foot of the ladder and bent on a hauling line which he uncoiled as he climbed the ladder. Once on the platform's summit he hauled the jerry can to the top and lashed it on. He pushed a plastic pipe into the jerry can's nozzle and fed it down towards Adele. He then descended and, using gaffer tape, fastened a small booklet around the leg of the ladder nearest Adele, but just above the line of seaweed.

'You have a water supply. I've given you the 10 gallons I keep spare aboard Carpe Diem. Just suck on the tube when you are thirsty. The dry suit will keep you warm when the tide's in. This is a tide table. From it you will see that the tides are quite small at the moment. They are called neaps they come in slowly and not very far and go out slowly and also not very far. But in two days' time they start to pick up. They come on to springs. Then they come in quickly and come in a long way.'

Adele swallowed: 'Please do not do this. I am very scared. I am begging you to release me…'

'I fully intend to,' said Hervey, 'once you have spent the last six hours on the cross before the new moon. Then I will return for your resurrection. You can contemplate your own demise because from the tide table you can tell exactly when it will be. How many people can say that?'

'How many people WANT to say that? I don't want to say that. Please do not leave me here.'

'Christ couldn't say that. He knew he was going to die. But he didn't have that luxury: knowing WHEN.'

Hervey, squatted on his knees and started writing in the sand with a finger.

'It's all very well being told to live in the minute, but what if you cannot use that minute for anything other than reflection? Is that wasting time? But is it possible to ignore the past? If it's long past then maybe your reflection is nostalgic, many would argue that IS wasting time. If it's regarding family then maybe it's sentimental reflection, many would regard that, too, as a waste of time. But if it is the immediate past then perhaps your reflection is analysis. Most people would regard that as time well spent.'

'I'm sorry but I really do not follow you. I am not a student of philosophy. But I am appealing to you and your considered approach to all things. You are a deep thinker, my husband is shallow. Please take me back ashore. I'll live in your chapel. I'll become a disciple. Don't waste me out here.'

Hervey stood up. He scratched a line of sand with his foot as he continued his mantra-like soliloquy: 'Forget the name of my boat, I didn't choose it. It's crass. Live every day as though it's your last? How depressing. Surely it's better to live every day as though you are going to live forever? That's LIVING! That's how Christ lived . Six days before he died in this world he befriended Zaccaeus the cheating tax-collector who made a fortune from others. Zaccaeus was so pleased to be acknowledged with love instead of hate he promised to pay back four times what he had cheated. For that he was given eternal life.

'Whether you have eternal life or not we cannot know. But because, unlike Christ you have the luxury of knowing WHEN you are going to die, you can ignore living every day as though it's your last until this, your final day!'

He stepped aside and Adele could see he had written a date in the mud 11 June. Six days away.

Adele watched him walk away across the sand towards Carpe Diem. There was nobody else to appeal to so she screamed.

He turned back and said: 'Jesus spent six hours on the cross, but don't take my word for it, it's gospel. According to Luke anyway,' then he guffawed with laughter.

He continued across the bank and casually stepped onto the boat's bathing platform, brushing the sand from his feet before disappearing below.

Adele's screaming echoed within the upperworks of the beacon returning to her ears the futility of her appeal. So she stopped. She was also becoming short of breath in the heat. The dry suit had sealable cuffs and a pliable rubber chest piece which had been attached last after Hervey forced her into the suit. He had then screwed on a metal clip which fastened the chest seal to a ridged lip around the suit's opening through which Adele had been obliged to enter. The elasticised rubber piece gripped her neck in a watertight seal.

She took stock of her world.

The legs of the beacon were encrusted with tiny barnacles which fought for living space. So congested was the adhesion room below sea level that they even grew on top of one another. In places the curled black shell of a winkle had found a patch of timber to attach itself. Barnacles had taken no notice and had glued themselves to the backs of their competitors too.

The water slithered across the sand again. The line of ripples stopped momentarily at Hervey's beachcombing before cresting the letters and trickling slowly into them. Erasing the legend forever. The tide crept around Carpe Diem's hull and she began to float. Eventually the hull turned and faced the incoming tide.

Adele felt terrified of being left alone.

'Please don't leave me,' she yelled, 'if I'm going to die at least be here with me.'

But the only sound was water lapping the beacon's legs.

And then in a sudden impulsive rage, she shouted: 'At least stay and enjoy your fucking killing.'

At this Hervey appeared on deck, hauled up the anchor and turned the ignition. Carpe Diem puttered gently towards Adele. He put the boat on autohelm and walked forward and leaning on the pulpit, said: 'I'm not killing you. I'm keeping you alive. You will be baptised in six days' time. At least that's the way I see it. In secular terms, in terms of care, you will be force fed a saline solution. But by then you will be a redeemer.'

The water slapped her boots and climbed up her legs. It was a huge relief to feel the cool tide against her overheated body.

'And you will die with my curse upon you,' she yelled with bravado. Hervey climbed back onto the flying bridge and conned the boat away. Once clear of the shallows he opened her up and roared towards the unseen land.

Carpe Diem's wash came towards Adele like a small standing wave. It splashed over her legs, passed through the beacon, and was gone.

She craned her neck up towards the tide table. Today was the 5th June, high water was at 18.15. It was 4.88m in height. She was only 1.68m tall.

Standing on the bolt raised her but she could not calculate by how much.

The washed out number on the sand had been the 11th June.

Six days' time.

_____

The last habitation of any note was a line of state-owned houses surrounded by fields. One pink, another yellow, yet another pastel blue, the occupants defying their semi-terraced status with paint. The road then narrowed between hedgerows of ivy-covered thorn bushes with flat fields either side and a line of tall trees running along an intersecting ditch, and a three-storied, isolated house appeared which supported a sailing boat wind-vane high up on a cupola lookout.

'The sea must be somewhere nearby,' said Dippy as Rod's car passed the lonely house. The ploughed fields had been hard baked into cracked crusts, like over-done pies, by the relentless sunshine. Black-faced sheep stared suspiciously before bolting as the Toyota cruised by. In the middle distance a flock of 30 or so swans made a blaze of white against the dun-coloured fields, like wrong-coloured flamingos on a shrinking Serengeti lake. A black-bladed water pump stood rusting and obsolete in a distant copse, like a dead sunflower.

'What we need is a monsoon,' said Rod, 'and we'll probably get one now this drought is official. But to you this must be chicken feed.'

'Funny thing the perceptions people have about the Dark Continent,' said Dippy, 'Do you know people say to me "I suppose you are used to the heat. I suppose you don't notice it." Brits aren't racist deliberately. They're just clumsy. They look at my dark skin and think I'm born with Factor Four pigmentation.'

Rod laughed, 'You're right. We apply the same exotica to the Arctic. We expect Eskimos not to feel the cold.'

A weatherboard pub with low eaves appeared at the end of the road.

'The Plough and Sail, eh?' said Rod, as he turned right and started bouncing down a rutted lane, his suspension grinding on pot hole ridges, 'bit more sail and a little less plough would do me. It seems Farmer Giles is trying to cultivate the road and all.'

'Should we let Essex know we're on their turf?' asked Dippy.

'You must be joking. Half of them are villains anyway.'

He parked in front of a padlocked five-bar gate which was bedecked with signs: 'Accept no liability for damage or theft', and 'Boarding of vessels is entirely at your own risk,' and 'Danger of flooding.'

Beside the gate ran a signposted public footpath next to a line of decrepit boats covered in plastic sheeting which had been shredded by winter gales into no more than hanging blue string. The pair climbed six steps and up onto the sea wall. There at last was the glittering river. Rod and Dippy had enough elevation to look for miles across the flat Essex marshland. The sun burned down upon the already scorched fields. The tide was high and the saltings appeared as a water-filled maze, like the grounds of Hampton Court flooded to hedge-top height with pathways of liquid light winding through the sedge. Part of the saltings was cut into symmetric squares: old oyster ponds like carved paddling pools in the marsh, but no longer used. Along the shoreline several hulked boats lay scattered, abandoned, finished. Dilapidated after a lifetime of voyaging. Like old shoes, worn, and holed, they'd been kicked-off after journey's end.

Out on the sparkling river a few neglected yachts sat motionless in their own reflection. Their mildewed halyards rattling loosely in the sea breeze. Downstream the snaking sea wall turned to knee-high parched grass and protected fields of corn, shimmering in the heat, from the flat, mirrored sliver of North Sea which had been drawn into the heart of the countryside. Up river the distant high-rise skyline of Southend threatened the rural arcadia like some brooding Gotham City. Here at Paglesham the emptiness seemed surreal: how could such wilderness exist, alongside suburbia? It was an abandoned No Man's Land of useless marsh. And even on a broiling high summer's day the sense of desolation was palpable.

A large black dog lay in the dust of the deserted Gunfleet Boatyard its belly heaving in and out, its pink tongue lolling as it gasped for air in the heat. The exhausted canine suddenly found a burst of energy as it spotted the two invaders and leapt to its feet and cantered like a small horse toward them.

Rod dangled his hands at his side and let the hound's dry muzzle explore them. Dippy did the same and the beast manifest its approval by trotting back and collapsing in the hardened earth in the shade of a sagging old boat builder's shed which sat on stilts on the marsh the seaward side of a large steel sea defence gate. The front end of the shed nudged up against the river side of the sea wall, the back end of it was lapped by the tide. A line of drunken telegraph poles ran drooping cables, which almost dipped into the river, from the rutted lane to the shed. Reinforcing mesh for concrete flooring had been used as a crude fence to corral scores of old heavy duty batteries, rusting oil drums and engine blocks.

It was the sort of place where you could imagine you had sovereignty. In the backwoods, the boon docks as the Americans say, forgotten, forlorn with no need to appeal to passing trade. Gunfleet Boatyard was a place with no corporate ostentation, no Health & Safety, and, if only it didn't have that pesky public right of way, no rule of law. The shed had been excluded, literally, from the Environment Agency's war against the waves. Its scabrous tarred planking, and russet-coloured sheets of corrugated iron roofing, its crooked stove-pipe and rotted slipway had been left to the inexorable tide of rising sea levels. It wasn't worth repairing, but neither was it

251

worth ripping down. One day it would collapse of its own accord and float away.

Rod peered through the salt encrusted windows of the shed, but could not see beyond shelves of rusty tins, boxes of shackles, and jars filled with used paint-brushes. He climbed two steps of railway sleepers to the barn-style door, which sported, incongruously a lion's head door knocker, better suited to some mock Georgian mansion, 'He's got a sense of humour anyway,' he said and tried the handle. It was locked.

On the land side of the sea defence gate cannibalised automobiles lay scattered among laid up boats, some wooden hulls had dried into dessicated planking and would not float again, others were charred from engine fire, and some fibreglass hulls were torn open like crushed fast food boxes.

'Insurance jobs,' said Rod, 'write-offs. Not a bad trade, you take the wreck off the hands of the Norwich Union or whatever, for which they pay a healthy fee, and save them facing the hefty cost of environmentally friendly disposal. Then you re-build them and knock 'em out cheap. Or sell them as they stand as "projects"'

'It's a scruffy eyesore,' said Dippy.

'That's just how they like it. No point in encouraging nosey parkers with an aesthetic sense of disapproval.'

To one side of the yard was a pound where some 20 or so dinghies, used as tenders for bigger boats, were kept. Some, filled with evaporating puddles of stagnant rain water, sat on trolleys like drought-struck ponds on wheels, others were upside down to keep the weather off. A small corrugated iron shed sat on concrete mushroom-shaped pillars. This was the lock up where boat owners kept oars and rowlocks, outboard engines and other dinghy paraphernalia.

On the far side of this was an area of rutted field used as a car-park. A solitary white van was parked there.

Dippy wandered almost randomly around the vehicle and then stopped aghast.

'Look,' she said and pointed at a dusty smear on the van's offside rear lower panel.

Grime had stuck to the bodywork in a faint oval shape.

'Very fishy,' said Dippy.

'Drawing in the net in or what?' Rod replied, bending down to rub the surface.

Just then Dippy's mobile rang. She wandered up onto the sea wall to get a better reception as Rod tried the car door. It, too, was locked. After a few minutes taking notes with the phone pinned to her ear, Dippy clambered back down into the car-park.

'OK, boss listen to this. I got someone at the Missing Person's Bureau to cross-check the name Hervey Lamb with any outstanding cases.'

'Go on.'

'Apparently six months ago one Gascoigne Cory left South Ken to pay a visit to his half-brother Hervey Lamb.'

'Didn't anyone visit Mr Lamb at the time?'

'Yes. Officers from Southend.'

'Don't tell me, they treated it as a domestic?'

'Must be something like that. Lamb told them a man had turned up claiming to be his long lost half-brother, news to Lamb, apparently. He said the mystery visitor had claimed he was from Galway and that he eventually went back there. He was known as an itinerant anyway.'

'Who reported him as missing?'

'A Miss Beth Jewson. She confirmed he was a bit of a wanderer which is why she didn't report him missing for three weeks and even then apologised in case she was wasting the bureau's time.'

'Silly cow that's what they're there for,' said Rod. 'So what have we got two missing people and a van with a smudge...?'

'And a name. A name of a man who's been linked to one of those missing and indirectly associated with a home owned by the hubby of the other missing person,' added Dippy.

They crunched back across the gravel to the boatshed.

'I'm going to need to cool off,' said Rod, 'this heat is unbearable.'

'But just chicken feed to me, right?' laughed Dippy.

The sun, now overhead, had produced a glare across the boatyard's pebbled ground and had burnished the river silver which made the eyes water to behold. The police officers climbed over the sea wall and sought the shade produced by the shed's north facing gable end. Here Rod sat on the concrete slabs of the sea wall and undid his bootlaces.

He pulled off his police issue sneakers and peeled off his socks.

Dippy wrinkled her slender nose. 'I'll try to put this the best way I can: if your feet were kippers they should have been consumed last month,' she said.

Rod laughed, 'You're right. I don't know why I insist on wearing these chockers. They're all synthetic and my plates need to breath.'

'Don't we all,' said Dippy moving away from Rod's stark, white, mummified toes.

He rolled up his trousers and walked down the slipway and into the river.

'Ahh, lovely.' He paddled in and kept going. The water was such a blissful relief. He padded down the submerged slipway, his toes negotiating little soft patches of mud and slithery fronds of weed.

'Who needs the Med?' said Rod.

He moved slowly down the slipway as far as his rolled up trousers would allow.

'You don't get sea anemones in Essex, do you?' he said suddenly as he peered at the rotten stumps of mooring posts.

'Global warming?' Dippy offered, 'what have you found?'

Rod rolled up his shirtsleeve and plunged his arm up to the bicep into the murky tide. He pulled out a pair of dripping knickers.

'Shocking pink,' he said.

Rod stared up at the steel girder which protruded from the shed. The lip of the steel was shiny. Unlike anything else about the dilapidated boatshed it suggested recent use.

The boatshed was raised on concrete supports at its seaward end and the main timbers of the rotting jetty which dropped from the shed's closed doors at a 30 degree angle into the river outside, went up into the shed through the floor. At the top of the tide sea water would enter the shed presumably by design to make the launching of craft possible.

'I can get inside if I pretend I'm a boat,' said Rod.

'What about a warrant?' said Dippy from the bank.

'Warrant abhorrent,' said Rod, ' here take these panties and stick 'em in an evidence bag.'

He threw the soggy ball of cloth to Dippy and bent over to climb in among the jetty supports.

Rod heaved himself up through the open floor behind the padlocked doors of the gable end and found himself staring at a pile of animal skulls and hooves beneath a giant cross. In front a row of old-style leather car seats had been placed.

As his eyes got used to the gloom he carefully avoided the bones and padded barefoot along the wooden boards which were clear of remains.

Along the side of the shed he noticed the door he'd tried earlier was locked on the inside with the key in the mortice. He unlocked the door and swung it into the sunshine.

'Hey Dips, over here. We're open for business.'

Dippy climbed the wooden stairs and entered the shed.

'Our born again boyo has built his own cross, over there look. And he's laid out the pews with car seats.'

Dippy saw the Christian cross at the far gable end. From the rafters a rubber glove had been suspended over the top of the cross and was hanging fingers pointed downwards.

'From the feathers stuck on it it looks like he's used it to hang game, we've seen plenty of pheasants in the hedgerows and in winter it must be a great wildfowling area for teal, widgeon and geese, although most of the latter are protected these days. But these bones are a puzzle, I think they're sheep.'

'The lambs of God, eh?' said Dippy, bending down to look along the line of car seats.

'Certainly bizarre. But don't they bless boats when they're launched?' he said, 'God bless this ship and all who sail in her? Could be innocent enough.'

'That's true but they normally bring in a minister for that. The shipwrights back home would not waste good timber on building their own chapel, and I've never heard of lambs being slaughtered for launch day,' said Dippy, 'and what's the significance of the suspended glove? The hand of God?'

'Maybe Adele has become a Born Again Christian, too?' Rod wondered aloud.

'Lord God, or Sir Keith? No contest, I'd convert, too,' laughed Dippy.

The pair walked through the shed to the opposite end, the landward gable end. Here there was an area with a makeshift kitchen. There was a sink and draining board against the window, with a small table and one wooden chair. Adjacent to that was a chest of drawers with tea stained rings on its top and a camping gas stove.

Dippy tried the drawers. The first one was full of chipped cups, a wire cage full of rusty cutlery and a mildewed cardboard box of teabags. The second was stuffed with dish-cloths, an apron and serviettes. The third was stacked with folded folios.

She pulled one out.

'What's that?' said Rod.

'A chart,' Dippy explained, 'to you, a map of the sea.'

She dropped the fold and spread the opened Admiralty chart on the table top.

'North Sea, Southern Part,' Rod read out the title, 'that's a big area.'

'It's out of date,' she said, 'look "last corrected 1993" it's stamped here on the bottom.'

'What else has he got in there?'

They rifled through the charts until at the bottom of the drawer they found a plastic portfolio. Dippy heaved it out.

'Admiralty Leisure, Thames Estuary – Essex and Suffolk Coast, that's us,' she read out the cover title, 'there's 12 separate charts in here, so the area's covered in fine detail.'

'These are better, they're in colour,' Rod leafed through them, 'pretty as a picture: look yellow for land, green for mud, er why's it got and blue and white for sea, Dips? You're the pirate here?'

'Blues are shallows, the white is deep water. Look this is where we are.'

Rod peered at an archipelago of marsh islets: Wallasea Island, Foulness Island, Potton Island, New England Island, Havengore Island, Rushley Island.

'Doesn't Essex look different from the heavens? I had no idea all these islands were on my doorstep. It's a bloody Caribbean of mud.'

'He's been scribbling on them,' said Rod, running his finger along some pencil lines.

'They look like course marks,' said Dippy.

'Course marks?'

'Yes, lines along which to steer a boat, based on tide direction, leeway and compass bearing.'

'If you say so Captain Cook.'

Dippy read out the names: 'Maplin Sand, Gunfleet Sand, Foulness Sand...'

'And they fly all the way to Spain for beaches,' said Rod.

'Outer firing danger area,' Dippy continued, 'experimental firing is frequently carried out in the area...'

'OK maybe not bucket and spade land after all,' said Rod, 'it must be these sands where the MOD test new ordnance for the benefit of burgeoning tyrannies.'

'Yeah and when they aren't blasting shellfish to that great seafood bar in the sky, the tide's in,' said Dippy.

'You mean all that lovely sand is underwater most of the time?'

'Well for two or three hours each tide anyway,' she answered, before falling silent.

She pointed her finger at a large patch of green: 'Look, someone's pencilled a circle here.'

'So he likes to doodle…'

'It's a position mark, I think from these figures next to it. It looks like a time 01.45…'

'And what's the other figure mean? Next to it. What does 6.12 mean?'

Dippy looked closely at the chart. The circle encompassed a feature which carried the legend 'Bn (unmaintained)' depicting a small black line with two triangles on the apex on an area of shallows called the Dengie Flat.

'This is a beacon and the fact it's unmaintained means it's no longer used. It's obsolete. Why would anyone want to go there? It's up on the sand, in the shallows, there aren't many boats which could get to it anyway, at least not keel boats,' said Dippy thinking aloud.

'See the figure 1 which is underlined nearby?' she asked Rod, 'well that's what's called the drying height.'

'Come on then, Canute, what the hell's that?'

'That is how high the sand is when the tide is out. That's to say how much sand is showing at Low Water. And before you say it, "Yes we do have charts in Somalia"'

'Hey, hey, I wasn't going to say anything. I'm impressed. I will recommend you to the marine unit.'

'You'll do nothing of the kind. I've seen enough salt water to last me a lifetime.'

Rod rooted through the chest of drawers again, 'There are more maps here, look'

'Charts, Rod, charts. Maps are for landlubbers.'

'Here's another version of the same chart,' said Rod, 'Outer Approaches To The River Blackwater. He's been at it again, look, but this time somewhere else.'

Dippy spread out the chart. On it a second unmaintained beacon had been circled and also with what looked like a time 08.46, and with the figures 6.02 minus 2.7 = 3.32.

'I thought so,' Dippy said, tapping the chart, 'the second figure is the tidal range.'

'The what?'

'The range, the height, the distance it comes up and goes down. Look, see the second beacon is closer inshore and the drying height is consequently greater: 2.7, here look it's marked. So at the time in question the 2.7 – the height the sand is exposed above the Low Water mark – is deducted from the range, the maximum height of tide, will give you the depth at that place at High Water.'

'You've lost me Nautilus, what are you going on about?'

'OK. Let's put it in simple terms: the ocean is the ocean is the ocean and how deep it is matters not to navigators. But when the ocean gets near to land it gets shallower and that does matter to navigators. They need to know how shallow it gets. And they work this out from tidal predictions – or tide tables – these tell us how far the tide will rise, on a certain day. That's a useful start. But the navigator still needs to know how DEEP it's going to be at a certain point and that depends on how close to the surface of the water is the land that water's covering.'

'OK, OK got you'

'So to work that out the Admiralty, with help from the Royal Navy, make what are called "soundings", simply measurements made with – in the old days a piece of lead dangling from a string - to computerised sonar today, these give the depth of water over the area in question. The soundings are then printed on the chart as numbers of metres. If that number is underlined it means the tide – at Low Water – exposes, the bottom to the height of that number. In other words what was the sea-bed when the tide was in is dry land when it's out.'

'If you say so Archimedes, if you say so, but what does it all mean?'

'No idea but whoever's been scribbling this has been working out the amount of water he's got at these beacons at High Water for the one further east and at Low Water for the one further west.'

'The second one has got the little triangles on it, too, but the other way up,' said Rod.

'Yes, they are Cardinal marks. They tell which side to leave the obstruction, so you are in clear water. The beacon further out on the sand has the triangles base to base which means leave to the east, and the one further in has them point to point which means leave to the west.'

Rod noticed the second chart was also out of date. He tapped it.

'Sailors are careful with their pennies and are loath to throw away old charts. They can be corrected with updates known as Notice to Mariners,' Dippy explained.

'But what changes anyway?

'Well on rocky coastlines nothing much: a few new buoy positions, or the erection of a wind farm, but in estuaries the mud, sand, and even shingle is always shifted around by the tides,' Dippy pointed to the great fingers of sand running in 45 degree bars from the mouth of the Thames Estuary out into the North Sea.

'I remember as a kid back home there was a dangerous offshore sandbank which was great for fish but which ocean storms repeatedly altered and so it became a menace for those trying to avoid its shallows. One calm day at low tide dad and I landed on it and went for a stroll. He stubbed his toe on a block of wood. When he bent down to examine it it turned out to be the truck of a ship's mast.'

'The truck?'

'Yeah the top. The rest of the mast – some 40 feet – was buried. That's how much the sand moved about. So in areas like these it's advisable to buy new charts every so often. Most mariners keep the old ones for reference, or sometimes decoration. My folks used them to wallpaper the house,' said Dippy.

Rod searched the drawers yet again and pulled out a third edition of the Blackwater approaches chart. 'This one is bang up to date,' he said 'and look, more markings from our second time around Christian, if that's what he is.'

Dippy looked at a further set of unmaintained beacons to the north of the others.

The one positioned closer inshore had been circled and a question mark positioned next to it on a stretch of submarine sand called St Peter's Flats.

On the top of the chest of drawers was a tin chest, with a key in its lock. Rod lifted its unlocked lid and found inside a tattered A5 notebook.

There were pencilled sketches of beacons, but without the Cardinal topmarks identified by Dippy.

'He's got drawings here of beacons with more figures.'

Dippy took the book.

'They are Lat and Long readings,' she said, ' they will give the beacon's exact position.'

The first sketch depicted a beacon with a bar across its apex, so did the second.

The rest of the book was empty, but as Dippy flicked through the pages, a cut out piece of chart dropped out.

It showed the northern-most set of beacons on St Peter's Flats. Both of them and a third solitary beacon further offshore, had been circled in pencil. A line from the circles had been drawn which crossed the chart to the data panel. Here had been sketched another question mark alongside a crucifix.

The heat of the day had finally dissipated and Adele had stopped sucking greedily on the pipe which drew the tepid water down from the jerry can. Surprisingly her perch was not unbearable. With the weight of her body partly held up by the ropes around her waist and her crossed feet braced on the rusty protruding bolt, there was no weight on her spread wrists. And as the sun dropped behind vermillion cloud in the far west, she dozed in fitful bursts.

As night fell there was so little moonlight she could not see the tide's final approach towards High Water. She could feel it climbing up her body. Its cool, clammy embrace slowly enveloped her but stopped rising just above her chest. Here it stood, slapping occasionally with the dying wake of some unseen distant ship passing through the offshore channels.

Some strange lights appeared: first of all a red and a white, then just a white, then a green and a white, then a red, a green and a white then back to red and white. Adele did not realise it was a small fishing boat hoping to net some summer bass by zig-zagging through the warm waters of the Ray Sand Channel. But she could hear the throb of an engine and she yelled into the darkness. But the lights simply continued their mysterious maritime pirouette until they all shut out leaving just a single white light receding into the distance as the engine noise faded. And as Adele's chance of deliverance headed away north.

Her thoughts returned to her immediate circumstances. She thought about the water-pipe which had sustained her crucified life for five days. There must be a water supply on the platform above her head which she could not turn upwards to observe. For the water to remain fresh, it must be in some sort of tank clear of the sea. Whatever container was being used must, logically, have a limited amount of water in it. Once the water was gone it would be replaced by…air.

———

Few upright features marred the prairie-like aspect of the Dengie Peninsula: an abandoned barn here, a square stack of straw, like a giant blockhouse there, and the white delicate fingers of 10 distant turbine plants, stilled in the windless heat. Rod and Dippy stopped the car on a rare hill by an old church, St James of Dengie. They looked down on a flat, monotonous expanse of vegetable fields which broiled under the sun, and ran eastwards to a far off low ridge, beyond which lay the sea.

'Their name liveth for evermore,' Rod read from a bronze plaque on the church wall, He ran his hand over the plaque which the sun had made almost hot.

'The Men of Dengie who gave their lives in the Great War,' he read out the names, 'Skeats, Ryan, Hammond, Heard and Nunn. Just five in this whole vast plain. Just shows you how unpopulated it was and still is.'

Most of the roads which led out towards the sea wall were private and were emblazoned with unfriendly signs: Private, Keep Out, or You will be prosecuted. Most of them anyway fell into footpaths or petered out into lost tracks down which vehicles – other than tractors – would get stuck.

But there was one service road which ran out through a land-based wind farm, snaking almost beneath the blades, to a 1950's built brick pumping house used to prevent the fields becoming waterlogged.

They drove along it, and stopped to open a five-barred gate. Suddenly a noise like a cross between a whistle and a whirr reached their ears and then a great swooshing vibration as the scimitars of the renewable world started to slash the air. Dippy looked up. The great blades swooped down towards the scorched earth then arced upwards again. On top of each towering pole, in front of each giant three-bladed foil was what looked like the pilot's cabin of some surreal, unmanned aircraft with the prop on back to front.

'Breeze is getting up,' said Rod, 'the sabres of green power have replaced the blades of invading Saxons,' he mused, 'followed by the Danes.'

'Meaning?' asked Dippy.

'This was their country. For Dengie read Dane, this is where they settled after mullering the locals. Essex man was Danish bacon back in the day.'

'So we have that in common then,' said Dippy, 'we've both suffered at the hands of pirates.'

'And now the wind fills the sails not of invading ships, but of invasive turbines,' Rod grinned.

'Very poetic, but that wind will be most welcome,' said Dippy wiping her sleeve across her brow.

They rumbled over a cattle grid, and wove through fields of beetroot, summer cabbage and turnips all laid out in rows converging in perspective across acres of agriculture a mile or two wide.

The road wound into a straggly copse of bent alder trees, crippled in their efforts to afford some shelter from the east winds off the North Sea to a crooked white-painted, weatherboard farmhouse. The road performed an S between a black barn, with a half collapsed roof, and an overgrown brick- walled garden in front of the farmhouse. It, too, looked abandoned. But there was a light on.

They stopped the car momentarily.

'Crafty. It's a security light, a desk lamp,' said Rod staring through the front room window, 'on in broad daylight. But I don't think it would fool many. Especially all these miles out across the marsh with no parked car in evidence.'

They drove on for another mile and reached the edge of the sea wall at a house-sized brick structure: the Marsh House Pumping Station, according to a shiny Environment Agency sign. 'Danger do not climb on structure' said an adjacent notice board.

Suddenly two loud pops made Dippy jump.

'Don't be nervous,' said Rod, 'it's just a field gun to keep the frigging birds off the crops,' he pointed at a blue bazooka-shaped gun aimed across the field and fed with a red bottle of propane gas, 'See?'

Away to the north Dippy spotted a little square edifice with a red roof and grey stone walls, standing completely alone on the marsh. A simple construction like a child's depiction of a house.

'That's St Peter's on the Wall. Oldest church in England, some say,' Rod said as they climbed the sea wall.

If it was a prairie of land behind them, it was a prairie of sea in front of them. The sea wall, was just a grassy caterpillar crawling north and south between the two elements, a crude dam of sods first laid down by Roman civil engineers. There was nothing but the sea to bring the vast, bright blue sky down to size which confronted the lonely pair with two-dimensional infinity. The third dimension was the sea, a puckered plane of coffee brown wavelets which was not infinite, it had a border: the sky.

Dippy stared out across the water.

'There,' she raised her arm, 'look just south of east,'

'Where? What?,' said Rod.

'Here stand in front of me,' commanded Dippy.

He did so and she put her arm alongside his head and turned it to point seawards.

'Look out, in line with that corner of sedge on the saltings. See it? That little black stick. That's one of the beacons.'

'Oh yes, I can see it, out in the middle of the sea.'

'Damn,' said Dippy, 'I should have checked the tides. It'll be an hour yet before we can walk off.'

'Well let's get a boat,' offered Rod.

'It's too late for that. Not even the shallowest draughted boat could get here in time, now. The chart shows us that the nearest boat will be at Bradwell – that's too far now to get here before the tide runs out, even for a high-speed RIB.'

'So it's too deep for us and yet too shallow for a boat?'

'Correct.'

'OK, Dips, we've got an hour to spare. As there's only one abode I'll spare you the onerous task of house to house enquiries, I'll knock the door you can make a Google search for the best bacon sarnie in the area.'

Unsurprisingly there was no response to a hanging bell outside the crooked door of Sandbeach Farm and the pair drove back along the service road until they reached The Black Buoy pub.

'This place does food,' said Dippy, 'according to TripAdvisor "better than average pub grub"'

'That'll do us.'

A white horse had his muddy snout poking through the beer garden fence, trying to reach unchewed grass on the car park side of the barrier.

The pub door was open as was a door at the back, the landlord was trying to encourage a through draught. Dolly Parton was singing Jolene from a cassette radio standing on the bar. The pub was deserted and smelled of yesterday's ullage.

'Coo-ee,' Rod called and tapped the bar, 'when you're ready.'

No-one appeared.

'Yes please,' Dippy tried.

'Anytime today will do,' said Rod loudly, just as a door holding the hanging spirit bottles opened and a tiny old, bespectacled lady stepped through.

'You're early,' she said, 'you shouldn't be drinking this early.'

'Well it's food we're interested in. Can you rustle us up some of your better than average pub grub?' asked Rod.

'Kitchen's not open yet,' the old woman said as she wiped the bar down.

'Not even for a humble sandwich?' pleaded the detective sergeant, 'name your price, we're starving.'

'Don't know what you're doing out here if you're not from round here,' she said looking straight through Dippy, 'but I'll see what I can do. What do you want to drink?'

'That's very kind. We do appreciate it. Well if the kitchen could be persuaded to make us some tea, that would be marvellous,' said Rod.

'We don't serve tea as a rule, but as I'm about to make one myself. I'll make a pot.'

'You are most kind.'

The landlady disappeared behind the optics again shutting the mirrored door behind her.

'How peculiarly English is that,' said Dippy laughing, 'an entrepreneur doing us a great favour by taking our money.'

'I know, it's a joke, we've violated her front room. She just wants a cuppa while listening to Radio 2,' said Rod wandering around the bar looking at framed photographs on the wall. Faded snaps of unremarkable mud roads and unidentifiable hedgerows with in one, a horse and cart, in another a thatched clapboard cottage, in yet another the church they'd stopped at earlier. Local views with folks in Edwardian clothing. But then on a back wall something later in the century: a picture of an aeroplane flying low. Looking closely Rod could see a little black stick in the background.

'Here's your tea,' said the landlady reappearing through the mirror, 'you can have ham sandwiches if you like. And I've got fresh tomatoes.'

'Thank-you. Just the job,' said Rod.

'Could I just have tomatoes?' said Dippy, 'I'm vegetarian.'

The old woman stared.

'What, you don't eat ham?'

'I don't'

'Well that's all I've got.'

'No but tomatoes will be fine.'

'What tomatoes on their own?'

'Yes please.'

'You've got some interesting local historical pictures on the wall here,' said Rod, 'I was wondering about this Spitfire...is this a local view, too?'

'That's not a Spitfire it's a Hurricane, that was taken by my father. Yes that was local all right. Just off on the Dengie. It was a practice for World War Two.'

'Really? How fascinating. What were they practicing on exactly?'

'Still out there. Old Thames lighters stuck out on the sands with markers on them. They practiced machine gunning them and also bombing – not real explosives – but dummy bombs filled with sand.'

'So this picture of the Hurricane shows it over the target?'

'Yes. That's just made an attack on the target. You can see the beacon in the background. There's four of them still out there. They cleared away the wreckage of bomb shells and the like, in the 1960s, but the sunken lighters are still there and so are the beacons.'

'You must have seen some changes,' said Rod but the old woman had disappeared through the hidden door again.

But when she came back with the sandwiches she carried on the conversation as though she'd never been away.

'Yes, I've seen many changes. Even the pub's changed,' she set the generously filled sandwiches on the bar before them, 'it was called the Black Boy, as in a person. But we had to change the name in case it upset someone,' she glared at Dippy, 'we had to get the sign re-painted.'

'I did wonder,' said Dippy diplomatically, 'because a buoy is something put in place to mark a hazard and black is probably the

273

last colour you'd paint it,' she smiled sweetly at the old crone who surprisingly grinned back in admiration.

'You must be a sailor,' she said approvingly.

'Done a bit,' said Dippy.

Once the tide had run off it revealed a vast desert of sand which ran away to the horizon. Rod and Dippy removed their shoes and rolled up their trousers to negotiate the prickly marsh grasses at the foot of the sea wall.

The pair struck off across the firm, wet sand towards the beacon which appeared to be about a quarter of a mile off the coast.

'What's a Thames lighter by the way?' asked Dippy.

'It's a barge, a dumb barge, ie one without its own motive power. It's towed in other words. Towed by a tug. They're used, or they were, in the docks to tranship cargo from ships.'

After 15 minutes walking the beacon did not appear any nearer.

'It's a mirage,' said Dippy, ' the wet sand is reflecting the pole making it look much longer and nearer than it actually is. It's more like half a mile off I'd say.'

As they trudged nearer they could make out that the top half with the two triangles pointing towards each other was yellow, the midsection black.

'Yellow, black, yellow,' said Dippy, 'the livery for a westerly Cardinal mark. It might be unmaintained, but you can still see the colouring quite clearly.'

As they came up to it they could see the black hull of the lighter almost completely submerged in the sand. Its rail was encrusted in

274

weed and barnacles, and under its angled swim head a small lagoon had formed in the sand.

A length of weed-covered rope hung from the beacon's lower triangle top-mark, but otherwise it was naked. They clambered onto the tilted deck of the barge and peered into its hold. There was nothing to see except mud and pools of water. A crab scuttled away under the deck.

Suddenly, CRUMP, the still air was rent by a massive shock-wave, a thumping noise up in the heavens.

'What the hell was that?' said Dippy, but as Rod started to answer a second huge CRUMP assaulted their ears.

'It's the MOD over on Foulness,' said Rod, 'must be that firing danger we read about on the map.'

'Chart,' corrected Dippy, as two more great CRUMPs whumped the air, 'it sounds like God slamming shut his chest freezer. I hope they're not still using this as a target.'

The great expanse of sand was now drying under the fierce sun. It had turned a warm brown colour and the sea was far off, at least two miles distant, a line of silver sparkling on the horizon.

Offshore a second black pole stood pointing at the sky a further half mile or more across the emptied sea scape.

It was tempting.

Rod could tell what Dippy was thinking. 'This beacon thing could be a wild goose chase,' he said.

'Well we're in the right place for that,' replied Dippy, whose mobile bleeped with an incoming message.

'It's from Sir Keith. "Adele never wore pink, she associated it with Barbie Dolls," yeah right, like he'd know,' Dippy said.

'OK don't get down-hearted, we're not just following our instincts, we're doing our best not to jump to conclusions. We're out here now we might as well check out the second beacon. How long have we got before the tide starts coming back?,' said Rod.

'Ages,' said Dippy, 'it's still going out. It won't be Low Water for another two hours.'

As they moved away from the front end of the semi-submerged lighter, Dippy turned and looked back.

'What's the hold up?' said Rod.

'Just lining up this beacon with the land behind. It's good practice to use a transit if possible. Give us a sense of our position in a featureless world, which the open sea is. Mind you the coastline here is virtually as featureless as the ocean.'

Dippy lined up the beacon with a dark kink in the far off sea wall. It wasn't much of a mark, but there was nothing else.

As she tried to memorise the image of the lighter with the distant wall behind she noticed a gold flash against the stern of the black hull.

'What's that?' she pointed.

The pair walked back towards the hulk and there lodged in a corroded plate of the wreck was a gold boot.

Dippy bent down and pulled it free. It was a woman's fashion boot with the heel missing. She tipped it upside down and poured out seawater, along with a tiny crab. But it was still weighty. She

276

unlaced the tongue. Inside were the skeletal remains of a human foot.

'Oh my God,' she said.

'Well it can't be the Lady Adele's, not so soon...' said Rod.

'So what are we dealing with?'

'Could be a simple drowning. Someone fell or jumped off a ferry...' mused Rod.

'You know the first things to go are the hands and feet on a body in the sea,'said Dippy, 'we found several bodies off the coast: victims of pirates. We thought they'd had their hands cut off to prevent identification, but their feet were gone as well. And that's when we were told the extremities break away first.'

The second beacon was on a salient of sand which nosed out into the shallow water of the Ray Sand Channel. It would be 'enfiladed' by the sea upon its return.

As they approached the black pole they noted once more the triangles on its summit. This time they were base to base and black. The middle section was yellow.

'Black yellow, black,' said Dippy, 'leave to the east.'

The near side of the abandoned lighter was higher out of the sand than its inshore sister, and was tilted over even further. This far offshore the tides ran harder and scoured more of the bottom away around objects which impeded its ebb and flow. Such tidal action had left the barge high up in the air on one side and its eastward facing side buried. A mini gorge had formed around the barge's front end. The mud sides of this hollow were craggy and terraced like the crater of some lost planet and to get to the barge's lower side the police officers had to scramble down into the gorge and climb up the far side. The ooze was much softer in the bottom of the mud ravine and sucked at their limbs. Dippy managed to cross the rill without difficulty, but Rod being much heavier sank up to his knees and struggled to pull each foot free. But nevertheless crossed to the far side.

Not until they scaled the grotesque mud cliff could they see the full length of the beacon.

At its base was a human figure standing bolt upright. It gave them a start. Both halted momentarily, instinctively waiting for a response at their sudden trespass.

'Hello?' greeted Rod.

The figure did not reply but nor did it move and as the officers approached they noticed its arms hung loosely by its side with strange bulbous bags where its hands should be. And the figure had only one shoe. A golden, knee-high fashion boot.

Mrs Laidlaw's titian wig hung damply over the bone of her brow, the fringe disappeared into her eye sockets. She appeared to be smiling, but then so do all skulls. A steel necklace held her vertebra to the barnacled post. A length of silt-stained rope was wound around her waist and bound to the post.

'Good God,' said Rod, 'what a way to go, miles out at sea, all alone, and yet denied the dignity of Davey Jones' Locker.'

Dippy said nothing.

'What the hell is a woman doing out here dressed to party?' added Rod as he surveyed the limp PVC skirt and the torn fishnet stockings which held fine strands of green weed.

'And what woman wears boxing gloves?' asked Dippy, as she lifted one of the sodden mitts.

It came away in her hand.

'Ugh,' she dropped the mushy pad on the sand, realising it was only the lacing holding the hand to the arm.

Rod gently fingered Mrs Laidlaw's mud-laced hair piece. 'This is nylon.' He tugged it off. On one side Mr Laidlaw's male pattern baldness was still in evidence, some tufted grey hair on a patch of scalp not yet consumed by shrimp.

'It's a tranny,' he said.

'Rod, a little grace, please,' Dippy requested, ' transsexual. Tranny sounds so dismissive of this poor man.'

Surprised at his inferior's sensibility, Rod felt a little ashamed and obliged to defend himself.

'It's an abbreviation, Dips, not a classification, but point taken. A killing as fussy as this suggests a ritual of some kind, but I'm no expert on cross-dressing.'

The ribbed sand was changing again,it was darkening. The cow brown tan was turning to a purple ash shade. The tide had turned it was making a comeback beneath the sand, first, raising the water table.

'Why should the cross-dressing be anything other than circumstantial?,' said Dippy, moving around behind the corpse and staring up at the beacon's topmark. The black paint of the Cardinal triangles which once advised craft to leave the beacon to the east, had flaked off and given way to scales of rust. Being further offshore the beacon had weathered less well than its inshore sister.

'This Gascoigne character. He's a youngster right?'

'True,'said Dippy.

'So this poor devil is someone else. We'll have to get Essex to send their pathologist, I doubt the seawater's left much for forensics to find. They can have the corpse. But let's keep the Gunfleet Boatyard, Mr Hervey Lamb and his strange maps to ourselves for now, OK?'

'Charts,' said Dippy, 'yes Mr Lamb has got some explaining to do.'

They turned away from the beacon and re-traced their footprints in the sand back to the mini-gorge. It was now half full of water.

'The tide's coming back in,' said Dippy, splashing through the rill. Suddenly she dropped down up to her waist in water.

'Bloody hell, watch this bit,' she said, 'the sand's shifted. It's like porridge.'

She wrenched one leg free, but in doing so pushed the other deeper and sank in further. The more she struggled the deeper she went.

'Help me Rod. I'm sinking.'

Rod tore off his uniform jacket opened it up and floated it across to Dippy.

'Here try and lay on that,' he said. He noticed the canyon-like sides of mud were collapsing as the tide pushed up beneath the sand. Great fissures appeared along the whole ridge as the sun-caked mud calved from the sand edge.

Dippy leaned forward and got her chest onto the jacket. But he couldn't reach her.

'Hang on, Dips. I'll get a line.'

Rod ran back to the beacon and feverishly tried to untie the knots which bound the coil of rope around Mrs Laidlaw's waist. But the bowlines were swollen with sea water and hard to budge. He tore a large oyster shell off the barnacled hull of the lighter and used it to bash the underside of the knot's lay.

'For God's sake hurry,' he heard Dippy shout, although being on the seaward side of the lighter he couldn't see her. The jammed bend would not budge so he smashed the shell open and began to use a jagged edge to saw through the rope. One lay parted white, frayed, stranded and Rod frantically heaved at the line and snapped the remainder of the lay open. As the line parted he fell backwards sprawling across the sand. He leapt up. Two to go. He sawed furiously and eventually cut through the knots and unwound the line. No longer supported at the waist Mrs Laidlaw slumped a few inches down the pole and was held solely by the chain snorter around her neck vertebra. The sudden tension made her skull lift up and stare skywards.

Rod ran back to Dippy who now had water up to her armpits. He noticed that even the sand he was standing on was beginning to wobble. He hurled one end of the line to Dippy.

'Dips. Take this line. Get it around your back, under your arms and tie it to you.'

She leaned forward on Rod's jacket which started to sink beneath the morass, but managed to get the line around her, under her armpits and she then made fast with the bowline she'd used as a child when hauling pots with her father.

'OK, Dips. This ground is starting to liquidise, too. So I'm going to move back to the stiffer ground by the beacon.'

He ran back round the front end of the lighter uncoiling the line as he went.

He got a turn around the beacon, below Mrs Laidlaw's remaining foot and heaved.

He got a few inches.

He took another turn and heaved again.

'You're coming, Dips' he shouted, 'how's it your end?'

'I've moved nearer the side of the bank, but I still can't lift my legs clear.'

Rod heaved again. This time he got a foot or two.

'Stop, Rod, the rope's just cutting into the bank edge.'

He made the rope fast and ran back round to Dippy.

The rope was cleaving through the bank edge as the water filled the gorge almost level with the sand.

At least Dippy was secured to the rope and had not sunk any further. Rod got down on all fours and padded, like a dog, towards her through the jelly-like mud. He spread-eagled himself in the slurry and heaved the line at a lower angle to prevent it cutting through the bank edge.

Suddenly she was free. The rope had held her up and as the tide rose she was able to get her legs clear of the liquid mud.

Rod pulled and she swam into the slurry and pulled herself ashore on her belly like a seal.

'Christ we're becoming marine mammals,' laughed Rod.

They retreated behind the lighter and climbed up onto its angled deck.

'OK. We can't get across the gully. But if we cross the lighter and lower ourselves down the landward side we can avoid it,' said Rod.

Mrs Laidlaw's legs were now awash. The tide was lifting her PVC skirt. The officers clambered up the crazy deck of the lighter, to the high landward side. Standing on the rail put them eight feet or so above the sand which, to their dismay, the sea was rapidly covering.

'We'll have to jump. Don't worry Dips. There are no more rills to cross it was all flat sand until we got to the gully. That was just caused by the tide scouring round the lighter.'

They took one more look back at Mrs Laidlaw but she had changed. The tousled titian wig was swirling away on the flood, the skull had slumped sideways causing the jaw to open askew. It had parted company with the vertebra and her trunk had dropped below the surface of the rising sea.

Both jumped onto the wet sand and started running westwards, but the tide was cutting in around their advance.

Three quarters of a mile away the beacon nearer the sea wall was shorter, it's length no longer reflected, mirage-like, on the wet sand. Already its base was surrounded by water. Rod turned and looked back. The tide had encircled the lighter. In the gully which had almost trapped Dippy the glistening head of an inquisitive seal was watching them.

To seaward a rolling white smoke had started to blur the horizon.

'What the hell's that, Dips? Scotch mist?'

Dippy turned and looked: 'Flash fog. It's so hot the sun's evaporating the incoming tide.'

Soon the fog overtook them, following the shallow skin of water towards the land. At first it was just scraps of driving mist drifting past them at knee height like some ghostly tumbleweed.

For a while it gave the beacon they were heading for a profile. It made it look bigger, nearer. Then the beacon disappeared completely and the officers found themselves wading through calf-high water, their splashing noises deadened by the moist blanket which now enveloped them.

A long, low horn sounded very far off.

'Foghorn,' said Dippy, 'there's a ship out there somewhere.'

'In that case we're headed the wrong way,' said Rod, 'that should have been behind us, right?'

'Stop and listen carefully. It will come again and we must determine it's direction and go the opposite way,' said Dippy.

The pair halted and listened.

The dead sound came again: the same long, low myopic plea of warning.

It came from where they were headed.

'You're right Rod, we're heading back out to sea. We've become disorientated. OK turn and walk directly away from the sound.'

They hastened on, stopping momentarily each minute as the horn sounded to check it was behind them.

Soon a long, low-lying dark line appeared ahead.

'The lighter. Can't be anything else, the beacon should have been this side of it. We must have passed it without seeing it.' said Rod, but there was something unnervingly familiar about the angle and the water was much deeper.

'We'll have to swim. That tide's coming in faster then we reckoned,' Rod said grabbing Dippy's hand. They struck out for the black line and reached the lighter's side with ease.

They clambered aboard. On the down side of the now semi-submerged lighter they could see the black perpendicular of the beacon, mist swirling around its length.

Six foot up the pole was a skull.

'Shit. We're back where we started,' said Rod.

The ship's horn sounded again. It was nearer. A few seconds later it sounded again, this time fainter.

Dippy bent her neck and looked directly up into the heavens. Overhead the sky was open. Across the clear, blue firmament a jet, very high, had its belly lit up by the bright summer sun. Like a shark it went straight across the blue, purposeful, on track, indifferent.

'Damn. It's echoing off the sea wall. We were responding to the echo and not the original blast,' said Dippy, 'that plane's heading west for Heathrow. We were going the wrong way.'

Just then the fog lifted and they could see the inshore beacon quite clearly.

'We've no choice but to swim,' said Rod, 'and to remember we're mammals, too.'

They stripped to their underwear, rolled up and tied their uniforms into a bundle with Mrs Laidlaw's rope and towing their clothes behind them, struck out for the shore.

The water was warm, at least, from the relentless sun's heat and relieved the fog had disappeared and assisted by the tide's movement, albeit obliquely, towards the shore, they made good progress.

By the time they were able to get their footing again they had been swept half a mile south of the pumping station towards Tillingham, where the spiky marsh extended further seaward than anywhere else on the Dengie Peninsula.

Once up on the sea wall, they collapsed in the soft grass and dried off in the sun.

'We've got to get out to those set of beacons further north,' said Dippy lying on her stomach.

'Well our boots are still ashore and bone dry, but our uniforms are soaked and though you'd look very fetching in your smalls and Doc Martens, I wouldn't go as far as to say arresting,' said Rod.

'Ha, ha. Detective Inspector McKay. So let's get them dried off.'

With staves from a broken paling fence they made two scarecrows of their uniforms and waited for the hot sun to steam them off.

At close to High Water they heard the murmuring of an engine and looking seawards Dippy could see a small white motor-boat well out beyond the scene of their adventures.

'That's strange,' she said, 'that channel is no longer marked because it's silted up and no longer used.'

'Says who?' said Rod.

'Well that's a fair point. Just because the Admiralty don't consider it worthy of navigational attention any longer doesn't mean to say it's not ACTUALLY used. But it would have to be by somebody who knew the sands intimately. Somebody who didn't need nav aids to assist them.'

'Somebody who believes they can walk on water, maybe,' laughed Rod.

'Or at least somebody with local knowledge,' Dippy added.

The little boat was powering southwards at speed, but slowed as it neared the Mrs Laidlaw beacon, then its windscreen flashed like a brilliant mirror as it reflected the sunlight.

'It's coming in,' shouted Dippy, 'look.'

Both officers stood atop the sea wall and squinted out to sea. The motor-boat changed course and turned to starboard motoring towards the beacon. The distant purr of engines died away as the boat stopped. The windscreen flashed a golden light as the boat rocked gently, flicking the reflected sunlight on and off as it was obscured by the beacon.

287

Suddenly the boat turned south again moving quickly across the horizon, the roar of the engines coming to the officers' ears just a few seconds later.

It lifted, bows first, and sped away. Even at that distance the officers could see a tiny quiff of rooster tail coming from the boat's stern.

'Something's put the wind up him,' said Rod.

'Checking on a victim that's disappeared?' Dippy said fingering her nearly dry uniform jacket.

'That's what I'm thinking.'

They watched the boat arc away across the silver sea until it almost disappeared, but the windshield continued flashing in the afternoon sun. The boat had turned westward and became a fast moving dot heading up the distant River Crouch before finally vanishing completely behind the smear of coastline at Shore Ends.

'There must be two more,' Dippy said suddenly.

'Two more what?'

'Two more victims. Remember what Mrs Lamb said: "When he's finished Calvary"'

'But she was away with the Christian fairies, surely?'

'I don't think her discourse is based on pure fantasy. That's what he's doing, he's creating his own kingdom out there, out in that forbidden place, the place where no-one ventures anymore. An unmaintained world. This is a place where you could construct your own Golgotha.'

'Part-time Golgotha,' added Rod, 'mostly its seal territory.'

'Then it's appropriate we're mammals, too,' said Dippy, 'we need to check the other beacons, but it's too late today, the sun's already down.'

LAST FLOOD

11 June

HW (am) Time 11.54 Height m 5.49

As the tide swelled around her feet, Adele started to drink. Once she had slaked her thirst, she sucked on the tube again and still the water ran through it. She started sucking mouthfuls until her cheeks blew outwards. Then, taking her lips off the tube, she spat the water out into the rising sea. In this manner she kept drawing water until the tube started gurgling. As the tide came higher, she sucked hard once more and cleared the tube completely of water. She was sucking in air.

She braced herself as the tide rose and lapped under her chin.

'Will power,' she said to herself, 'it's not really will power it's just the knowledge that yielding is another form of behaviour, less satisfying than not yielding.'

She bit on the tube and drew it into her mouth before compressing her lips around it.

The water climbed over her mouth. She breathed in through the tube and exhaled through her nostrils blowing out the sea water. She willed herself to keep her nose closed, but it was tough, wrinkling her nostrils to clamp shut her nasal passage and then opening to exhale. She occasionally swallowed water as she fought to get her submarine respiratory system synchronised.

Just before the water covered her eyes she shut them and concentrated solely on her new breathing exercises until the rising sea turned to something glutinous. Through her rubber suit she felt lumps of soft matter bouncing off her legs, then off her chest and then it was as though the water had turned to acid as she felt a searing pain across her face. All around her jellyfish were swimming in their peculiar manner: turning themselves inside out and then re-enveloping their intestines as they girned through the sea. The pain had been caused by one of these creatures in disembowelled mode brushing its purple fronds of poison across her face. Adele kept her eyes closed and worked out what was happening. Fortunately the pain soon abated and she became immune to further contact.

Rod and Dippy drove eastwards through Bradwell Village out as far as the road went until it succumbed to wheat fields. A muddy car park was provided for pilgrims making their way to the rudimentary church, St Peter's-on-the-Wall, which stood isolated out on the marshes. The ground was covered with a sprinkling of greenish frosted glass from a smashed car window. And a sign from Essex Police warned the pious not to leave valuables in their cars.

'Some folks still need converting,' smirked Rod as they parked up.

'Meaning?'' asked Dippy.

'These local toe-rags could do with some of the fire and brimstone that was once on offer here. See the little building at the end of the track?,' said Rod.

Dippy looked ahead across the dusty wheat fields and saw a stone gable end with a single window and a high-pitched tile roof.

'That's St Peter's-on-the-Wall,' Rod continued, 'allegedly the oldest church in England.'

'Really?,' said Dippy, genuinely interested, 'and if my hunch is correct it overlooks our Mr Lamb's Calvary.'

'Well maybe, but even its builder couldn't walk on water: St Cedd arrived here by boat to spread the word and by Christ, if you'll pardon the blasphemy, did it need spreading.'

'Bad manor was it?' asked Dippy.

'Not many, whatever the Romans had done for Essex man, it had worn off long before. He was no better than a bestial bandit, even the King approved of incest.'

'How come you know so much about it?'

'My old man used to bring us here for summer pic-nics. I still dream about the big brass eagle which held the bible on a stand in that church. Long since been nicked by an opportunist scrap man.'

291

A chocolate brown Labrador came snuffling along the path towards them and stopped at a particularly arresting scent to squat.

'Theodore, Theodore,' cried the pooch's owner, a middle-aged woman in shorts, walking boots and sun-hat, 'No, Theodore. No. Not there, Theodore.'

But if the dog knew its name it ignored the command. Theodore's owner bent down, her hand enveloped in a green plastic bag, to retrieve the creature's steaming evacuation.

'Morning,' she greeted gaily.

'Morning.'

As they passed Dippy said quietly to Rod: 'Man's best friend, eh?'

'Picking up stools from the face of Mother Nature ain't my idea of friendship,' he replied.

The church had an oak door studded with iron bolts. They entered a simple ragstone walled chapel with flagstone floors and wooden benches. It was cool.

'Such a relief to get out of that sun,' said Dippy looking at a Byzantine–style crucifix high up over a stone altar.

'That's Cedd there, praying at the foot of the crucifix,' Rod said.

'Should have been called St Cedds-on-the-Wall,' said Dippy.

'It was a political move naming it after a saint buried in Rome because Cedd's role included merging Irish Christianity with his preferred Roman version. The Paddywacks versus the Papists you might say.'

'And look at the hand of God protruding from the cloud over the top of the cross,' said Dippy, 'where have you seen that before?'

'When I fill in a lottery ticket... "It could be you"' said Rod.

'Seriously, think about it...the rubber glove?,' said Dippy.

'Bloody hell, you're right. Mr Lamb's chapel.'

'Perhaps he had pic-nics here too' said Dippy with a grin.

The officers closed the heavy door behind them and walked around the towering chapel walls towards the marshes. The frenetic sound of larks twittered overhead.

Summer bees buzzed over the long grass which ran out towards the sloping sea wall. Off to the right was a small copse of Spanish oaks and a few lichen-covered elder bushes growing in a dip of the sea wall. Through the branches of they could make out a single storey timber cottage with a moss-covered slate roof built around a single, crooked brick chimney. They climbed down into the copse and Rod peered through a window. He could see a small kitchen table and chairs. Behind which was a set of bunk beds. He knocked on a green wooden door which faced out over the marsh.

No one answered.

Around he back of the cottage was a long, kayak-like boat stored bottom upwards on some wooden frames.

'Last of the Mohicans?' said Dippy.

'Close, but no, it's a gun punt,' said Rod, 'they were once used by wildfowlers to shoot geese and other water fowl by the score. You could make a living from it.'

To get on-top of the sea wall again they climbed some mud steps with plank risers and with the elevation Dippy stared seawards across the marsh. In the far distance she could just make out a bold black line on the horizon and beside it a black pole.

A small wooden post marking a public bridleway had been hammered into the sea wall bearing the legend St Peter's Way with an image of cross keys marked on it.

'The keys to heaven,' said Rod, 'that's what St Peter had on his key fob.'

'Well that must be the nearer of the northern set of beacons. Let's hope we're not too late to beat the next Ascension,' said Dippy grimly.

'Can I help you?'

The officers turned to see that a scrawny crow of a man carrying an easel and basket of paint -brushes had crept up behind them.

'Hello, Sir. You might be able to. We are investigating the disappearance of a woman. We think she might have visited these parts,' said Rod.

Jackson Smith looked puzzled.

'There's few folks ever bother going any further than the chapel,' he said, 'what makes you think she's disappeared here?'

'No she disappeared somewhere else, but might actually be here,' said Rod, ' we are checking.'

'But there's nowhere to check. There's the chapel, the cottage, which I rent, and that's it. Otherwise it's just the sea and the sky.'

'Do you mind if we take a look inside your cottage?'

'Well it's not mine it belongs to the RSPB, but I'm sure they won't mind. Help yourself.'

The officers entered the Spartan cottage. The wooden floors creaked, a pile of unwashed plates sat in an old butler's sink, the sheets and pillows of one bunk bed were left unmade, but in contrast to the domestic chaos, a vase of marsh flowers sat in the hearth.

'Nice flowers,' said Dippy.

'Yes,' answered Jackson.

'You live here alone then?'

'Yes, well I don't actually live here. I'm only here on certain days. To paint. My family home's in Brentwood.'

'What do you paint?'

'I use the flats – the mudflats – for inspiration. They are my canvas, as it were, they are my stage. For my daubings,' said Jackson with a dismissive modesty he hoped wouldn't go unchallenged, 'here take a look if you like.' He led them towards the back room where piles of stretched canvasses were stacked against the wall. The smell of turpentine hovered.

'My studio,' Jackson ushered them through. An easel was set up in front of a large picture window. The canvas set upon it showed a crude, child-like drawing of a figure on a cross.

Dippy's heart jumped.

'This is interesting. What is it?'

'Oh that. I call it "the stigmata of capitalism"'

'Very unusual. What inspired it?'

'Do you know what, I don't know! I just get out there, set up and these things happen. I mean obviously I'm wielding the brush, but sometimes it seems to move itself,' said Jackson warming to his muse.

'You mean like a ouija board?' said Rod.

Dippy suppressed a smile.

'Well I'm not saying I'm in a séance or anything, but I think, like most expressionists I'm in touch with my sub-conscious…'

'So why do you need the mud?' asked Dippy, 'the great outdoors?'

'The sands are a physical void onto, no actually INTO, which I pour my mind. I then capture what comes out on a smaller plane, the canvas,' said Jackson.

'But it's not completely empty,' said Dippy, 'there are objects out there, beacons for example.'

'Yar right, and they may or may not be included in the work. But they are never mise en scene, you know, meant to be there. Dali often used the cliffs of his Spanish home in his surrealist works, but they were more as he dreamt them than as he saw them.

They kind of got in the way,' said Jackson.

'Like the beacons?'

'Absolutely.'

'Well if you say so. I'm no artist,' said Dippy, 'but it might interest you to know that we have found a corpse tied to a beacon out on the sands.'

Jackson blanched, 'You have to be joking…'

'I'm afraid not, this crime scene is further south than where we are at present, but it's out on the same sand,' said Dippy.

'Which makes your painting, as an expression of personal hidden depths, a bit like the Virgin Mary's birth,' said Rod, 'hard to swallow.'

'This is amazing,' said Jackson, 'absolutely amazing. Do you know what, you are never going to believe this, but when I made that work it's true I had looked out towards the far beacon. And it did seem to look different...but, no, no it can't be...'

'Can't be what?'

'This sounds insane but I did hear a scream...'

'You what?' asked Rod.

'Yar right. You know I was out there, the beacon did look a little different, but I paid no attention to it, it was just...'

'Just something which got in the way?'

'Yar, yar. I mean I'm not saying it was ignored completely. Something must have registered in my sub-conscious, I mean I was here to express the materialist shallowness of a painter I know. Dreadful fraud paints just narrative, so commercial...'

'And the scream?' asked Dippy.

'Yar. I thought I'd imagined it.'

'Like you imagined a crucifixion?'

'Absolutely. I mean there was no-one out there. There is never anyone out there. Why would there be anyone out there?'

'When did you paint this? When did you hear the imagined scream?' asked Dippy.

'I come here on Mondays and Wednesdays, so last Monday, three days ago.'

'Would you show us where you were working when you heard the scream?' asked Dippy.

'Of course, but you'll have to wait now for the ebb. The tide's making and we can't get out on the sands.'

'What about the kayak?' Dippy asked.

'The gunpunt,' corrected Rod.

'Help yourself,' said Jackson, 'there's even an old mast and sail with it in the cottage.'

'Can you sail Captain Bligh?' asked Rod.

'No I can't' replied Jackson.

'I'm not talking to you, sir.'

'I can as it goes,' said Dippy, 'but there's paddles, too, isn't there?'

'There are, under the boat.'

'Would you come with us?' asked Dippy.

'Well I've never used the punt, but I'm told it's a two-man craft,' said Jackson.

They lifted the punt up onto the sea wall and turned it over. Sure enough there were two seats and a little decking around the access for each sitting position. It was fitted with drop-boards each side and a tiny rudder. Every surface of the boat including the two paddles were painted grey.

'Just as well it's a flat calm this thing's lethal. It's freeboard is negligible,' said Dippy.

'Negligible freeboard, me hearties, what's fricking freeboard Skips?' said Rod.

'The depth of the boat's sides.'

They slid the hull across the tufty marsh and launched it into a creamy brown foam speckled with bubbles lifted by the sea from the burrowings of creatures entombing themselves in the mud as the tide rose.

They climbed aboard and started paddling through the cream towards the beacon.

After 50 yards the cream gave way to a mirror-like surface which the sun burnished into molten light.

The glare made their eyes water.

By the time they reached the beacon, the hull of the lighter it marked, was under water. They could see its dark decks clearly just a few feet beneath their keel as they glided over the top towards the solitary pole standing out of the sea.

A large black bird was perched on the lower Cardinal triangle occasionally pecking at the pole beneath. It was not a sea-bird.

'What's a bloody crow doing out here?' said Rod.

'It's found a food source of some kind,' said Dippy. As they neared the beacon they could see the bird was tugging at some streamer wrapped on the pole. It would tug, swallow, then stop, survey the world suspiciously, then continue.

This beacon was unlike the others they'd seen. It had a small box-like float attached to it, a sort of landing pontoon on slides which went up and down with the tide.

They paddled alongside the pontoon and Dippy reached up from the low-sided punt to try and attach a rope to it. But she could not reach the weedy cleat on the pontoon's deck without standing up.

Carefully, with her feet either side of the cockpit, so as not to unbalance the punt, Dippy stood up.

'Too late,' she said and dropped back into the punt.

'What's up, Dips?,' Rod lifted himself up slowly, hooking his feet beneath the fore-deck to hold the punt against the pontoon.

Slumped against the foot of the pole was what looked like a Guy Fawkes dummy. A figure with outstretched legs and the remains of a head with a shock of black hair dropped forward onto its chest.

Spooling out from the figure's back was a scarlet pipe, which was draped around the beacon like a maypole ribbon.

'I don't know about the stigmata of capitalism,' said Rod, 'more like evisceration. One thing's for sure it ain't the Lady Adele.'

'And another thing seems certain,' said Dippy.

'Yeah, I know. Calvary had three. She's out here somewhere,' said Rod.

A light sea breeze was filling in and the police officers in their makeshift patrol boat set up the mast which had been lashed to the deck. The furthest beacon was another mile offshore and too far to paddle. Dippy hoisted the spar which held the spritsail, a small cotton sail, and sheeted it in.

'Those boards on the sides,' she said, 'act as keels. You drop the one furthest from the wind and the boat presses onto it. It acts as a lever and the hull, instead of blowing sideways, will go ahead.'

'So this one then?' said Rod patting a small block and tackle on the starboard deck.

'That's it. Untie the line and lower it down.'

'Aye, aye Skips.'

Soon the punt was scudding across the flat sea.

'The breeze is from the north east and we're heading south-east, so we can reach across the face of the wind,' said Dippy, coming into her own.

Rod had found a small scale chart in a locker under the foredeck. It depicted the whole of the Thames Estuary coastline.

He flattened it on the deck and ran his finger along the coastline. 'Bradwell-on-Sea, Clacton-on-Sea, Holland-on-Sea, Frinton-on-Sea...Essex man is proud of his nautical links.'

'They can add another...Calvary-on-Sea,' said Dippy grimly.

The far beacon was more than a lone pole. It was a lattice-work structure. It had four legs, cross beams, a platform on its summit supporting the northerly Cardinal triangles on a pole. As they closed with it they could see a metal ladder, half submerged in the sea.

Dippy nosed the boat up to the ladder's rungs and ordered Rod to slip a line around the frame. Once moored, they dropped the sail and Rod climbed the rungs to the platform.

'Nothing up here, except bird shit, and an empty jerry can covered in more bird shit' he said, then looking around the whole horizon over the glittering sea, added, 'Nothing anywhere for that matter. Even Essex has disappeared...wait I can just make out the chapel, but that's about it.'

Dippy climbed up and joined him.

'That's not the chapel. That must be the power station on the other side of the point. We're too far off to see St Peter's.'

They stood there in the middle of the sea.

'Makes you feel kind of insignificant, out here,' said Rod, 'with just the sea and sky. The world is epic, isn't it? We never see the big picture scuttling around the metropolis. How could anyone besmirch this?'

'That's the problem,' said Dippy, 'insignificance. Some people can't handle being nothing. They have to act. Violence can be creative, in a perverse way.'

'It can be conscience that makes a killer justify his actions,' said Rod.

'How's that?'

'A guilty conscience won't allow him to accept culpability, he has to rationalise what he's done. Make it the victim's fault, otherwise how can he continue with the every day?'

'So once he transforms into victim instead of perpetrator, there's no stopping him?' asked Dippy.

'Especially with exceptionally egotistical people. They have no humility. Humility, in the east they understand it, in the west we are repelled by it, but I say it should be on the school curriculum. The sooner kids get humility the better.'

'That comes with religion – or should do –' said Dippy, 'it is taught in the Koran, but sadly our book has got a dirty name these days.'

'I gave up on Christianity years ago,' said Rod, 'once I realised it's just another rationale for crims to use to avoid taking responsibility for themselves.'

They fell silent and became aware of an odiferous smell.

'You cleaned your teeth lately, inferior?' said Rod.

'Listen,' said Dippy, 'that ladder's got a pulse.'

They stood in silence and could detect a faint murmur from the ladder.

'Must be the tide.'

Rod put his ear to it.

'Something's breathing!' he said in astonishment.

He climbed down the rungs until they disappeared beneath the sea.

At the surface he peered down through the water and could see fronds of hair waving in the oscillating tide.

'There's someone down there,' he said. Rod climbed back to the platform as quick as a monkey and tore off his clothes. Dressed only in his underpants, he inched his way down into the sea. Taking a deep breath he closed his mouth, put his fingers over his nose and submerged himself.

Just two rungs beneath the surface he opened his eyes and despite the salt water saw a blurry face, of what he immediately thought was a woman. Her hair was floating around her head, sweeping across her face, then away again.

Rod surfaced.

'It's her,' he gasped, took a breath, then dived again.

He could see her eyes were closed, and her mouth was pursed around a small plastic pipe.

He surfaced again.

'She's alive, Dips! She's breathing. Breathing through a tube.' He swallowed more air and went under again.

This time he tapped the figure on the shoulder. She opened her eyes. Rod gave a thumbs up. She closed her eyes again.

He burst out of the water once more.

'She knows we're here,' he gasped.

Rod went under again. He tapped Adele, her eyes opened again. Rod pointed at her then himself then upwards. She nodded, then closed her eyes again.

He re-surfaced.

Breathing in again he went back down and this time noticed the victim's left arm was fastened to a cross beam at the wrist.

On the surface, he panted: 'You were right. She's had her left arm stretched out as though on a cross. I can't see the other arm, but I assume it's the same.'

On his next dive Rod went down head first and swam down to her legs. He could see they were fastened around the ankle. He ran his hands up her thighs and found the ropes around her waist.

On the surface again he said: 'She's been tied to the leg. We need a police diver.'

'I'll call the Coastguard,' said Dippy looking at the water washing around the beacon's legs, 'it's slack water, now, look the tide's stopped making. It's almost high water. Then it will start to drop. How much water is over her head, roughly?'

'Only about six inches.'

'In that case her head will be clear in around 40 minutes.'

Rod climbed out onto the platform. 'The bloody sea's actually as warm as bathwater,' he said.

'The sun warms up the sands and as the tide slides over them the heat exchanges from sand to sea,' said Dippy, 'off the Puntland coast in the height of the dry season you could dig your hands in the sand when the tide had gone out and it would still be warm.'

Rod was rifling through his police backpack. He found a packet of chalks which he used to demarcate stopping distances on the tarmac at road accidents. On the back of his patrol vest he scrawled:

'Police Rescue'

He submerged himself and tapped Adele again. Her eyes opened and he held the vest in front of her, again with what he hoped was a reassuring thumbs up, before bursting to the surface again.

Dippy watched a clot of weed almost imperceptibly start to drift north-east beneath the beacon's cage-like structure. 'The tide's away,' she said as the ebb started to pick up speed and soon streamers of tide were crinkling around the beacon's legs.

More of Adele's hair became visible as the tide dropped. Rod was able to mop her hair from her brow.

An engine noise throbbed far away to the north and the officers stared at a fast-moving boat heading their way.

'Looks like rescue's at hand,' said Rod.

'I'd have thought the Coastguard would have sent a chopper,' said Dippy, 'not a lifeboat.'

They watched the boat with a moustache-shaped bow wave getting nearer.

'Hang on a minute that's no lifeboat,' said Dippy, 'that's a sports boat.'

Rod looked back to Adele. The water had now dropped below eye-level and she appeared only semi-conscious.

The roar of the boat got louder and as it closed the beacon it seemed to accelerate.

'Slow down,' yelled Dippy waving furiously.

But as the boat got within 15 feet of the beacon it made a sharp turn and Rod watched in disbelief as a three foot wave, almost perfectly sculpted from the sea by the boat's manoeuvre, came curling in towards them.

The wash broke over them, swamping the gun punt and Adele's head which was thrown against the leg with the impact.

As it subsided her head cleared the surface, but by then the boat had turned again and was cutting another sharp turn around the beacon. A second wave slapped in coming as high as Rod's chest as he held onto the ladder for support.

The wash carried the tube away from Adele's mouth and although her head was now just clear of the water, the boat was coming back for another pass.

'Some maniac from the Romford Navy, having a laugh,' said Rod, 'plonker.'

'I think it's a bit more than that,' said Dippy.

Rod grabbed his patrol vest and formed a makeshift cofferdam around Adele's head as a third deluge hit the beacon spilling over the vest.

The speed-boat had black tinted windows and whoever was driving it was at the controls inside the cabin not up on the flybridge. It turned again and leapt across the sea like some wild beast heading straight towards the beacon. From its PA system a song was blaring, reminding Rod of the speeding fairground rides of his youth. But Eddie Cochrane didn't sing: 'For Those In Peril On the Sea.'

The boat was yanked into a 90 degree turn once more sending another deluge over Rod and the semi-submerged Adele.

But this time, as the boat circled, the air was buffeted by the sound of an approaching helicopter. As it hovered overhead the sea was now flattened: agitated by another force: the downblast of the red and white Coastguard Search and Rescue helicopter which lowered a man wearing an aqualung and flippers on a wire.

The boat turned away and sped off towards the south-east.

Dippy helped the diver alight onto the platform.

'Her mouth's clear of the water now,' shouted Rod over the rotor roar, 'but if you could cut her free. I'll support her head.'

The diver made short work of cutting the cable ties, and unlashing the ropes and Adele was lifted onto the platform.

'She's breathing,' said Dippy, 'but she's barely conscious'.

'She may be hypothermic, certainly without the dry suit she'd be dead,' said the diver who radioed for a stretcher to be dropped.

'Where will you take her?' asked Dippy.

'Colchester General,' the diver replied, 'the Clacton lifeboat has been tasked too. She should be here soon.'

Adele was strapped into the stretcher and both she and the diver were taken into the belly of the helicopter.

The officers watched the aircraft flutter away towards the coast. As the tide continued to drop, Dippy noticed a sodden booklet taped to the leg next to the ladder.

She climbed down to get a closer look. 'It's a tide table taped open. It's showing this month's tides.'

'Considerate,' said Rod.

'Today's date is highlighted in red...and you said, Rod, that there was about six inches above Adele's head?'

'Correct, thereabouts,'

'That's about point one five of a metre, so last night's tide, at 5.25m was point two four metres lower, which, in theory, would have left her head just about clear of the water.'

'So she's been subjected to a death in instalments?,' said Rod.

'Well, I think so. Working backwards there has not been a tide as high as this morning's since...the 1st of June when the afternoon tide was 5.51m.'

'That's the night she went missing,' said Rod.

'So the abductor held her captive ashore until the tide time was right,' said Dippy.

'The dry suit would have prevented her becoming hypothermic, as the coastguard man said. And you can survive without food for a good while, but she would have needed water. You can't survive without it for much longer than four days.' Dippy mused.

'The pipe...' said Rod, he followed the pipe up the ladder, noticing how it had been taped to the rail nearest the position in which Adele had been tied. 'It leads into the jerry can. There's still eight inches or so of water in the bottom.'

'So he wanted her to survive, at least for a while,' Dippy said to herself.

'He's imposed a sort of mental torture. Here you are wear this suit, we don't want you getting cold now do we? Here you are have some water, we don't want you going thirsty now do we?'

'Of course…it's a perverse act of care!' said Dippy, 'an eye for an eye and all that. As retribution for the abuse of his old mum Hervey Lamb has punished a Memory Lodge executive…'

'So "Here have a look at this table, you're going to drown on the 11th" is a mercy killing?' asked Rod.

'Who knows, but it completed his Calvary, I suppose,' said Dippy.

'Calvary only had three crucifees, right?' said Rod.

'Right.'

'So, apart from nabbing our born-again boyo, it's job done, yeah?'

'I think it must be so…' said Dippy absent mindedly, 'but then those crucified at Calvary were all men…'

'Don't. I wanna get back to dry land,' laughed Rod.

The hum of a distant engine sounded from the north and there skimming towards them was a fast-moving orange and blue craft.

'Lifeboat?' asked Rod.

'Got to be with those colours. A RIB.'

'RIB?'

'Rigid Inflatable Boat.'

'What, a bloody high-speed lilo after all the cash those RNLI tin-rattlers raise?'

'There's not enough depth of water for the bigger boats, in these parts,' said Dippy.

They watched the RIB approach, slow to a halt and a lifeboatman climbed onto the ladder with a rope. Rod looked at the smart lettering of the boat's name: Geraldine and Arthur Johnstone-Rodgers.

'That's a mouthful,' he said.

'Yeah 'tis a bit,' said the lifeboatman, 'named after the boat's benefactors.'

'If you left the name off you'd save a healthy donation in paint. Don't take your helmet off we need you to chase a speed-boat,' said Rod.

The coxswain looked southwards, 'Only so far, the tide's running out fast even in an Atlantic 85 we won't get across the Ray Sand for much longer.'

'He might not either,' said Rod, pointing to the disappearing speck.

But Hervey knew the ground. He had walked out on the low tide mud and marked a low way across the sand with withys: willow saplings jabbed in the mud every 100 yards. He used his makeshift pathway to cut the corner, save fuel and lessen the tedium of the longer route out to the all tide channel known as the Spitway.

Now as he approached each withy, he slowed, plucked it from the sand, and sped on to the next one ensuring his 'deep' water route could not be followed.

The lifeboat headed off at high speed between the Dengie Flats to starboard and the Buxey Sand to port.

'This is the Ray Sand Channel,' shouted the coxswain over the engine roar, 'once upon a time you could take it right through into the River Crouch, but it has silted up and there's very little water at the southern end even at high water.'

Hervey slowed his boat to a walking pace to ensure the hull lifted out of the sea: at speed it sucked down increasing its draught. He scraped across the last half mile of sand with barely inches beneath his keel and, once in the deeper River Crouch, altered course to west-south-west and accelerated away.

Rod watched the fugitive through the coxswain's binoculars.

'He's cracked it,' he said.

'We've only got three metres under us, now' said the coxswain, 'keep a sharp eye on the depth,' he commanded his crewman, 'and call it.'

'Two point seven,' said the crew, reading the digital display console, 'two point six, two point seven, two point seven….two point five…'

The sea was getting browner in colour the closer they got to the bank. Rod watched the wake of the boat boiling as the twin outboard propellers stirred up clouds of mud between the rubber tubing of the hull.

Hervey's boat had now disappeared between the sea walls of Shore Ends. Rod willed the RIB on, ignoring the muddy wake.

'Two point one, two, two,' the crewman kept up his litany of impending impact, 'one point nine…'

'That's it,' said the coxswain, shutting down the throttle, 'that's us, we've run out of water.'

'Go on,' said Rod, 'don't give up now, Geraldine Johnstone-Rodgers would be proud of you.'

'She wouldn't thank us for beaching the lifeboat out here. We're no good to anyone stranded miles offshore on the Buxey,' said the coxswain turning the boat round and heading back north-east.

'Where we headed, skipper?' asked Rod.

'Clacton,' said the coxswain.

'Which unlike here is on sea,' muttered Rod bitterly.

The winding creeks of flat marshscape embraced the fast-moving Carpe Diem as she carved a white-foamed wake up the ebbing waterway. The wash ran to each bank and slapped the glistening ooze sending up clouds of turnstone, which wheeled then settled again to their mud-drillings. Hervey looked ahead at the daymarks he knew so well. The tall Scots pine and the jib of the yard crane at Gunfleet Boatyard were the only perpendiculars in a brown-grey horizon of creek and salt marsh, the six-sided, concrete pill box with the blind windows on the corner of Paglesham Pool, where he'd acted out childhood war games, and the little oyster pontoon with the incongruous structure of a garden shed erected on its deck. All so familiar and yet now no longer reassuring, now objects he realised would be denied him. Hervey passed his boatyard and steered instead for an opening in the marsh of Potton Island. Up into a side fleet called The Violet he nosed and then into a mud-hole called Potton Creek. He slowed the boat and crept slowly up until he could see a disturbance in the water ahead. It was the tide running over a submarine road used by the military as a ford at low water.

There was just enough tide to get over it, although he had to tilt the engines to make sure the props cleared the weedy concrete causeway. Once south of it, he anchored. Nothing could get at him here. Ahead the creek was muzzled with drying ooze, astern the underwater road was already surfacing as the tide fell. Soon it would act as a dam behind which Carpe Diem could ride in impregnable security until the night tide. There was no sign of life with the exception of a large horse standing on the island sea wall, his tail brushing summer flies from his rear.

Once the road was clear of the water it barred the current and the ebb stopped running out. Hervey pulled on his rubber waders and climbed off the back of his boat. The water was still deep enough to climb almost to the top of his boots, but the bottom was firm and he waded ashore to the marsh edge. He climbed the grassy sea wall watched attentively by the horse, and made his way along the west side of Potton Island but along the tide line using the sea wall to hide behind. When he knew he was on the same longitude as his boatyard he climbed the sea wall and before he got to the top lay down on his stomach in the long grass and slid upwards until just his head was proud of the wall. He immediately could see revolving blue lights over on the Paglesham side of the river. He twirled his world into focus through his binoculars. A police vehicle was parked at the top of the slipway between the flood barriers. Several uniform police officers were unrolling blue and white tape around the old shed, and a well-built man with a slim woman sporting an afro hair-style were questioning residents in the old lighters. Moose was wagging his tail. 'You stupid mutt,' Hervey muttered prosaically even though he knew he would never see him again.

Hervey crept back down the sea wall and along the marsh to Carpe Diem. His recce had served him well. He could not return by way of Paglesham Reach, he would have to make his way back out to sea through the archipelago of marshy islets to avoid being spotted.

Hervey was exhausted. He made some tea and then lay out on his bunk and slept.

When he woke the tide was back and Carpe Diem was floating in glittery moonlight. The moon was waxing gibbous, 13 days old and just one night away from being full.

Hervey hauled up the anchor through the rapidly filling creek.

Barring Carpe Diem's route to enter the maze of creeks, which was now Hervey's only alternative route to the open sea, was an old iron swing bridge. It was used by the military to access Potton Island and no other traffic was permitted to cross it. But ancient navigational by-laws obliged the MOD to allow water traffic through the bridge and it was swung for vessels whose skippers made the command with three hoots of a foghorn. But this was during daylight hours only.

Hervey reckoned he could just squeeze beneath the bridge's span which was an inverted V-shape, the point of which pivoted on the central buttress. Where the span connected with the shore bridgework, on both sides of the creek, there was clearance at the top of the V. But it would be tight. If he left it too late the tide would be too high to get beneath it, if he tried too early he would run aground.

The black ironwork of the bridge stood out in stark profile in the moonlit creek as Carpe Diem probed towards it. Her engines, echoing off the girders, sent a heron up from the marsh, it flew crookedly across the moon, as though its wings were not quite yet in synchronisation from its sudden awakening.

The boat's bow disappeared beneath the bridge as Hervey put the boat on tick over allowing the tide to carry her way through the bridge. But the current suddenly stopped, and came against him: the flood tide was coming in around the island from both directions. Hervey had reached the watershed and had left the flood tide driving south to meet the flood coming north. Before he had time to power up again Carpe Diem swung athwart the creek her fly bridge jamming under the span.

Hervey tried a burst of reverse power, but the boat would not shift. The swift running tide lifted her still further up under the bridge's upperworks. Carpe Diem was now being pressed bow down under the lower point of the V, her stern was therefore being pushed up towards the higher part of the span.

315

'Bastard,' muttered Hervey, pressing the button of his automatic fog-horn. A rasping blast rent the peace of the night three times.

A light came on in the little hut on the mainland side of the bridge. The silhouette of the bridge-keeper showed at the window which he opened.

'Good morning,' said Hervey sheepishly, 'sorry to disturb you so early. Could you give me a swing? I thought I could get through without one.'

'You thought wrong.'

'Fool,' Hervey said under his breath.

'This bridge only opens during daylight hours. It's in your pilot book, that's if you've got one,' said the bridge-keeper dismissively.

'Yes, I am aware of that and I'm sorry. I have to make a passage tonight and obviously misjudged the clearance,' said Hervey anxiously listening to the increased rush of tide around the bridge supports.

'You should have gone north about round the island,' the bridge-keeper continued, and as if Hervey's pilotage skills had not already been ridiculed enough, added: 'there's normally no-one here.'

Hervey's skull-like face flattened and a terrible concentration communicated itself through the darkness, like that of a panther before leaping upon its prey.

'You're lucky I'm here,' said the bridge-keeper, switching on his console, ' as I say this bridge isn't manned at night, as a rule.'

Hervey's face relaxed, 'And I'm very grateful to you bridge-master,' he said looking nervously as the bridge span silently started to move dragging Carpe Diem with it, the stainless steel push-pit on the stern buckling under the fixed part of the bridge.

The bridge-keeper stopped the span.

'Don't worry about that,' commanded Hervey, 'keep it going, I'm not worried about that.'

The span started moving again and activated an emergency light as the metalwork crumpled and a life-buoy ripped clean off.

The bridge-keeper's face opened and closed in the flashing light. It wore an expression of smug schadenfreude.

'Looks expensive,' he said as the wreckage of Carpe Diem's rail hung over the stern. Hervey's own occulting visage was one of muzzled hatred.

'Yes, as I say, you're lucky,' the bridge-keeper continued his narrative, a running commentary part of his day job, 'we had a leaving do last night, few bevvies too many for me to drive home. So I'm kipping at me work station. Or I was.'

The span had now swung clear of its shoreside buttresses and the creek was temporarily unimpeded by a bridge.

Carpe Diem's waterline aft showed about six inches of bottom and as Hervey applied stern throttle the propellers just shredded the water: the blades weren't deep enough in the creek to get a purchase. He eased her back into neutral and walked forward along the deck.

Squatting into a kneeling position he pushed both palms against the bridge upper works and tried to stand up. Carpe Diem was only of light displacement and under her skipper's efforts her nose see-sawed further and sank deeper into the creek. Once in this depressed position Hervey shoved her bodily astern and she hopped up, clear at last of the infernal bridge and floating level.

'You got away with that, mate,' crowed the bridge-keeper, 'it's your lucky night,' he added as the span silently started to move back into line.

Hervey looked back. 'Thanks,' he said, but the bridge-keeper had already closed his window. He was in silhouette. Using a telephone.

Hervey could not open up Carpe Diem yet. He had to nose her carefully through the narrow, winding creek. A dog started barking over on the Wakering shoreline. It echoed across the creek. Hervey knew it was the hirsute orange-haired Alsatian kept in a cage at the local breaker's yard there. He motored on past a creek which was a short-cut inside Rushley Island. He knew it could take his draught, but there were reed islets in the middle of the stream which covered after half tide and he was not going to chance stranding on one of them at night. He'd taken enough risks. So it meant his route took him close to the main crossing onto Foulness Island, the Havengore Bridge which barred passage out to the wide Maplin Sands and eventually the River Thames. This, too was not manned at night. But he did not need to get through this bridge. His passage was the other way up through Narrow Cuts a ditch-like creek which led back to the River Roach, but downstream of the Gunfleet Boatyard.

But before he could enter Narrow Cuts he had to approach Havengore and as he did so someone up in the bridge control cabin flashed a torch-light over Carpe Diem's deck.

'What a nothing job,' Hervey said to himself, 'more than his job's worth,' and then he stood up and shouting, added: 'Hey Torchy, that IS all your job's worth, you are ruining my night sight.'

He had already masked the boat's name on both sides of the wheelhouse with gaffer tape, and unnecessary move as she'd not be returning.

Hervey turned to port into Narrow Cuts and opened her up.

He steamed northwards until his chart-plotter threw up the position of the north-west beacon on the Dengie Flat. The closest one to shore which he had so far not used.

Slowing Carpe Diem to tick over mode, Hervey trained a powerful searchlight towards his goal. The beacon's stark presence showed the two triangles pointing toward each other as its topmark. This was the beacon he needed: the one on St Peter's Flats nearest the chapel.

He looped a mooring line around the post and hauled Carpe Diem as tightly to the beacon as he could. Then, standing on the fly bridge, he attached his chain snorter to the lower of the Cardinal triangles and in the bight of the chain shackled two steel blocks, through which he threaded two long lines of strong sisal rope. On the end of one rope which had an eye splice in it, with a galvanised thimble, he shackled Carpe Diem's anchor and then looped all the boat's chain over the anchor's flukes. Using the boat's anchor windlass he then winched the anchor and chain to the top of the beacon. And made the other end of the hauling line fast to a cleat in the boat's cockpit.

Hervey then cooked himself bacon, eggs, mushrooms, tomatoes and baked beans and ate up on the fly bridge in the balmy night air. He watched the first streaks of dawn high in the eastern sky and sensed a change in the weather. As the sky lightened it was covered with cold, navy blue cloud, with a tamarisk-shaped swirl of darker cloud playing over it.

Once Carpe Diem was hard aground on the tide-deserted mud, Hervey stepped off the bathing platform onto the sand. The line holding up the anchor and chain he now made fast to a bolt at the foot of the beacon. The second line, which led through the second pulley, and which was bent to the anchor stock at the top of the beacon, he led down to the sand and left it there in a coil.

Beside the coil he left his Green River stainless steel knife in its sheath.

The sun was now above the horizon, but Hervey did not enjoy its golden presence for long as soon it climbed into the fern-shaped cloud bank now stretching across the whole eastern horizon.

Hervey looked at the glossy, expensive topsides of his powerful boat which sat on the damp sand. He'd done well. He thought about the leaky old ex-Naval pinnace his father had bought from the widow of a Gunfleet Boatyard resident who'd died of pneumonia. It had to be pumped out each tide to prevent it sinking.

'You never did anything properly, dad,' Hervey said, 'you were a great ducker and diver, you ducked every challenge life threw at you and you dived when it caught up.

'You gave me no lines not to cross, not because you didn't know where they were, but because you couldn't be bothered to demarcate them,' Hervey walked across the sand to the water's edge the tide had stopped ebbing. It was low water. He looked eastward, the dark cloud bank was thickening, lowering and heading slowly westward swallowing up the blue sky.

'Your seed was just teenage spunk, you spilled it as though it was lager. So I discover your other son. What am I supposed to do? It was a father he needed, not a half-brother. But that was all he had, all he could turn to and once he got it he fouled up. He was bound to. No loving father leaves a son coming from nowhere…to face the inevitable melancholy unequipped.'

Hervey looked at the distant North Sea, little white flecks were appearing. The wind was picking up for the first time in over a week.

'Your love for me was guilt,' Hervey continued, 'that's the thing I get…that's what I'm left with, not love but guilt.'

Hervey walked back across the drying bank. Particles of sand were starting to lift and twirl towards the beacon. The windward side of the lighter was speckled with drifting sand.

'Mum knew you. She knew what mums have to do…stand by their beast. She also stood by me. But it wasn't enough. It wasn't the drinking, not even the violence… I never cared about that. It was the fact you were so nice to everyone on the street side of our front door. It always seemed strange. I didn't know what it was I was missing.

I know now that your public face was part of your cajoling survival tactics, but then I wondered why it didn't extend to me.'

The rope under tension started rattling against the beacon in the rising wind. Hervey could no longer look eastward as the dried sand blew into his eyes. With his back to the wind he could feel it stinging his bare legs.

'Why wasn't my father nice to me? I wondered. He was nice to everyone else, well apart from mum, but you were even nice to her when you were sober and mum could handle your rubbish behaviour because she had your affection, at least she believed she did.'

Herring gulls curved across the sky riding the wind effortlessly on outstretched wings.

The loose mud particles had now been converted into a mini sand storm which was like a rolling mist across the bank. Stripped of the top layer of sand the banks now had a cracked surface like the bark of an oak tree.

'Here I am,' Hervey shouted, arms outstretched, 'stronger than you. Stronger than you because my behaviour has always been the same on both sides of my front door. I grew up and I knew the only person who was ever going to abuse me and get away with it would be you. No-one else would.'

The flood tide was now returning, the little wavelets bounding across the ribbed sand like an army of lemmings.

'So that leaves me here…a serial snuffer-outer of wankers like you and a man who meted out judgment in a serious manner, not on some personal whim, not as a pathetic gesture of personal inadequacy.'

Hervey made up a bowline on the bight with the coiled rope and laid it on the sand. He stood in the knotted circle he'd made and watched the tide approach.

'I'd rather it wasn't like this, but I couldn't live like you. What was it like, the last hours? No one there for you? Did your philosophy of taking no prisoners work? Did you laugh in death's face? I hope so but I doubt it somehow.'

Hervey knotted the bowline tight around his ankles.

'I bet you will have been using your weasley charms on some poor Macmillan nurse. I bet you would have been positive about your disease, like all those scared of death who practice self-delusion. I bet you were well behaved. I bet you were nice. What was it you used to say: "Come in like a lion and go out like one too, let life make no lamb of you". What wonderful bollocks.'

As the tide washed around his feet, Hervey unsheathed his knife and cut the first rope holding up the anchor and chain. As it crashed to the ground the second rope yanked Hervey off his feet and held him suspended upside down from the beacon.

The soles of his feet were jammed hard up against the block. The wind increased with the flood tide and Hervey was blown at an eight degree angle off the beacon, as a gust caught one side of his shoulders he spun one way and then the other.

Carpe Diem floated and with no anchor to hold her the rising easterly gale quickly blew her in to the shoreline where she was pinned beneath an obsolete jetty close to a service railway line once used by the operators of the nuclear power station being decommissioned at Bradwell.

The isolated tracks had once proved popular with those for whom Beachy Head was too far a drive. A rusting metal sign proclaimed:

'We're in your corner. Whatever you've done. Whatever life's done to you. No names. No pressure. No judgment. We're here for you. Any time. Call the Samaritans on 01621883456.'

As he dangled watching the world upside down Hervey recalled the time Joe had dropped an adjustable spanner in the lazarette locker on his old rotten pinnace. He was too big to retrieve it so he lowered Hervey, then aged six, head first down into the bilge to grab it.

Hervey laughed.

He recalled his father's warnings to him about wearing sea-boots on a boat: how it was not uncommon to find dead anglers floating upside down kept afloat by their waders strapped to their belt loops.

'Damn you,' Hervey shouted and laughed again as his head dipped into the rising sea.

The End

Author Biography:

Lifelong sailor and former Fleet Street journalist, Dick Durham, has combined his experiences of both to produce a crime thriller, set in London and the Thames Estuary. The story tracks the events surrounding a serial killer who creates a half-tide Calvary on the vast shoals off the Essex coastline by utilising obsolete navigational beacons to crucify his victims.

Dick, who covered many crime stories during his 25 years on national newspapers, including the Brinks-Matt robbery, Operation Circus, The Met Police investigation into paedophiles, Myra Hindley jail scandals, the IRA Baltic Exchange bomb, and the Chillenden Murders, has also sailed the creeks, rivers and swatchways of East Anglia.

'The idea came to me one day while I was on board my boat waiting for the flood tide to lift her. As I watched the film of water come sliding towards me, filling my boot-prints, climbing the weedy legs of a nearby beacon and gradually floating the hull of my boat from the sand, I imagined what it would be like if I had no boat to save me from the rising sea,' he says.

Dick has written eight books on maritime subjects, including two biographies, but this is his first foray into fiction.

'Essex has a mysterious, low-lying coastline where land merges almost imperceptibly with sea and it has long been associated with extreme violence, from the Vikings, through bombing from the Luftwaffe, to modern-day gangsters. Even the Kray Twins came down for caravan holidays.'

Dick, who covered Ronnie Kray's funeral for the Daily Star and Reggie Kray's funeral for CNN.com Europe, added: 'Much of the coastline of East Anglia is a half-tide world denied to man when the tide is in and denied to the finny tribe when it's out. This peculiar characteristic is what adds to its mystery.'

Printed in Great Britain
by Amazon